Blessings!
M. Lyn Walker
△ζ☺

HIS TREASURE
A McGregor Novel ───────────

M. Lyn Walker

LifeRich Publishing is a registered trademark of The Reader's Digest Association, Inc.

LifeRich Publishing books may be ordered through booksellers or by contacting:

LifeRich Publishing
1663 Liberty Drive
Bloomington, IN 47403
www.liferichpublishing.com
1 (888) 238-8637

ISBN: 978-1-4897-0969-1 (sc)
ISBN: 978-1-4897-0970-7 (hc)
ISBN: 978-1-4897-0968-4 (e)

Library of Congress Control Number: 2016916722

Print information available on the last page.

LifeRich Publishing rev. date: 11/8/2016

Dedication

To Morgen, imagination and right thinking are both gifts from God that help to open the doors to your dreams. Only believe!

For where your treasure is, there will your heart be also.

Matthew 6:21

ACKNOWLEDGEMENTS

Again, I acknowledge my Lord and Savior, Jesus Christ for being the head of my life, along with the Holy Spirit who once again was such a fabulous co-author. I give all praise and honor to you!

Dwayne, to say that I couldn't have completed this second manuscript without your loving support is an understatement. You are the best proofreader I know. You are my rock and an invaluable business partner. I have been blessed beyond measure to have you in my life, these past twenty-nine years.

Kids, I love you from the bottom of my heart. Watching you step into your calling is a delight. Always give God honor and glory. Nicholas, enjoy the journey, but stay focused on your goal. Amaris, proofing the manuscript helped move this project forward. Your assistance was immeasurable. Christopher, your witty humor and personality are a joy. My love and respect grows deeper, daily. Melvin III, Gra Gra loves you dearly. Cynthia, as usual, your perfectionism and keen eye for detail was priceless. Thank you all for loving me.

To my pastors, Ronald and Roxanne Harvey, working along side you in ministry is an honor. Love truly abounds at RLCC. Watching God's promises overflow for faithful believers who remain obedient to His Word is exciting. Thank you for providing a spiritual environment where lives can be transformed.

To the crew, Minister Roderick, Minister Avis, Minister Victonia, Minister Liz, the entire RLCC family, my parents, siblings, and everyone else who prayed over this project. Thank you, thank you, and thank you for your faithfulness and love. I am who I am because of you!

CHAPTER 1

⸙ ✝ ⸙

MORGAN TRAVERSED THE WINDING STAIRS OF THE MANSION'S VESTIBULE. SHE WONDERED whether Edward was home, but not wanting to bring attention to herself, she gingerly walked down the steps before resting on the landing. Then she continued down the remaining stairs with her shoes off. Anxiety caused her broken heart to pump erratically. Adrenalin surged. Waves of blood swooshed to her brain, producing a tingling sensation in her ears.

Acknowledging a housekeeper as she walked down the hallway, Morgan held her purse tightly in one hand and her expensive shoes in another. She held them close, keeping both items from brushing the pricey artwork that lined the corridor's walls. Morgan's pulse raced. Hearing movement in the kitchen, she ducked into the butler's pantry to regroup.

Knowledge of Edward's latest dalliance had been the last straw. But she knew from their years together, that he would neither tolerate nor accept drama or theatrics from her. So she took a deep cleansing breath and composed her emotions. Giving his staff fodder for gossip was unacceptable. From the pantry, she heard Edward speaking with someone from his security detail. Now she knew with certainty that he was near.

Feeling less confident, she straightened her shoulders and plastered a smile on her face. Leaving with dignity was important. Edward had taught her well. She exited the tiny room. This would be her grand performance, her final curtain call. Walking boldly into the massive gourmet kitchen, she greeted her lover.

"You're up early, darling," she said.

Edward was drinking espresso. The morning paper was opened flat on the counter. He never looked up.

Morgan leaned against the Italian marble counter and slipped her feet into buttery soft leather mules. "Did you just get home?" Her bold challenge forced his hand.

Edward put the cup down and stared. His appreciative glance was welcomed. A sly smile formed on Morgan's face, acknowledging his admiration. Her long flowing weave had cost him handsomely and her make-up was flawless, as required. The simple, yet tasteful slacks and top that she wore screamed of money, as they should since her outfit hadn't come cheap. Morgan knew that he still found her attractive, although they hadn't been intimate in some time. She carried herself with the quiet sophistication, a more wizened male appreciated. Edward was over thirty years her senior, having just turned sixty-five on his last birthday.

He finally responded. "No, I returned about an hour ago." The skin surrounding his eyes crinkled as he spoke.

Morgan's face remained neutral. She searched his eyes for approval. Even in this final hour, it meant a great deal to her. He'd always applauded her poker face, an air of detachment that she'd perfected over a lifetime. When he nodded, ever so slightly, she relaxed. His acknowledgment of this attribute lessened the pain.

For Edward, the dissolution of their arrangement was nothing more than a business transaction. Morgan knew that he'd spent the evening with her replacement, a younger version of the cocoa brown wonder that stood beautifully before him. He wouldn't hide the romance. He didn't have to. She'd been his muse, not a wife. And their relationship was now over.

"I hope you enjoyed yourself last night," she said nonchalantly.

"I did." His smile was crooked, but his answer was honest and sincere.

She appreciated his directness, always had, although his answer hurt. Noise filtered down the hallway. Other houseguests were slowly awakening. The mansion was always teaming with rich and famous friends, whether Edward was home or not. She heard the faint sound of a vacuum cleaner. The corridor that she'd just traveled was now being cleaned. Morgan also heard indistinct voices coming from the attached garage. It was time to leave.

"My bags are packed and I'm flying to the states with Jeffery," she said.

Edward nodded again. His business partner had flown in for a series of meetings on one of the company jets over a week ago.

Morgan was happy that Jeffery was accompanying her home.

"How long will you be gone?" he asked. His eyebrows arched, letting her know that he was truly interested in her response.

Searching his face for a glimmer of regret, but seeing none, she replied. "I'm not coming back."

He took another sip of his espresso. His Adam's apple moved slowly as he swallowed. "I didn't think so. Do you need anything?" he asked.

"No, I came to you with nothing and that's how I'll leave."

Edward sighed in resignation before speaking. "I'll make a final deposit into your bank account. My gifts are yours to keep."

This time Morgan's eyebrows rose. He was being more than generous. She walked closer and searched his weathered face for understanding, still amazed that he'd never had cosmetic surgery or dyed the silver strands that liberally streaked his hair. She kissed his cheek.

He held her hands in a hardened grip. "I never planned to marry you."

"I never expected you to," she said.

He squeezed gently. "Be safe, call me when you're settled."

Morgan's grin expanded. "*Au revoir,*" she said, affectionately kissing his forehead.

"*Au revoir mon amour,*" he said tenderly.

Morgan left the kitchen and walked down a small hallway. She nodded to two employees who smiled back as she passed. The door leading to the garage opened. The man standing on the other side startled her. She quickly descended the steps and flew past another employee, never acknowledging his equally surprised expression. Her heels clicked on polished concrete. She greeted the limo driver, who stood beside the open passenger door.

"Your bags are in the trunk," he said.

Jeffery, Edward's business partner and her dearest friend remained quiet until she was comfortably seated. Morgan noticed his tightened jaw.

"How did it go?" he asked.

Her eyes welled. He handed her a monogrammed handkerchief. Mindful of her false eyelashes, she patted the area surrounding her lids carefully.

"As well as could be expected," she said, controlling her emotions.

He leaned back against the plush leather seating. "Once you're back with family, life will become brighter," he said.

Morgan stared out the window and dazedly observed the passing scenery as the limo headed towards the airport. Europe had been her home for five long years. She'd intermittently visited the states, but hadn't traveled back to Michigan in a long time. She'd even missed her grandmother's funeral. "I hope I haven't caused a permanent breach in your friendship?" she said.

Jeffery shook his head. "No, Edward will understand why I didn't come into the house. As you're well aware, we haven't been close for awhile."

A sob caught Morgan off guard. Jeffery patted her hand. Then he closed his eyes. She wondered if he was praying. Pent-up emotion finally broke and hot tears flowed liberally down her cheeks.

Jeffery held her hand tightly, as Morgan wept.

CHAPTER 2

☙ ✝ ❧

PETRA TOOK ANOTHER SWIG AND THEN SLUMPED INTO A MASSIVE CHAIR THAT WAS COVERED by a faded sheet. Even in her alcohol-induced fog, she asked for another bottle. It was downright depressing that she couldn't even get drunk in peace, without thinking about her grandmother.

Grandma Rosemary always knew stuff. She'd always been able to sniff out Petra's lies. Her father couldn't. Too busy working, he rarely took the time to dig deeper into her half-truths. But Grandma Rosemary always got to the bottom of any story that Petra told. Her mother's untimely death and her father's ineptness were two reasons why the teen was drinking warm beer with a stupid boy, in a cottage located in rural Michigan.

Petra was well acquainted with the house. She and her grandmother had visited Grace Harding often over the years. But for some reason, the cottage had remained empty since the woman's death. Now, because her father's work plans had changed, she was being forced to spend the rest of the summer with her grandmother. She'd almost slit her wrists when her dad had given her the news.

The teens in Indigo Beach were lame. At fifteen, Petra was far too old for the play dates that her grandmother would probably make her attend. Since she wasn't going to be in Chicago for the next month, driver's training classes had to be postponed until October. She was livid!

The boy passed the bottle. Frustrated with her life, Petra took another long gulp and then belched. "That's pretty disgusting," he said.

Petra glared at her dumb friend. She took another long swig for good

5

measure. Then she tried standing and staggered. The teen became alarmed. Beer normally didn't affect her this way. The floor moved and the cottage walls began swaying.

"You probably should have stopped three bottles ago," he said, before looking at his cell phone. "I've got to get home. You coming?"

Petra plopped back down and stared. "Yeah, in a minute," she said. Her words were slurred.

The boy shook his head. "No can do, if we don't start walking now, I'll never make it back before my dad gets home. Besides your grandmother will be really upset if she gets home from church and you're not there."

Petra sat on the arm of the chair, willing her legs to work. They wouldn't. She sucked her teeth in disgust. "So what'll happen if you don't make it back on time?"

"It ain't worth finding out," the boy said. Dazed, Petra watched him don a baseball cap. "You comin'?" he asked again.

"Just leave. I'll be fine. I'll get home before dark." Petra's words were garbled.

The boy looked doubtful, but nodded. "Do you know how to get back to her house from here?"

She nodded.

"All right, then I'll see you at church on Sunday," he said, before leaving through the front door.

Petra's lids grew heavy. She vaguely heard the screen door slam against the doorframe when he departed. Then she snuggled comfortably in the soft oversized chair and promptly fell asleep.

CHAPTER 3

✝

JACOB HAD ORIGINALLY PLANNED TO DRIVE TO INDIGO BEACH ON SATURDAY AND SPEND TWO relaxing days in his hometown before flying to Mexico, but his travel plans had changed that morning. His flight now left in a few hours. He would just have to catch up with his mother and daughter later in the week.

Furious and disappointed, Petra had ignored him on their drive into Michigan. As usual, he'd overlooked his daughter's insolence. Jacob didn't understand adolescence and had no idea how to relate to his only child. His deceased wife had made parenting look easy, but it wasn't.

When Lillian got pregnant, Jacob married his college sweetheart even if marriage at twenty-four had felt a bit too young. Thankfully, completing undergraduate studies, in international business and then earning an MBA had meant that he could financially support his small family. His hard driving, type A personality helped fuel success.

Intensely driven as well, Lillian had completed her degree and delivered their daughter within the following year. With Jacob traveling back and forth between Mexico and other parts of Central America, he'd eventually coerced his wife into full time motherhood, since he was rarely home.

This arrangement had worked beautifully, or so he'd thought until the night of the accident, when long held truths began unraveling. He still didn't understand the events of that fateful evening. Lillian was legally drunk when she'd wrapped her sport's car around the base of a tree. Thankfully, Petra had been with their housekeeper. Unbeknownst to him, the woman's responsibilities had expanded to include childcare.

He and Lillian had grown apart during their ten-year marriage. Her idealism and high energy had turned into stoicism and restlessness. The woman lying in the morgue had been a stranger. Regardless, he'd mourned.

Now, Jacob was faltering at single parenting. He was floundering and failure was inexcusable to him. Petra blamed him for her mother's death. He blamed himself too. His only child was strong willed and repeatedly rebuffed his parental control, but every now and then, she yielded to pressure. Jacob loved showing photographs of his perfectly coifed family. Photos that painted a picture of family life that only existed in his imagination.

He was dad, but had never really been a father. He'd been a spouse, but rarely a loving husband. Jacob drove himself hard, because his personality demanded nothing less, while his young daughter grew angrier. He placed his travel bags near the front door. A car service was waiting. Taking the service elevator down to the garage, he walked past highly priced vehicles. Jacob's neighbors were all movers and shakers. His residence had an enviable address, overlooking Lake Michigan. He'd worked hard and success was his reward.

The driver opened the back door. Jacob entered and inhaled. The aroma of expensive leather was robust.

After placing Jacob's luggage into the vehicle's trunk, the driver sat behind the steering wheel. "Good afternoon, Sir."

"Good to see you again. I thought Griffin would be driving me to the airport today," Jacob said, buckling his seat belt.

"This is his day off, Sir."

Jacob cringed at the oversight. "Obviously, my days have gotten away from me." He hated being wrong about anything.

The driver chuckled. "That can happen when you work long hours."

Deep in thought, Jacob stared out the window as the car merged into traffic.

"Will you be gone long?" the driver asked.

Jacob shook his head. "No, I'll only be out of the country for a few days." As the car zoomed towards the airport, Jacob pushed thoughts of Petra and his failings aside. He would deal with her issues later, because he didn't have time or the energy to address them now.

CHAPTER 4

✝

"HAVE YOU PRINTED THE AGENDA FOR TOMORROW'S MEETING?" DEON ASKED HIS ADMINISTRATIVE assistant. Wednesday night service had just ended and the pair was exiting the sanctuary.

"Thank you for reminding me, I completely forgot."

Deon was surprised. Rosemary rarely forgot to do anything. The woman had worked for New Life Full Gospel Church for over thirty years. She'd been the office manager during his father's tenure and now she kept him out of trouble.

Rosemary's family had migrated to Indigo Beach four generations earlier. She was deeply rooted within the community. Although nieces and nephews lived far and wide, four of her five children still resided in Michigan. Jacob and his daughter lived in Chicago. Deon had been praying for Rosemary's second born and his family for years.

When Deon stopped, Rosemary smacked into him from behind. "Rosemary," he barked.

"Pastor, I'm so sorry."

He shook his head. "Woman, your mind has been elsewhere all day. Come into my office."

Faint lines surrounding her eyes deepened. She was clearly worried about something.

"Now, what's got your bustle all bunched up?" he asked.

Rosemary sat on the arm of Deon's leather couch. Emotions washed across her face. "Pastor, Petra is coming to stay with me for the rest of the summer. You know that my granddaughter is a handful."

"Most teenagers are, get to the point," he said, sensing that there was more to the story.

Rosemary sighed. "I don't want to be tied down."

Deon understood her dilemma. Rosemary had parented, fostered, and helped raise more children than he could count. God had used her nurturing spirit mightily. She was justifiably tired. "When is she arriving?" he asked.

"Saturday morning, and I have so much to do before then."

"I've never known you to avoid a challenge."

Rosemary stood and walked towards the doorway. "And I won't now, do you want me to lock up before I go?" she asked.

"No, I'm waiting on Summer."

"Then, I'll see you tomorrow," Rosemary said, before she left.

Through the doorway, Deon watched his administrative assistant retrieve her cell phone from her purse and listen to messages. She dialed a number. Deon grew concerned when he saw her frown. "Is there a problem?" he asked.

"I'm not sure, Jacob dropped Petra off earlier than planned, but she isn't answering my house phone."

"Call her cell."

"I don't have her new number."

"Then call Jacob and see if he knows what's going on," Deon said.

Rosemary called her son. Deon became alarmed when he heard her angry retort. "I haven't had time to check my messages and I always turn my phone off during service. You know that." Then she grabbed her purse and sweater from her desk.

"Is everything all right?" he asked.

When Rosemary looked up, her eyes were stormy. "It will be when I get home. Please give Summer my regards and I'll see you tomorrow."

"Call us, if you need anything."

Rosemary half smiled. "If I need you, I will."

From the outer office window, Deon watched Rosemary stroll across the parking lot and enter her car. He said a quick prayer for Petra, Jacob, and his dear friend because something felt off and his instincts were rarely wrong.

CHAPTER 5

✠

MORGAN STARED OUT THE WINDOW OF THE CORPORATE JET AS IT FLOATED ABOVE THE CLOUDS. She was far too anxious to sleep, so her thoughts wandered. Jeffery was reading. His glasses hung precariously low on the bridge of his nose, but she resisted the urge to push them higher.

The years had passed quickly. She'd left Indigo Beach thirteen years earlier, earned a degree, and started her career. Morgan still remembered the day that she was contacted by the headhunter. She was working for a small manufacturing company in Chicago at the time. Three interviews later and quite unexpectedly, she landed her dream job in New York.

With impressive grades, and solid skills, a company owned jointly by Edward and Jeffery retained her services. In her first year of employment, marketing savvy helped propel her division forward. The next year, the company out paced the competition by using a masterful strategy that she unabashedly created. Soon after, she caught Edward's eye. Their affair began explosively. Five months later, Morgan left the company and moved to Europe. Their relationship wasn't good for morale and besides; she was now wheeling and dealing at a higher level, one better suited for her highly analytical mind.

Morgan loved the excitement. In the beginning, life was thrilling. Edward taught her business principles while she watched a master entrepreneur execute lucrative deals. He clothed and housed her in luxury. In return, he expected hard work and loyalty. They were a formidable pair.

He respected her deeply ingrained Midwestern work ethic. She applauded his power.

But, all too soon, their relationship changed. High passion turned into domesticity and with it, the predictability of familiarity and routine. Morgan was a realist and she knew that the relationship would end, just as quickly as it had begun. Then Edward became sick and leaving him wasn't an option. Soon, good intensions left her feeling trapped and drained.

When Jeffery found out about their romance, the men argued bitterly. To date, they remained professional, but their friendship had never been the same. During those difficult months, Jeffery and his wife took Morgan under their wing and offered unconditional love. From the beginning, Mona knew even if Morgan couldn't at the time, that she'd found a father figure in Edward to replace the one that she'd never known, who'd never claimed her as his own. The older woman taught her new paradigms. Now, years later, Morgan revered Mona's wise words and she was eternally grateful for the woman's friendship.

Mona was now deceased. Breast cancer had claimed another victim. Jeffery was by her side the day she died. That same morning, Morgan was out of the country, finalizing a deal for Edward. Not being present for her dear friend's death was just another regret that was piled high on top of so many others.

Morgan wasn't proud of her past. When her brief affair eventually became public, newspaper articles maligned her character. Every printed untruth was hurtful, but the title of mistress was valid. Now, it was a badge that she no longer wished to wear.

Prior to her death, Mona had implored Morgan to return home. Regretfully, she hadn't. She'd made one false promise after another to the dying woman, but once the jet landed, Morgan planned to honor her word. She was confirmed on a commercial flight from New York to Chicago. From there, a bus would deliver her to Indigo Beach. Arriving by a car service was far too pretentious for the folks back home.

Morgan looked up when she felt Jeffery staring. His eyes were warm, almost paternal. Then the lights came on in the cabin of the plane. Apprehension mingling with fear had her heart racing. The plane began its descent. Morgan understood men, even one as steady as Jeffery. Her mother had loved freely. All of Mamie's children had different fathers. Two of her sisters knew their dads, but three didn't. She was the oldest and her mother had schooled her, the longest. Mamie Harding would be proud of what her first-born had accomplished, but she wasn't so sure that others in town would agree.

A short time later, the plane landed smoothly. Morgan and Jeffery gathered their bags. Going through customs at the private airstrip was uneventful. She was grateful that Jeffery would remain by her side until her second flight boarded.

Later that evening, she flew to Chicago. Morgan thought about her four sisters and their children. She'd missed out on so much, having been gone for so long.

She finally relaxed when the plane reached its cruising altitude. Morgan flipped through the pages of an international newspaper, eventually finding the article that she sought. For a few months, she'd been following the rise of a particular Swiss company. Morgan knew a solid business opportunity when she saw one. The company wasn't on the market yet, but everyone and everything had a price. This, she knew with sureness.

Morgan glanced out the window one last time before she resumed reading. Beautiful Indigo Beach was beckoning. In her childhood, Lake Michigan's sandy beaches had always been a place of solace and peace. She desperately needed reconciliation, but more importantly, she hoped that Michigan's intense summer sun would burn away years of shame.

A short time later, the fasten seatbelt sign came on. Morgan lifted her tray table and prepared for landing. Mamie Harding's oldest daughter was finally going home.

CHAPTER 6

✝

"BUZZ, BUZZ!" PETRA'S PHONE VIBRATED. SHE STIRRED. "BUZZ, BUZZ!" THE TEEN FELT DISORIENTED. Petra used her shirtsleeve to wipe spittle from her mouth. A deep rumbling vibrated in her belly. She also felt sick, but there was no need to go to the bathroom. The water in the cottage had been turned off. Besides, her legs weren't cooperating. Her phone vibrated again. Petra pulled it from her back pocket and looked at the caller ID. Her dad was calling. She let the call go to voice mail, just like the others. Having missed eleven calls from her father and grandmother combined, she knew that she was in big trouble. Petra's stomach rolled again and then she vomited all over the chair and the floor. Tears now flowed freely. She wiped her mouth again and dialed her father.

"Petra, where are you?" he shouted.

The teen moaned.

"Talk to me! Are you okay?"

Petra stuttered. "I'm sorry, so sorry." Her stomach rolled again.

"I'll send your grandmother to get you. Now tell me where you are?"

Petra moaned again.

"I need to know what's going on."

Petra could tell that her father's anger was rising. "I'm at Grace Harding's cottage," she whimpered.

"Who's there with you?" he demanded.

Petra focused on her surroundings. "No one."

"How'd you get there?"

She ignored her father's question.

"Are you hurt?"

"No." Petra squeaked out, before another wave of nausea had her doubled over.

"I'm calling your grandmother. She'll be there shortly," he yelled, before he hung up.

Petra slumped in the oversized chair. She heaved one last time before her stomach finally emptied. More tears cascaded down her face. A short time later, she heard cars pull into the driveway. Only when she felt a presence, did she open her eyes. Grandma Rosemary stood in the doorway of the parlor.

Bottles littered the floor. She felt intense shame as she watched her grandmother glance around the room. She groaned when she realized that Pastor Deon and his wife were standing behind her grandmother. Embarrassed beyond belief, Petra squeezed her eyelids closed.

"Summer, I need to get my granddaughter out of these soiled clothes. See if you can find something for her to wear."

Petra vaguely heard her grandmother's request. In a haze, she watched Sister Summer walk towards the back of the cottage. Her humiliation grew.

"Pastor, would you please call Jacob and let him know that Petra is safe," Rosemary asked.

Pastor Deon left the room, giving the women privacy. Limply, Petra allowed her grandmother to remove her clothing.

Sister Summer soon arrived with a folded sheet. "I couldn't find anything else," she said.

Shameful tears continued to flow.

"No sense crying now," her grandmother said, as she removed Petra's shirt.

"The water is off," the teen said weakly.

Rosemary sighed. Then she made a toga to conceal Petra's slight frame. "We'll come back tomorrow and you'll clean," Grandma Rosemary said angrily.

Petra felt even worse as she watched Sister Summer sop up vomit from the floor with another sheet. Then Grandma Rosemary guided her out the front door. She gripped the thin fabric tightly. Her grandmother rarely lost her temper, but something told Petra, that she would tonight. Taking a deep calming breath, she walked across the yard.

Grandma Rosemary opened the backseat car door and Petra climbed in. Pastor Deon and his wife stood near. "How'd you get into the house?" Grandma Rosemary asked.

Petra didn't know what to say, so she remained silent.

"Young lady!" Her grandmother's voice turned serious.

"We . . . uh, I climbed in through the bedroom window."

The three adults looked at one another.

"I'll check it," Pastor Deon said, turning back towards the house. Summer and Rosemary stood patiently beside the car. He soon reappeared "Rosemary, let Mamie know that the window latch in the master bedroom is broken. I locked the front door from the inside, but the house isn't secure." Pastor Deon looked pointedly at Petra, who shamefully looked away.

"Do you need us to do anything else for you?" Summer asked.

Rosemary sat behind the steering wheel. "No, the two of you have done more than enough tonight."

Petra closed her eyes and reclined against the back seat.

Summer spoke in a hushed whisper. "Rosemary, how would Petra have known about the broken latch?"

Rosemary shook her head. "I don't know, but the bigger questions are, who bought the beer and who was with her? I don't believe for one moment, that she drank all of those bottles alone."

Petra pretended to be asleep.

"My youngest daughter abused alcohol. So I know first hand how scary underage drinking can be," Summer said.

"Ladies, every closed eye isn't asleep," Pastor Deon said, glancing into the car.

Petra felt three sets of eyes staring at her and she squirmed.

"I raised five saved kids by myself. My granddaughter doesn't know who she's messing with," Grandma Rosemary said crossly. Then she slammed her car door shut. "Pastor, what was Jacob's response when you reached him?"

"He was justifiably furious."

"I'll call him when I get home," Grandma Rosemary said, as she started the engine.

"It's going to be an interesting summer," Summer said.

"I believe my wife might be right," Pastor Deon added.

Petra heard the couple walk towards their car. Then her grandmother backed out of the driveway. Soon, exhaustion took over and she slept.

CHAPTER 7

✝

JACOB WILLED HIS MIND TO SETTLE, BUT IT WOULDN'T. IMPOTENCY HAD HIM GRIPPED IN FEAR. He cursed Lillian with unfiltered venom. Then he choked back embarrassment, thankful that his shameful behavior hadn't been observed.

He'd always played by the rules and couldn't understand why Petra wouldn't. Without complaint, he'd helped care for his younger siblings when his older brother had gone off to college. Graduating with honors, he'd never let obstacles of any kind get in the way of personal success, but unlike him, Petra refused to cooperate. To date, his only child was his most formidable opponent, and that list included powerful and well-heeled diplomats and business industrialists. In truth, Petra scared him, because she was winning.

Since her mother's death, the teen had gone through countless nannies, but at fifteen, she was far too old for a sitter. She needed help and sending his only daughter to his mother seemed like a logical choice given that Rosemary had successfully raised her own children alone. Jacob hoped that his mom could figure out what was troubling his child, because he was spending far too much time worrying about her and his job performance was suffering. He'd actually considered sending Petra to boarding school.

Physically fatigued and mentally exhausted, Jacob just wanted to forget about the day's difficulties and get some rest. He burrowed deeply under the warm cotton blanket and plush duvet that covered his over sized bed. Earlier, his mother's and Pastor Deon's calls had interrupted delicate negotiations. Once again, personal troubles had wrecked havoc on an otherwise productive day. Truly at the end of his rope, Jacob prayed. He also asked for God's forgiveness. His earlier outburst, although done in private, was humiliating. Praying aloud felt awkward at first, but he continued. Then his phone rang. Jacob looked at the caller ID before answering.

"What now?" he asked, far too sharply.

"Am I bothering you?" His mother sounded as irritated as he felt.

Jacob counted to ten. "Ma, it's been a long day."

"This won't take long," she said.

He sighed, resigned to hearing another lecture.

"Son, you stopped leading your home years ago and Petra is living proof of its spiritual bankruptcy."

His mother's words cut deeply.

"Petra wants to speak with you," Rosemary said.

"I have nothing to say to her right now, but I'll call when I do."

Rosemary's silence spoke volumes. "Procrastination won't fix your problems or make them go away."

"I'm tired and I don't feel like dealing with any of this right now," Jacob said.

"I'm tired too, but I don't have the luxury of ignoring your daughter. She's in my house."

Jacob cringed. Her point was well taken.

"I'm going to make a cup of tea. Then, I'm going to let the Holy Spirit have His way. His guidance is really all that I need," Rosemary said, hammering her message.

Jacob bristled at the inference. "I'm sure that everything is under control," he said, just wanting the conversation to end.

His mother hung up.

Jacob willed his turbulent emotions to subside. It took awhile before they did. He knew that Petra was better off with his mother. He didn't have the temperament for single parenting, nor did he have any desire to sort out his daughter's issues. But timing in business, as in life was everything, so any discussions about boarding schools would have to wait until his mother was calmer and this storm had passed. With a possible solution in hand, Jacob settled comfortably under the expensive bed covers. Then he promptly fell asleep.

~~~~

Petra still felt dirty even though she'd taken a long hot shower. The stench of embarrassment clung to her damp skin. She wrapped a towel around her slight frame and padded back into her bedroom. Then she began dressing for bed. Pipes clinked and clanked as water from a downstairs faucet flowed through old plumbing. The house sounded and felt wonderfully familiar. She quickly ran down the stairway to see what her grandmother was doing. Once she entered the brightly lit kitchen, she observed blue and yellow flames flickering under a kettle on the stove. Her grandmother indicated for her to sit. Then the older woman took eggs, butter, and milk from the fridge.

"Are you hungry?" her grandmother asked.

Petra nodded.

"Your stomach should tolerate scrambled eggs and dry toast. A cup of hot tea might also help. I know it will definitely settle my nerves," Grandma Rosemary said.

Petra sat quietly while her grandmother fixed dinner. The older woman placed a simple meal on Petra's placemat. After fixing a cup of tea, Grandma Rosemary sat next to Petra at the counter. Not normally a tea drinker, the teen found the beverage surprisingly calming. Petra ate while her grandmother drank two cups of the beverage without uttering a word. After she finished eating, Grandma Rosemary gathered their dirty dishes and placed them in the sink. Then the older woman turned and leaned against the counter. "Now start from the beginning and don't leave anything out."

Petra's eyes watered.

"I've never been moved by tears," Grandma Rosemary said.

"Do I have to do this now?" Petra whined.

Grandma Rosemary glanced over her reading glasses. "Do you have somewhere to go that I don't know about?" she asked.

Petra moaned, "No Ma'am."

"Then start talking."

Petra knew she couldn't lie or could she? Maybe, telling a half-truth would work tonight. Weighing the odds and with nothing else to lose, she plunged headfirst into her story. The truth was there, somewhere.

CHAPTER 8

☩

THE SLEEPY COMMUNITY OF INDIGO BEACH WAS JUST TOO SMALL FOR A TERMINAL, SO BUS riders were dropped off at the local drug store. Having sat behind a raucous family of four during the entire three-hour trip, Morgan was more than ready to get off. She was tired from riding, but at least she'd slept soundly the night before, in her Chicago hotel. Between a crying baby and its cursing father, her nerves were frazzled. Not wanting to experience more of the same at any of her sister's homes, she'd already decided to sleep at her grandmother's cottage, regardless of its condition.

Somehow, the nuances of bus travel had faded from her memory. Jeffery would find humor in this new adventure, but at the present moment, hilarity was lost. She needed a hot bath and a good meal to change her disposition. From letters that her mother had written, she knew that Mamie routinely cleaned the tiny house. Morgan couldn't wait to go home.

The family of four exited first. Morgan grabbed her purse and proceeded down the aisle. She graciously accepted the bus driver's hand when she reached the last step. Her luggage had already been removed from a storage area, beneath the bus. A lone taxi waited in the parking lot. She waved to get the driver's attention. He pulled forward. Morgan didn't recognize his face, but a few questions later she realized that he was locally born. The man and his family lived in a neighboring community.

Morgan leaned back against worn hard seating. This was how she remembered rural living, worn out people living hard lives. It was the very reason that she'd left in the first place. She'd always wanted more. More options. More stability and definitely more money than the area could provide. Now she was home. Streets passed in a blur. The cab driver rambled on about nothing of importance while Morgan stared out the back window wondering whether she'd be tolerated or welcomed by family and friends.

It didn't appear as if much had changed. Blue Star Memorial Highway was still as prosaic as she remembered. Was this an omen? Soon, the taxi maneuvered down the private road and then pulled into her grandmother's driveway. The driver parked. Fresh tire tracks were visible. Morgan smiled. Apparently, her mother had recently visited. After the taxi driver deposited her bags on the front porch, she tipped him generously. Then using the key that she'd had since childhood, she unlocked the front door. The smell of lemon permeated the interior, a good sign.

Morgan heard movement. She frowned. Then she called out. A youthful voice answered. Confused, Morgan walked into the parlor. A young girl was crouched on the floor. The teen's arms were submerged in a bucket of water.

"Who are you?" the teen asked brashly.

"And who might you be?" One of Morgan's delicately plucked eyebrows arched dramatically. "More importantly, why are you scrubbing the floor?"

The girl threw her sponge back into the bucket and leaned back on her thighs. The teen ignored both questions, snapped a wad of gum, and glared.

Realizing that she'd left the front door open, Morgan turned and retrieved her bags. The girl looked familiar, so she tried another approach. "Do you live around here?" she asked.

The adolescent shook her head. "No, I'm staying with my grandma for the summer."

Tired and annoyed, Morgan played the game of cat and mouse begrudgingly. "Who's your grandmother?" she asked.

"Rosemary McDonald," the teen said, between gum snaps.

Morgan grinned. "And your mother?"

"She's dead." The teenager's words were meant to shock, but they didn't.

"Ah, you must be Jacob's daughter," Morgan said.

"You know my dad?" the girl asked surprised.

Morgan nodded. "I know your whole family. And by the way, you still haven't told me why you're hand mopping my grandmother's floor."

The girl's expression remained shuttered.

"I'm sure your story is interesting." Morgan waited for the teen to speak.

"I got trashed and threw-up, right over there," she said, pointing towards the over sized chair. A slight smile crossed Morgan's face. "So cleaning the floor is your punishment?" she asked.

The girl nodded.

Morgan peered closely at the adolescent, sensing a kindred spirit. "Well, since I've wasted precious time asking ridiculous questions, I'll help. Do you have another sponge?" The teenager threw a grocery bag. Morgan caught it easily and removed a sponge. Then she plunged her hands into deceptively cold water. "Whoa, that's freezing."

"Yeah, I know," the teen said.

Morgan gritted her teeth, refusing to become any more irritated than she already was. The duo worked in uncomfortable silence until the adolescent finally spoke.

"I'm Petra."

"Nice to meet you. I'm Morgan Harding."

The girl half grinned. "You're the one who lives out of the country."

This time, Morgan smiled. "I'm surprised that you've heard about me."

Petra looked away, revealing nothing.

"So, why are we using cold water?" she asked.

"The pipes are blown out. It was warmer when we brought it, but it's cold now," Petra said, pointing towards four empty jugs.

"Oh, the cut off valve is in the crawl space," Morgan said.

Petra's eyes grew larger.

Morgan chuckled. "Don't worry. I won't make you crawl under there."

The teen looked relieved.

"So, tell me how you got caught."

"I fell asleep."

"What were you drinking?"

"Beer."

"You got wasted on beer. That was stupid."

The teen became angry. "Whatever," she fired back.

"Well, I've definitely made a few bad decisions in my life," Morgan said.

Petra stared wide-eyed. "And you can admit it?" she asked.

Morgan chuckled. "The only people who can't admit their failures are totally deceived or dead."

Petra huffed in amusement. "Wow, that's deep."

"So, who are you mad at?" Morgan asked.

"My dad."

"Figured as much."

Petra looked quizzically. "Why would you say that? You don't even know me."

"It's a familiar theme. A father can screw up his daughter's life, whether he's in it or not."

"I never thought about it, like that."

"I think about it all of the time," Morgan said, as she plunged her arms back into the cold and lemony smelling water.

CHAPTER 9

✝

THE CORPORATE JET DIPPED AND JERKED FROM TURBULENCE. WHILE OTHER EMPLOYEES OF R. K. International worked quietly or prayed, Jacob gazed out his window, unconcerned. He'd already sent his reports to the home office and thankfully so, because his attention was clearly on other matters.

He and his mother had argued bitterly before takeoff. Miffed at being ignored for three days, she'd voiced displeasure and frustration at his apparent disregard. Having the last word, she'd challenged him to read his Bible and get his heart right before he set one foot into her house. He'd quickly downloaded a Bible application to his smart phone before the plane took off. Now, he was half-heartedly reading scriptures.

Jacob had begun questioning God's Word, soon after his father's death. Pastor Deon had just accepted leadership of New Life Full Gospel Church. At that time, the church membership was reeling from their senior pastor's death. Defiant and insecure, Jacob had become angrier when hormones and disappointment brewed toxicity. Needing comfort and guidance, but too prideful to accept either, he'd steadfastly refused the young pastor's help. Jacob wondered whether his life would have turned out differently, if he had.

The revelation caused him to moan. Alarmed by his behavior, he quickly glanced around the cabin, wondering whether his anguished cry had been heard. A colleague approached.

"You look deep in thought," the woman said. A highly respected member of the company's legal team stood near. She sat across from him in an empty seat. "I'm surprised, you aren't working?"

"I finished my reports last night while the rest of you slackers were drinking tequila at the bar," he joked.

She laughed. However, her sharp, intelligent eyes expressed concern.

"Usually, you join us. What kept you away?" she asked.

Jacob wondered how much he should share. His coworker was a mother. Maybe she could help. "My daughter has been acting out lately," he said, without revealing any details.

The woman grinned. "Daughters will do that, when they're attempting to get their father's attention." The woman leaned forward. "What did she do?"

"She got caught drinking beer," he said.

"How old is she?"

Jacob wanted to crawl into a hole and hide. "Fifteen."

"Probably going on thirty."

Jacob grinned sheepishly. "You know my daughter well."

The woman's grin expanded. "I raised one like her. My husband and I hired a counselor who helped us navigate adolescence. If you're interested, I'll forward the woman's contact information."

A calm exterior masked Jacob's stormy emotions. "I think I have things under control," he said, more confidently than he felt.

The woman chuckled. "I'm sure you do, but I'm curious. When did her behavior start changing?"

Jacob fidgeted. "Right after her mother's death."

"Didn't your father die young?" she asked.

Jacob felt exposed. "Yes, when I was in high school," he said, feeling more unnerved.

"Then you should understand her feelings of abandonment. How did your father's death affect you?" she asked.

Jacob glanced out the plane's window before answering. "I was hurt and angry, but I turned my anger into focus."

The woman nodded. "Well, your daughter is like you in many ways. She is hurt and angry, and she's focused on making your life difficult."

Jacob stared. "I hadn't thought of that."

"I'll text you the counselor's number after we land," the woman said. Then she stood.

Jacob watched the woman amble down the aisle. Then he glanced back out the plane's window. Funny how, he'd never put two and two together. Petra's rebellion mirrored his own. He saw the problem more clearly now, even if he didn't know how to fix it.

CHAPTER 10

✝

DEON MUNCHED ON A DONUT WHILE ROSEMARY DRANK COFFEE. THEY WERE SEATED AT MAMIE Harding's kitchen table. Although Rosemary was a few years older, the peers had known each other since childhood. In a small community, folks just knew each other well. Mamie hadn't always made good lifestyle choices, but Deon appreciated how Rosemary had steadfastly refused to judge. The fact that Mamie's children had different fathers had never mattered to either of them. Deon admired both women's strength.

He glanced around the room. Although, Mamie's furniture was old, many of the items were expensively upholstered. She'd always lived well, even if a man hadn't ever been a permanent fixture in her home.

At fifty-seven, his friend was small in stature, but voluptuously curvy. Dyed blond hair helped disguise her age, even though soft creases in her rounded face didn't. Thankfully, maturity had softened Mamie's appearance and her heart.

"How long is that grandchild of yours going to be with you?" Mamie asked, as she poured more coffee into Rosemary's cup.

"Most of the summer," Rosemary said.

Mamie topped off her own mug. "It sounds like Jacob is passing the buck again."

Rosemary sighed. "If I let him, he'd leave her until she got good and grown.

The friends laughed.

"I'm going to pray your strength in the Lord," Mamie said, waving her hands dramatically.

Deon finished his donut.

Mamie held up the half eaten box. "Want another?" she asked.

He ignored her question. Having already eaten three chocolate covered donuts, if he didn't stop now, the box would soon be empty. Deon whisked crumbs from his shirt and watched them fall to the floor. Mamie shook her head.

Rosemary rolled her eyes. How are the girls?" she asked.

"Well, Morgan is still traipsing in Europe. As you already know, Destiny and the kids are doing fine. Georgie just purchased a new hunting dog and Tonya is fit to tied. Did I mention that Meesha and Grayling are engaged?"

"How's Sara?" Deon asked. As usual, Mamie had neglected to mention her second born.

Mamie looked wistfully out the kitchen window. "I worry about that child the most. I suppose one failure and four successes ain't too bad?"

"No sense in worrying about something that you can't fix. Just keep praying like I do," Rosemary said.

"Deon, are any of my prayers getting through?" Mamie asked.

"A few."

She turned pensive. "I wish I had a do over."

"Me too," Rosemary said, clinking her cup against her dear friend's coffee mug.

"I also wish that I could be a fly on the wall. A couple of my grandbabies are going to give their momma's grief and I want to see it all." Mamie winked at her guests.

"You're preaching to the choir," Rosemary said.

Deon glanced at his watch and stood. "Mamie, I won't have time to fix your window, if I stay any longer."

"Then, let's get you out of here," she said good-naturedly. She led her friends from the kitchen and back into the living room.

"Will you ever sell the cottage?" Deon asked.

"I can't, the house belongs to Morgan."

"I didn't know."

"It's her inheritance. Although, I'm not so sure that she'll ever want to live there again. The Valley is so remote. Frankly, I'm surprised that Petra walked over there. It's at least three miles from your house."

"Three and a half to be exact," Rosemary said.

"How often do you and Morgan speak?" Deon asked.

Mamie closed her eyes. Hurt was visible when they opened. "It's been awhile. You know, Indigo Beach can't compete with Paris and Rome. I keep the house up though."

"We could tell," Rosemary said.

Mamie smiled reflectively. "I'll take care of it until she tells me otherwise."

"Mamie, what do you want to happen?" Deon asked.

"I want my baby to come home. I wasn't the best mother and we have some things to hash out."

"God will bring her home, you'll see." Rosemary said, hugging her friend.

Deon followed Rosemary onto the porch. Then the old friends walked down the steps together.

"Tell Petra I said hi," Mamie hollered, from behind the porch railing.

"I will," Rosemary yelled back.

"Pastor, please give my love to your wife," she yelled cheerfully.

Deon nodded and then entered his Lincoln, wondering how Petra was really fairing. She'd been alone for two whole hours, which was plenty of time for a rebellious teen to get into more trouble. He trailed Rosemary's vehicle closely, as they traveled towards the Valley.

Sparsely populated, the area was located near Lake Michigan's shoreline and contained cottages and large estates. He still had just enough time to fix the latch before his first appointment of the day. Summer had suggested that he accompany Rosemary that morning. She'd also encouraged him to make the repair.

Deon followed Rosemary's car down a private road. She parked. Then he maneuvered his car onto the grass and parked. After exiting her car, Rosemary waited at the base of the porch for him. They climbed the steps together.

"I sure hope that Petra finished cleaning," Rosemary said.

Deon smiled. "It doesn't take rocket science to scrub a floor."

Rosemary grinned. "Oh, I don't know about that."

Deon chuckled.

"How long will the repair take?" she asked.

"Not long."

Muted laughter filtered through the closed door. Deon was startled. Rosemary's face turned explosive. She banged on the door. Minutes later, a younger version of Mamie Harding stood under its threshold. A bright white smile, containing a small yet noticeable gap in the upper front teeth beamed back.

"Rosemary, Pastor Deon," Morgan exclaimed.

"Oh my goodness," Rosemary squealed excitedly. Morgan walked into the older woman's friendly arms. "Child, you look just like your mother," Rosemary said, giving the young woman a quick once over.

Deon gave Morgan a quick hug. Then he and Rosemary followed her through the parlor and into the kitchen. Petra was seated at a table. By the looks of it, more than the parlor floor had been cleaned.

"You turned the water on," Rosemary said, standing by a sink full of sudsy water.

Petra rolled her eyes.

Deon observed the teen's response with amusement.

"You've been busy." Rosemary slid her hand across the dust free counter.

"Rosemary and I just asked your mother about you," Deon said.

The younger woman's shuttered eyes remained neutral. "She doesn't know that I'm back yet."

"That's apparent," Deon said.

Morgan looked away.

Then Rosemary's eyes opened wide. "How long are you going to be in town?"

Deon watched the by-play with interest.

"I really haven't decided," the young woman said.

"Jessica Williams is looking for another part-time clerk." Deon quickly added.

Morgan tipped her head and laughed. "Oh my, I'm a little over qualified for a retail position."

"Well, I'm hiring. My granddaughter obviously needs a sitter and you'd be perfect. You're definitely not overqualified for that job," Rosemary said, as she glared at Petra.

Morgan's eyes twinkled.

Petra appeared guarded.

"You'd really be helping me out. It's either that or she'll have to go to work with me everyday."

Petra moaned. "I'm in the room."

Deon observed the exchange with interest.

"I don't need an answer right now. Just think about it," Rosemary said.

The women exchanged phone numbers.

Suddenly, the room darkened. Deon looked out the kitchen window. "I think a storm is rolling in," he said.

"Are you planning on sleeping here tonight?" Rosemary asked.

Morgan said, "Yes."

"I'd feel better if you stayed at the farm," Deon said, peering up at the sky. Swaying branches swung low and wide as strong winds whipped through the foliage. Trees rustled loudly and ominously.

"I know gas and hot water are turned on, but you don't have any electricity," Rosemary said.

Morgan held up a box of candles and pointed towards a lighter. An uncomfortable silence blanketed the room. "Really folks, I appreciate your concern, but I'm fine. I'll have Mr. Camden come over and check everything out as soon as he's available. I promise."

Rosemary looked skeptical.

Deon continued staring at the sweeping branches. A storm was most definitely brewing.

"Petra, did you apologize for trespassing?" Rosemary asked.

The teen rolled her eyes.

"She doesn't have to," Morgan interjected.

"Oh yes she does, Petra?" Rosemary waited for the teen to respond.

"I'm sorry," she wailed theatrically.

"Petra!" Rosemary snapped.

The fifteen-year-old scowled and then addressed Morgan, much too sweetly, "I'm sorry for entering without permission and for trashing your floor."

Deon stifled laughter.

Frustrated with her granddaughter's half-hearted apology, Rosemary sat down at the table and tapped her shoe on the floor. "Pastor, we'll wait until you finish."

Deon took the hint. "I promised your mother that I'd secure the window."

Petra's face turned bright red.

This time, Morgan refrained from laughing.

"I'll be done in a few minutes," he chirped, as he walked into the back bedroom. Minutes later, the latch popped off without much trouble and it was soon replaced with a newer version. Within minutes, Deon completed the task and reentered the kitchen.

Rosemary and Morgan were chatting quietly. Petra was sprawled across the kitchen table, bored senseless.

"Thank you for everything."

Morgan's graciousness and genuine sincerity contrasted greatly with the air of sophistication, her hair and expensive clothes exuded. Deon was pleased that a hometown girl still existed underneath her expertly applied make-up.

"I can't get you to change your mind," Rosemary asked, one last time before she stood.

Morgan shook her head.

Deon grabbed the young woman's hands in his massive paws. "Call my wife if you need anything."

Morgan grinned.

Deon jotted his wife's number on the back of a business card.

"Don't forget to tell First Lady that you gave her number to me," Morgan said cheekily.

"I won't."

As Deon followed Rosemary and Petra from the cottage, he sensed Morgan's overwhelming sadness. The poor child was troubled. He asked the Holy Spirit to mend her broken heart. Then he thanked Him for his wife. As a result of her simple suggestion, he now had front row seating to God's masterful plan of deliverance.

Deon entered his car, pondering Mamie's secrets. No doubt about it,

Morgan's return was ordained. With certainty, closely guarded confidences would soon be revealed. And when they were, Indigo Beach would never be the same. Deon drove back to his office, with a knowing smile plastered across his face.

CHAPTER 11

☩

MORGAN WAS WEARY. IT HAD TAKEN EVERY BIT OF FORTITUDE THAT SHE POSSESSED TO REMAIN cordial to Rosemary McDonald and Pastor Deon Bradford during their visit. When all she really wanted was a bath and her grandmother's feather bed. Thankfully, her mom had laundered and sealed Grandma Grace's best linens in airtight containers. They'd smelled fresh and familiar when she and Petra had taken them out. Morgan lit a candle and walked into the bathroom. Light barely filtered in through a dirt-covered window. Her mom had beautifully maintained the inside of the cottage, but the outside was a different story.

Pastor Deon was right. A storm was coming. Menacing clouds peaked through the canopy of trees that surrounded the tiny house. Dark shadows danced on the cheerless walls. In spite of it's dark and dreary interior, her childhood home felt peaceful. She could never sell this house. Too many memories were intertwined with hopeful longing.

Morgan had spent her childhood cocooned in isolation, a place where she'd been unconditionally loved. The men in her mother's life hadn't wanted perceptive eyes to witness their transgressions, so she'd been sent away. This tiny cottage had become her refuge.

No one understood why she hadn't come home for Grandma Grace's funeral. How could she explain that her grandmother's death had come on the heels of Edward's messy divorce and Mona's chemotherapy treatments? In the span of months, her well-organized life had fallen apart.

She'd hidden in Europe and clung tightly to Jeffery and Mona's friendship. Mona had begged her to return home. She'd rejected each and every attempt. Even while losing her own battle to cancer, Mona had comforted Morgan, as best she could. In those final days of her life, Mona taught Morgan that sin came with a price. A principle her mother had neglected to teach.

Thinking back, very little had ever-escaped Mona's shrewd observation. The older woman had instinctually known when she and Edward's affair had ended, mere months after it had begun. She hadn't been concerned when Morgan received a ten-carat diamond for the completion of the Beijing project. Nor was she surprised when Edward presented Morgan with a five carat ruby necklace for weeks spent finalizing the Singapore deal. Mona knew that the gifts were acknowledgement of long hours spent strategizing and planning. Unlike the press, which sensationalized the amounts of money Edward purportedly spent on his paramour. Mona always knew that Morgan had worked hard for the bonuses that she'd received and not from lying on her back. She and her mother were different in that regard.

Mamie had been the other woman multiple times, always associating with older wealthy men who didn't mind spending quiet weekends in the country with the honey brown knockout. Throughout Morgan's childhood, uncles came and went.

Grandma Grace parented all of her grandchildren until they reached adulthood. When middle age limited her options, Mamie morphed into Momma Harding as everyone in town called her. Just like her mother had done, she now lived peacefully in the country, helping to raise every child her own daughters brought home.

Morgan closed the faded bedroom curtains and walked back into the kitchen. Every room held memories, mostly good. A kitchen candle flickered yellow, white and gold. The house smelled of bleach and lemon. She soon found her favorite blanket, buried at the bottom of the linen closet. It's discolored fabric evoked happier times. The smell of fabric softener was soothing. Morgan curled up in the overstuffed chair that sat in the parlor. She draped the blanket across her lap. How many times had her grandmother rocked her fears away, in this very chair? Her phone rang. She answered.

"I've been waiting for your call," Jeffery said.

Smiling, Morgan pulled the blanket closer to her chin and snuggled comfortably under its weight.

"I'm sorry, I should have called hours ago, but I walked into the most interesting situation," she said.

"I can't wait to hear all about it, but first tell me about your bus ride."

"Oh my, where do I begin?" she said, still chuckling. Morgan told Jeffery about her travels and exploits. Their conversation was animated and relaxed. However, jet lag soon took its toll. She was tired, so very tired.

"So, what do you think about Rosemary's offer?" Jeffery asked.

"I don't know, what are your thoughts?"

"Pray about it."

"No, seriously, what should I do?" she asked.

"Ask God for guidance. It's time that you learned to trust Him."

"I've been let down by so many men. You can't possibly expect me to trust a Father that I don't know?"

"I do, because if you don't, you won't be able to trust any man."

"I don't know if I can."

"But you must."

"So now you're a coach," Morgan said sarcastically.

Jeffery sighed. "Whatever you call me, I'll thankfully answer."

Life was strange. Something quite good and wholesome had come from her brief but sordid affair with Edward. She valued Jeffery's friendship.

"I call you friend," she said.

"Good, let's leave it at that."

"You haven't given me an answer," Morgan said.

"I don't plan to, God will."

"All right, I'll pray and wait. *Au revoir Jeffery.*"

"*Au revoir Morgan.* I'll call you later in the week," Jeffery said, before disconnecting.

Morgan wearily stared at the wall. Rosemary's offer held allure, but did she really want to babysit a petulant teen for the better part of the summer. Morgan took Jeffery's advice and prayed. Her prayer was simple, heartfelt and pure. When exhaustion finally took over, she slept deeply. A flame flickered, danced, and bobbed in a lantern that set on the floor, by the overstuffed chair.

CHAPTER 12

✝

AS PETRA RODE IN HER GRANDMOTHER'S CAR, HER CURIOSITY WAS PEAKED. GRANDMA Rosemary appeared preoccupied and Petra wondered why. She hoped that Morgan was the reason and not that she'd angered her grandmother again. Petra wasn't happy about having a sitter, but if she had to have one, Morgan would do. She'd actually enjoyed their brief time together.

"Are you hungry?" Grandma Rosemary asked.

Petra nodded.

"Good, then you won't drag your feet about preparing dinner tonight."

Petra sighed. As punishment, she had to cook dinner for a month.

"I'll help you as soon as I locate Leroy's new number for Morgan. I forgot to mention that it had changed."

Petra now understood why her grandmother had been so quiet in the car. She flipped on the kitchen light, washed her hands, and then placed a bag of russet potatoes and a large pot on the counter, before grabbing a potato peeler from the drawer. She was busily working when her grandmother reentered the room a short time later.

"Do I really have to fix dinner every night?" she asked.

Grandma Rosemary ignored her question, washed her hands, and then proceeded to open the refrigerator. After grabbing steaks covered in brown paper, she closed the door. Then she said, "Yes." Grandma Rosemary placed the package of meat near the sink. "Finish what you're doing. Then I'm going to show you how to grill tonight."

Petra moaned. "Will I have to touch that meat?" she asked, noticing her grandmother's sly expression.

"Yes."

She moaned again.

Grandma Rosemary chuckled. "I suggest you fix your face. You brought all of this on yourself."

Sulking, Petra stomped to the sink, rinsed the peeled potatoes, and then trudged to the stove. She placed the pot of potatoes on a back burner and then asked, "What's next?"

"Season the meat." Her grandmother's response was succinct.

Petra stared at the raw beef in disgust, fully understanding why no one in the family ever crossed Grandma Rosemary. It just wasn't worth it. Less than an hour later, dinner was prepared and the two women were seated at the dining room table. Nausea churned, every time Petra thought about the bloody meat that she'd repeatedly touched. Grandma Rosemary had found the whole situation amusing. Petra sat at the table, scowling.

"Cheer up, the worst is over," Grandma Rosemary said. The older woman passed the platter of steaks.

The teen speared a smaller piece with her fork. "I think I'm going to become vegan," she said.

"You can make that decision when you're older, but for now, everyone living under my roof eats meat," Grandma Rosemary said, selecting a juicy rib eye.

Petra took a bite. "Wow, this is really good."

Grandma Rosemary smiled. "A good cut of beef doesn't need much more than kosher salt, cracked pepper, and butter," she explained.

Petra plunged a forkful of mashed potatoes into her mouth.

"Still want to be vegan?" her grandmother asked. Her eyes twinkled.

Petra shook her head. "No, not really."

Grandma Rosemary nodded. "So what did you think of Morgan?"

Petra had wondered when her grandmother would bring up this subject. "She's cool."

"How so?"

The teen shrugged. "She's easy to talk to."

"Really, what did you girls talk about?" Grandma Rosemary asked, between bites.

Petra hesitated, wondering just how much information she should share.

"I told her about yesterday."

"Did you tell her about all the drinking that you've been doing?" Grandma Rosemary asked.

Alarmed, Petra stared at her grandmother, wondering how she knew. "Wha, what are you talking about?" she stammered.

Grandma Rosemary peered over her glasses. "This isn't my first trip to a rodeo," she said straight-faced.

Petra glowered.

"I knew your mother drank heavily, but I looked the other way. There's no reason to believe that you haven't inherited some of her bad habits. Did you tell Morgan the truth?" she asked.

Petra put her fork down, realizing that there was no point in lying. She nodded.

But instead of getting angry, Grandma Rosemary looked pleased. "Good, if she accepts the job, she'll do just fine." Then she dipped another piece of meat in melted butter.

Petra sighed.

"Petra," Grandma Rosemary said.

"Yes."

"I love you."

"I love you too," the teen said. Petra was surprised by her grandmother's admission.

"I won't lie to you, I wasn't happy when your father decided to send you here, but I am now."

Petra was happy too, because in this moment her grandmother made her feel celebrated, which her father rarely did. Petra's face flushed angrily. She felt her grandmother staring.

"Is there something, you want to talk about?" Grandma Rosemary asked.

The teen groaned. The woman was too perceptive. "No," she said.

"I'm a very good listener." Her grandmother took another bite of steak and waited.

Grandma Rosemary's offer was tempting. Her mother's secrets were a tremendous burden and Petra was tired of being a secret keeper. She shoved another forkful of potatoes into her mouth. When she looked up, her grandmother was staring again. Grandma Rosemary always knew stuff and try as she might, the teen just couldn't figure out how, so she quickly looked away.

CHAPTER 13

☙ ✝ ❧

JACOB WALKED INTO THE CONDOMINIUM AND PLACED HIS SUITCASE ON THE FLOOR BY THE MAIN entrance. His housekeeper had left a stack of mail on the credenza. He thumbed through envelopes as he walked up the hallway. The house was silent and it felt odd tonight. He paused in front of Petra's bedroom door and peaked in. The room was awash in color. Purple and pink contrasted with teal and black. Dolls and high tech electronics coexisted.

Petra had always been a handful. Intelligent and impetuous, she was a typical only child. She was spoiled, assertive and opinionated. He loved her fiercely. When Pastor Deon had called from the cottage, he'd asked Jacob to alter his summer travel plans. Jacob had rejected the suggestion outright, but after mulling over the request, he was starting to rethink his decision. His career really wasn't more important than his daughter. The Kennedy Group could do without him for a few weeks.

His administrative assistant had rescheduled three different trips. Since Jacob was used to working from remote locations, conducting business from Indigo Beach wouldn't be a problem.

After emptying out his suitcase, he quickly began repacking for his trip to Michigan. His administrative assistant had also set up an appointment with Pastor Deon. They were meeting in the morning. He had questions for the preacher. Years ago, he hadn't allowed the inexperienced minister to help, but he was hopeful.

After ordering dinner from the concierge, Jacob sprawled across his bed and waited. The view of Lake Michigan from this height was breathtaking. He grabbed his Bible and began reading. Then his phone rang.

"Hey Ma, what's up?" he asked.

"I called to apologize. I was very short with you this morning."

"No worries, you told me to read my Bible and that's what I've been doing."

"Really," Rosemary said, sounding pleased.

"Yes Ma'am, I've even taken a few notes," Jacob said jokily.

"How's it going?"

"I'm not sure."

"Jacob, believers must hear, read, and do the Word of God."

"Ma."

"Keep studying and God will reveal solutions to all of your problems," she said.

"Is this another lecture?" Jacob asked, becoming irritated.

"Not from me, but when the Holy Spirit speaks, I suggest that you listen."

Jacob knew that his mother was right. Even his father had relied heavily on her spiritual advice. "Is there anything else?" he asked.

"No, drive safely tomorrow and Petra sends her love."

The call ended.

Jacob wondered about his mother's last comment. Did his daughter really love him? Her actions said otherwise, but maybe his did too. The doorbell chimed. Jacob's stomach rumbled loudly as he padded down the hallway. While he walked, he pondered something that he'd just read. The Israelites repeatedly turned their back on God, but God loved them anyway. Jacob didn't understand that kind of love, but it was something to consider.

CHAPTER 14

✝

FROM HIS OPEN DOOR, DEON WATCHED PETRA FILE PAPERS. ROSEMARY HAD PLACED A DESK IN the corner of the outer office, where the teen could work. Since Rosemary still hadn't heard from Morgan, she and her granddaughter came early and left around noon each day. Summer stopped by as soon as her farm tasks were completed. She answered the church phone, so that Deon could get a few hours of work completed without interruption. As usual, his wife was a blessing.

"Grandma, can we leave now?" Petra asked, clearly bored with her task.

Deon chuckled.

"We'll get out of here when Sister Summer arrives."

Deon heard footsteps. Which was odd, since his only scheduled appointment was later in the day. Minutes later, Morgan entered the outer office.

"Good morning Rosemary," she said.

"Morning Morgan, Rosemary greeted the young woman warmly.

Deon quickly walked into the outer office, not wanting to miss a single word of their conversation. "Blessings to you Morgan," he bellowed.

"Good morning Pastor."

Morgan looked rested and relaxed. She grinned at Petra who remained seated. Deon stared, trying to figure out why the woman looked different. Then it donned on him. Thick, naturally curly hair had replaced her long straight weave. Without false eyelashes and heavy makeup, Morgan actually appeared refreshingly young and unpretentious. Deon caught Rosemary's admiring smile. Apparently, she liked the transformation too.

"You look different," Petra blurted out.

"Child, don't be rude," Rosemary admonished.

Morgan just laughed. "It's okay, I'm still getting used to my new look too."

"I really like your natural curls. They're flattering and youthful," Rosemary said.

Deon nodded agreeably.

"Thank you," Morgan said, seemingly embarrassed by the attention.

"Morgan, why are you here?" Petra asked.

Rosemary cut her eyes at her granddaughter.

"I came to give your grandmother my answer. I'm just sorry that it took me so long."

"Are you going to accept?" the teen asked.

Deon leaned against the doorframe, enjoying the conversation.

"I won't take payment, but I'll gladly help out," she explained.

Deon's grin widened.

"So, you're accepting my offer?" Rosemary asked.

Petra's eyes glazed excitedly.

"Yes, I am."

"Can I at least reimburse you for incidentals?" Rosemary asked.

Morgan nodded. "That sounds reasonable."

"So we have a deal?"

"Yes we do," Morgan said. Then she turned and faced the teen. "Are you sure, that you want to spend the rest of your summer with me?

Papers scattered across Petra's desk, when she stood. "Yes, can we go now?" the teen asked.

Deon walked towards Morgan and clasped her hands. "It's good seeing you again," he said. Her shielded eyes hid very little from him. "Since you're going to be in town for awhile, I'll expect to see you at Sunday morning service."

"Rather pushy aren't you?" Morgan said grinning.

"Always, and by the way, you need to go and visit your mother. She's worried about you."

Morgan's face remained shuttered. "I'll think about it."

"Fair enough," he said, while rocking on the heels of his shoes.

"Can we leave now?" Petra moaned.

Morgan looked questioningly at Rosemary.

"You're free to go, just have her home by five. She's preparing dinner again tonight."

"Grandma," Petra groaned.

"Watch yourself," Rosemary warned.

Morgan appeared amused. "I'll have her back long before then." She waited for the teen to gather her belongings. "Cooking, huh, I want to hear all about it, once we're in the car."

Deon waited until he heard the back door shut, before he spoke. "Well, the plot thickens." His bushy eyebrows scrunched theatrically, as he talked.

Rosemary smiled. "Pastor, don't forget that I have a dentist appointment tomorrow."

"Take your time. I'm going to be in a meeting all morning, so you won't need to be in the office until around two o'clock. Now that Petra is gone, will you work your normal hours today?" he asked.

"I'll stay as long as you need me," she said.

"Perfect, I'll call and ask Summer to bring us lunch. Grab those fancy folders that you like using. We're going to assemble the Vacation Bible School handouts in my office." The pair worked until all of Deon's projects were completed. By four o'clock in the afternoon, Rosemary was preparing to leave. "I wonder how the girl's afternoon went?" he asked.

"I was just thinking the same thing. Pastor, do you have a moment?" Rosemary asked.

Deon walked into the outer office and sat. He faced his assistant. "Always for you."

Rosemary half-heartedly smiled. She hesitated before speaking. "As much as I enjoyed motherhood, I wanted all of my children gone from the house as soon as they turned eighteen, but I sometimes wonder if I pushed a few of them away too soon. After my husband died, Neville stepped up and helped me with the younger kids, but once he left for college, I expected Jacob to fill his older brother's shoes and he struggled. Unfortunately, I was so busy working, that I didn't realize my second born was floundering and losing faith."

Deon pulled his chair closer to her desk. "Rosemary, hind site is always revealing, but you can't live in the past. God is giving you an opportunity to fix a few things. Follow His lead. Things will work out."

She squared her shoulders. "I've been beating myself up over this mess."

"Wasted energy," Deon said, glancing at his watch. "You better leave now or the girls will make it home before you do."

Rosemary grabbed her purse and stood. "You're right."

Deon watched her scurry down the hallway. Then he leaned back in his chair. After rubbing his achy knees, he slowly stood, and walked back into his office. He grabbed his Bible and quickly looked over notes that he'd prepared. Deon thanked God for grace. It was a gift that he never took for granted. Then he waited patiently for his last appointment to arrive.

CHAPTER 15

✥

EDWARD FELT OVERWHELMED. HE LOOKED AT THE STACK OF FOLDERS ON HIS DESK AND SIGHED. He desperately missed Morgan. His life hadn't been the same since she'd left. For five years, she'd evaluated potential deals and made strategic recommendations. Now she was gone and he was lost.

He was also furious with Jeffery for escorting her back to the States. He'd left his business partner a scathing message. Now, his long time friend was ignoring his calls and he really needed his advice.

Although, he'd pushed Morgan into leaving, Edward hadn't expected her immediate compliance or the unbridled guilt that he was feeling. He slammed his fists on the bureau, frustrated with how things were turning out.

Admittedly, he was jealous of his friend. Jeffery had a wonderful relationship with all of his children. Each was training for leadership positions within The Kennedy Group, businesses that Jeffery independently owned. Sadly, Edward's own children hated him. He hadn't spoken with either in years. Morgan had tried intervening, but he'd refused any assistance. With maturity beyond her years, she'd seen things he hadn't. He had so many regrets.

His first wife was in her sixties, the quintessential grandmother, beautiful, stately, and serenely competent. His second wife was twenty years younger. She was a shrew that he despised. His wives were women he'd manipulated and come to hate. Morgan was different. Indifferent and independent, she kicked intimidation in the teeth, and was now besting him at every turn.

His new lover was dull and uninteresting, but he didn't care. She was young and he felt even younger laying beside her. Hedonism now ruled, but alas, he had a business to run, so Edward focused on the folders scattered across his desk. Behind the scenes, Morgan had helped mastermind R. K. International's explosive growth. She'd handled the European operations while Jeffery managed stateside accounts. Edward didn't trust his closest executives to give him the answers that he needed. Unfortunately, a decision had to be made today. He threw caution to the wind and dialed a junior administrator.

"Get the contract signed," he said.

"Yes, Mr. Rousseau, I'll take care of it right away."

Edward glanced at his watch. If he left the office now, he could spend time with Cherie before his next appointment. He closed his laptop and locked his office door. His administrative assistant looked up when he passed her desk.

"I'll be back in an hour."

"Yes, Mr. Rousseau," she said.

Edward walked down a lonely hallway. Then he entered his private elevator. It ascended to the penthouse apartment above.

CHAPTER 16

✠

PETRA WAS IMPRESSED WITH MORGAN'S SUV. ITS LUSCIOUS INTERIOR WAS SLEEK AND HIGH tech. More importantly, the car smelled new. Dry air stung her exposed limbs as it whipped through the open windows. Freedom felt wonderful.

"Did it cost a lot?" she asked.

Morgan looked sideways. "What did you say?"

"Did the car cost a lot?" Petra yelled.

Morgan smiled. "It didn't cost an arm or a leg, just a foot," she joked.

Petra giggled. "It's beautiful," the teen hollered.

Morgan chuckled as she lowered sunglasses to the bridge of her nose. "I have one more errand to run, but we'll need to hurry. I have to get you home by five o'clock."

Petra nodded. The duo had gone shopping in Holland, a neighboring community.

"Are you rich?" the teen asked.

"Does it matter?"

"No, I was just curious," she said.

Morgan smiled. "I've done all right for myself, but that's not why I won't take money from your grandmother."

Petra held her hair in one hand, to keep it from whipping into her mouth. So why aren't you," she asked.

"Friendship can't be bought," Morgan said, glancing sideways.

Petra watched farmland roll by as they traveled. "I'm really sorry about everything."

49

"I know, and that's why I accepted your grandmother's offer. I probably should have responded sooner, but I had to get my life together first," Morgan said, patting the car's dashboard affectionately.

"Where are we going now?" Petra asked.

"To a home improvement center, I've hired Leroy to remodel my kitchen and bath."

"I thought that Mr. Leroy worked for Mrs. Williams."

"He does, part-time, this is a side job for him," Morgan said.

"Grandma Rosemary says that he is really talented."

"Yes he is, and I can't wait to see how the travertine will look on the cottage's floor."

Petra frowned.

Morgan smiled. "It's an expensive stone that you, my young protégée are going to help me pick out. I can tell that you have an eye for color."

"How?" the teen asked.

Morgan chuckled. "I read people really well and your bold choice of orange and turquoise today speaks volumes," she said, glancing at the young girl's outfit.

Petra grinned from ear to ear. "My mom always said that I was creative. The teen watched soft curly tendrils whip across Morgan's face, as the wind circulated through the vehicle. "Morgan, how old were you when you started drinking?" she asked, truly curious.

Morgan momentarily took her eyes off the road. "About your age, why?"

"Just wondering."

"By eighth grade, I'd already smoked weed and run away from home," Morgan said. Her hands remained on the steering wheel and she continued looking forward

"You had?"

"Uh-huh."

"Did you get caught?" Petra asked.

Morgan nodded. "You bet I did and Grandma Grace tore my butt up. You better be thankful that your grandmother doesn't believe in corporal punishment. Because, if you'd pulled your stupid stunt with Grandma Grace, you'd still be feeling it."

Petra's eyes enlarged. "Really?"

"Yes really," Morgan said, as she parked her car. "Come on, we're short on time."

Petra climbed out, slammed the passenger door, and raced to keep up with her new friend.

Morgan entered the store and disappeared down an aisle. "Petra, I'm over here," she hollered.

Awe struck, the teen caught up with her. Morgan was commanding. Within minutes, sales associates and the store manager were scrambling to locate tile samples and paint color swatches. Petra had never experienced this kind of focused chaos before. Being with Morgan was exciting, and the exhilaration she felt wasn't like a buzz from alcohol. Thirty minutes later, the duo left the store with brochures and tile samples. Relaxed and happy, Petra languidly leaned against the car's seating as they drove home. "That was fun," Petra said, breaking the silence.

"Yes it was and we got a lot accomplished," Morgan said.

"Do you ever get scared?" Petra asked.

Morgan's answer was measured. "Absolutely, why?"

"You seem so in control."

Morgan appeared thoughtful. "Some people see snow covered peaks and become frightened, but mountains excite me. I always picture myself on top."

Petra pondered Morgan's statement as the SUV rolled down the highway. Her mom had lived fearfully, which wasn't living at all. Her father's chauvinism had strangled her mother's creativity. Petra grew angrier as she reflected on her parent's marriage and her mother's untimely death.

"What's the matter?" Morgan asked.

Petra blanketed her face, mindful that Morgan was as perceptive as her grandmother.

"Nothing."

"You can tell me," Morgan said, gently prying.

Petra slumped against the car seat. "I don't know where to start."

"The beginning is usually a good place."

Petra rolled her eyes. Morgan's offer held allure, but she hesitated.

"I'm waiting," Morgan said, with theatrical flair.

Petra turned sideways and faced her new friend. "My dad thinks he knows everything," she moaned, for affect.

"Most men do, it's in their DNA. How does that make you feel?" Morgan asked.

Petra hadn't counted on the older woman's level headed response. "It makes me angry," she said.

"Do you believe that men are smarter than women?" Morgan asked.

Petra shook her head vigorously. "No, but my dad does. He made my mom feel stupid."

Morgan covered Petra's hand with her own. "Sometimes people use degrees, titles and attitude to hide insecurity. I wouldn't be too hard on him. Everyone has failings."

"But he treated my mom horribly," Petra wailed.

"Your mother gave her power away. So she's partially to blame for how she lived. You're smart and creative. Don't let anyone, including your father tell you otherwise."

"Have you ever given your personal power away?" Petra asked.

Morgan's face clouded. "I've tried not to."

"But have you?" Petra asked, needing to know.

Morgan sighed. "I have," she said honestly.

Petra leaned back. "Let me know when you've figured it all out."

Morgan smiled.

Petra was a fighter. That's why she and her dad butted heads so often. Her mother had called her a wild child, often enough and Morgan was correct. Her mother had given up. Petra had no intention of following in her mother's footsteps. She would never abdicate control. Her dad would never break her spirit, ever.

CHAPTER 17

❦ † ❧

JACOB GRABBED HIS LUGGAGE FROM THE TRUNK OF HIS BMW. HE'D JUST ARRIVED AND PARKED in front of his mother's house. The drive from Chicago had been tolerable until he'd reached the city limits. Then negative memories assaulted him.

Thinking of Lillian usually provoked these feelings. He had so many regrets. He'd never given his late wife the opportunity to travel abroad. Instead, he'd religiously demanded that they make their annual pilgrimage to Indigo Beach. Dreams deferred had caused much of his wife's misery. Eventually, she'd stopped asking and he hadn't cared.

Remorse weighed heavily, as Jacob walked across his mother's front lawn. He glanced at the manicured yards and freshly painted houses that lined the street. His life had never mirrored the simplicity of his childhood, with its predictability and comfort. Jacob placed his bags on the front porch and unlocked the door. The house was silent when he entered. His mother, like many other residents in town didn't use a security system, so nothing beeped or chirped when the door opened.

After climbing the stairs, Jacob deposited his bags on a stand in his old bedroom. Twin beds balanced the room. He and his older brother's awards still hung on the walls. Walking closer, he read inscriptions. Neville had dominated sports. Jacob's academic recognitions hung nearby. Framed certificates and faded ribbons coexisted. Not much had changed in this room. Neville's effervescent personality was overshadowing his accomplishments. Even after all of these years, Jacob felt inferior.

Now, the brothers competed in other areas. Neville was a phenomenal dad and he had two great kids to prove his worth. Respectful and well mannered, neither teen had given their parents a moment of grief. The kids loved the Lord and the entire extended family routinely celebrated their successes.

As usual, Jacob fell short. Petra was an adequate student, who had little interest in areas he valued. Truthfully, he didn't understand his only daughter. Her weaknesses and strengths, likes and dislikes were a mystery to him. Much to his annoyance, Neville was still on top.

Jacob stretched across his bed. Then he plumped his pillows. The soft cushions felt heavenly beneath his head. The freshly laundered bed linens smelled wonderful and he luxuriated in their familiarity. After draping a downy comforter over his feet, Jacob settled back and relaxed. It didn't take long before sleep blanketed the room. A short time later, snoring reverberated down the hallway.

CHAPTER 18

✝

DEON PULLED SUMMER CLOSER. WITH FINGERS INTERTWINED, THE COUPLE HELD HANDS AS THEY drove towards the grocery store. The Lincoln cruised smoothly down the country road. Spending time with his wife was a rare treat. So Deon was taking full advantage of the bright sunny day and cloudless sky.

"Deon, I must say, I'm jealous of Rosemary's ingenuity."

"Did I miss something?" he asked.

Summer smiled indulgently. "Honey, I'm talking about Petra's punishment. Have you been listening to me?"

"Oh that," he said guiltily, because he hadn't been listening at all.

"I wish I'd thought of it when my girls were younger."

Deon parked in the lot. "Oh, I'm sure your punishments were just as creative." He walked around the car and opened the passenger door for his wife.

Summer held onto his arm. "Thank you darling," she crooned. Her voice was smooth and buttery.

Deon blushed.

"Honey, I almost wet my pants when Rosemary told me about Petra's aversion to raw meat. That story is priceless," Summer prattled.

Smiling wryly, Deon followed his wife into the store. "You and I both know that Petra will be whipped into shape very soon."

Summer pulled a cart from the rack. "I wish I could be a fly on Rosemary's wall."

"'That child has bitten off more than she can chew," Deon said, as he waved to a couple of parishioners.

"She'll figure it out soon enough," Summer said, as she pushed the cart towards the can goods aisle. As they approached, the couple saw Mamie Harding bending low. "Mamie, do you need any help? Summer asked.

"I just might, if I stay down here much longer."

"Deon, just don't stand there. Help the woman out," Summer squealed.

Deon reached down and pulled his friend to her feet.

"Phew, I wasn't sure that I'd make it," Mamie said, as she rubbed out wrinkles in her top. Today she was wearing an oversized button up shirt over black leggings. Black ballerina shoes completed her outfit.

Deon liked the ensemble and thought about buying something similar for his wife. "My arthritis bothers me when the weather changes, but my joints stopped hurting when I lost some weight," he said, making a point.

Summer glared.

Mamie ignored the dig. "Shouldn't you be working?" she asked.

Summer grabbed cans off the shelf and placed them in the couple's basket.

"Yes, but I'm spending the morning with my wife, which is far more enjoyable." Deon noticed dark circles were hanging low under Mamie's eyes. He grew concerned.

"You couldn't have found someplace more romantic?" she said.

He threw up his hands in surrender.

"Since I normally shop alone, I thought that his offer was sweet," Summer said, coming to her husband's defense.

Deon grinned smugly.

"Honey, don't forget to tell Mamie about Morgan's visit," Summer interjected.

Mamie looked questioningly at Deon.

"There's not much to tell. Your daughter dropped by the office yesterday."

Mamie appeared sad. "She's visited quite a few people in town, but not me."

Deon grew reflective. "Have the two of you ever been close?" he asked.

"When she was younger." Mamie's voice trembled. "You know, Momma really raised her," she said.

"That's what I remembered, she'll come calling soon."

Mamie looked skeptical. "I don't know about that."

"She will because I told her too."

"Deon, you're the best."

He grinned mischievously. "Mamie Harding, I think you just gave me a compliment."

"Deon, why did Morgan stop by the office?"

"Rosemary has her watching Petra for the next six weeks."

"Lordy, God is good!" Mamie exclaimed excitedly.

"Yes He is," Deon said.

Summer indicated that she was ready to leave the aisle.

"Mamie, it was good talking with you," Deon said, as the couple began walking away.

Mamie waved. Deon waved back.

"Honey, hiring Morgan was a stroke of genius," Summer said, as she pushed their cart towards the cereal aisle.

"Yes it was." Deon grabbed two boxes off the shelf. After reading their labels, he threw the sugary laden cereals into their cart.

"Really Deon," Summer said, shaking her head.

He quickly tossed an additional box of frosted covered oats into the cart, for good measure. Then he followed Summer as she maneuvered their cart towards the produce section of the store. Gleefully, Summer dumped bags of apples, oranges and pears on top of Deon's cereal. He smirked.

"What are you up to?" she asked.

"Nothing," he said innocently.

"Yes you are, I can feel it."

Deon walked towards a freezer and pulled out two containers of ice cream.

"Deon!" Summer yelped.

Disregarding her over-the-top response, he grabbed a third tub and gently placed all three containers into their basket. "Woman, my cholesterol is normal and I've lost five pounds."

"But it won't stay that way for long, if you keep this up," she snapped. Summer moved Deon aside, grabbed the cart's handle, and pushed it towards the cashier.

"We need to shop together more often," he said, purposely goading his wife.

Summer glared. "Is that so," she said, putting items on the conveyer belt.

"This experience has been rewarding and most enjoyable," Deon said, as he helped Summer empty out their cart.

The clerk rang up their order and bagged their items. Then Summer swiped her debit card. "It certainly would have been cheaper if you'd stayed home," she said, after glancing at the receipt.

"Probably, but think of all the fun that you would've missed."

Summer moaned.

Tickled beyond measure, Deon pushed their overloaded grocery basket out the door.

CHAPTER 19

†

MORGAN DROVE TOWARDS THE COTTAGE. SHE MUCH PREFERRED TRAVELING ON BLUE STAR
Memorial Highway than navigating the interstate. The tree lined road
meandered alongside Lake Michigan's beautiful shoreline. The scenic view
was even more breathtaking than she remembered.

Spending the afternoon with Petra had been both entertaining and eye
opening. The teen was smart and wise beyond her years, but hungered for
validation. Morgan could relate, but as the afternoon progressed, Morgan
also realized that they shared similarities in temperament and creativity.

As an only child, Petra had been needlessly burdened with the weight of
her parents' dysfunctional marriage. Lillian had blurred the lines between
motherhood and friend. She'd unknowingly saddled her daughter with
problems. Petra was still grieving and clearly, Jacob didn't know how to
help his daughter, since he didn't understand the depth of her anger or rage.
Imposing his unbending will on his strong-minded and defiant child was
making a bad situation even worse.

Morgan planned to offer friendship. It was the least that she could do.
She would offer Petra the same kind of unconditional love and kindness
that Mona and Jeffery had given to her years before. Morgan dialed Jeffery's
number. His voice came through the speaker system of her car.

"Dear friend, how are you doing?" she asked.

"I'm well today, thank you for asking."

Morgan smiled. Then she glanced at Petra, who had fallen asleep. The
teen's head rested comfortably against the window glass.

"Is everything all right?" he asked.

"Yes, I accepted Rosemary's offer."

"Wonderful!" Jeffery sounded pleased.

"I'm not accepting payment," she said.

"That's even better."

Hearing Jeffery's approval was all the encouragement that Morgan needed. "I believe that I can help."

"From what you've shared, I know you can," he said.

"How is Edward doing?"

Jeffery answered slowly. "We aren't talking at the moment."

"This is all my fault," Morgan said.

"Not this time."

"How young is she?" Morgan asked, knowing that only a woman could get Jeffery this upset.

"Barely legal," he said gruffly.

Morgan exhaled. "I'll pray."

"That's all that any of us can do." Jeffery's steadfast faith was encouraging. "Are you settled yet?" he asked.

Morgan happily regaled her mentor with remodeling plans, community gossip, and a few deeply held desires.

"Being home has been good for you. You sound happy," he said.

"So far so good."

"Have you spoken with your mother yet?" he asked.

"No, I haven't had time," Morgan said, telling a half-truth.

"When you're ready, you will. By the way, check your email. I want your thoughts on a business I'd like to purchase."

"This sounds intriguing. I'll read it when I get home, *Au revoir Jeffery.*"

"*Au revoir Morgan*, call if you need me."

"I will," she said, before disconnecting.

CHAPTER 20

✝

JACOB SLOWLY AWAKENED. ONCE HIS VISION CLEARED, HE SAW HIS MOTHER STANDING IN THE doorway.

"What time is it?" Jacob stretched and yawned.

"Almost five o'clock."

He swung his legs over the side of the bed. Then he rubbed both hands over his face.

"Tired?" she asked.

He continued massaging his chin. "It's been a long week."

Rosemary walked into the room and sat on the opposite twin bed. "How long are you staying?"

"I was thinking about three weeks."

"That's fine." His mother leaned forward and kissed his forehead. Her touch brought back a flood of childhood memories.

"Where's Petra?" he asked.

"She's with Morgan Harding. They're on their way home."

The name rang a bell, but Jacob couldn't place her face. "Isn't she on punishment?" he asked.

Rosemary stood. "Since you ignored us while you were in Mexico, I wasn't able to tell you about my offer to Morgan or her acceptance. We'll talk later."

Jacob ignored his mother's dig. He stood and began unpacking, but within minutes she called his name.

"Jacob!"

"Yeah, Ma," he shouted back.

"Morgan and Petra just pulled up. Please go downstairs and open the front door for them."

Jacob bounded down the stairs. Once he swung the front door open, Petra flew into his arms. She felt wonderful. He'd missed her terribly.

"Daddy, you're back," she squealed.

He held on tightly. Out of the corner of his eye, Jacob saw an attractive woman standing on the porch. He beckoned for her to enter. She made eye contact with his mother, who was now standing at the bottom of the staircase.

"Jacob, I'm sure you remember Morgan," his mother said, making the introduction.

He couldn't place her face, but he nodded anyway.

"Did you girls have fun?" Rosemary asked the woman.

Morgan nodded. "We got a lot done today."

"Did you mind your manners?" Rosemary addressed her granddaughter sternly.

Petra glared.

"She was no trouble at all," Morgan said, winking at the teen.

Jacob observed the by-play.

"I want to hear all about it," Rosemary said, motioning for Morgan to follow.

"Daddy, when did you arrive?" Petra asked, leaving his embrace.

"A few hours ago."

"You look terrible," the teen commented.

Jacob sighed. He knew just how bad he looked. Most of the previous night had been spent reading or staring aimlessly at the ceiling. His eyes were bloodshot and he hadn't shaved. "Thanks for the compliment," he said sarcastically.

The teen shrugged. "It's the truth," she said, leading him down the hallway.

"So tell me about your new friend?" he asked.

Petra rolled her eyes. "You'll probably hate her, but I don't care. She's cool," she said, with an attitude.

Jacob followed his daughter into the kitchen and sat on a stool. His mother and Morgan were already deep in conversation. The woman was culturally refined. Soft curly tresses hung loose from her ponytail. Full pouty lips were barely covered with color, but the rest of her exquisite face was devoid of make-up. Her jeans and tee shirt were expensively made. So were the Italian sandals that adorned her feet. Her look was inconsistent with anyone living in Indigo Beach. He wanted to know more about her.

"Jacob, stop staring, it's rude," his mother admonished.

He grinned impishly.

Morgan's eyes sparkled. "No harm done."

Her voice was low and seductive. Now, he was more intrigued than ever.

CHAPTER 21

✤

PETRA FELT OFF BALANCE. SHE LOVED HER FATHER AND HAD MISSED HIM TERRIBLY WHILE HE was gone, but she was also angry at his decision to leave her in Michigan. Morgan had helped her understand the complexity of her emotions. They'd even discussed dating. She was still a virgin. Her mother had begged her to abstain from sex until marriage. She'd never understood why her mom was so insistent, but she did now. The circumstances of her birth had drastically altered her parents' lives.

She'd always felt that her unplanned birth had been the cause of her mother's unhappiness. Her parent's endless arguments had only confirmed her mindset. Her mom's depression began when she turned eight years old. Petra did everything that she could to help, but with each passing year, the bouts of sadness became longer and more severe. In between these stretches of madness, her mom partied.

Petra still missed the get-togethers that she and her mother attended. She remembered the spicy smell of alcohol on her mother's breath and the euphoric gaze in her eyes when she took pills. So neither Mrs. Sanchez nor Petra was surprised when Lillian wrapped her car around a tree. A functional alcoholic for years, everyone, except her father knew about her addictions.

After talking with Morgan today, Petra was starting to understand her mother. Highly educated and industrious, her mom had yearned for excitement, but after years of downplaying her own creativity and intelligence, she'd lost all confidence. Petra couldn't imagine Morgan giving up on life.

"Daddy."

Jacob peered across the kitchen counter. "Yes."

Petra looked into her father's pale brown eyes, orbs that mirrored her own. "I'm sorry," she said.

"Your drinking brought back really bad memories."

Embarrassed, Petra looked away.

"Why'd you do it?" Jacob asked.

Petra breathed deeply. "I was mad."

Her father looked confused. "About what?"

Petra knew that she wasn't making sense. "You'd broken another promise," she said. Her eyes misted.

"Honey, I have a very important job."

"That always comes before me."

Grandma Rosemary stopped talking and glanced towards her son.

Her father grinned weakly at his mother. Then he moved his chair closer to his daughter. "Honey, I'm sorry, but my job pays the bills."

Petra's eyes welled. She was tired of hearing excuses.

"You have to understand," he pleaded.

But Petra didn't. She couldn't comprehend how any job could be more important than family. "I'm ready to start cooking," she shouted recklessly. Petra felt out of control.

Grandma Rosemary glared at Jacob, clearly holding him responsible for his daughter's impolite behavior.

Petra grinned. Her dad wasn't a big shot in his mother's house. She sashayed towards the sink and washed her hands. Then she waited for her grandmother's instructions.

CHAPTER 22

✝

"TEENAGERS," JACOB SAID AWKWARDLY.

Morgan smiled. "It's really nice seeing you again," she said.

Jacob was caught off guard. Clearly they were acquainted, but he didn't know how.

"Morgan, share your remodeling plans with Jacob. They sound so exciting," Rosemary said, while washing her hands.

Morgan's face became animated. Her eyes softened. "I've hired Leroy to gut the kitchen and bath. That's why Petra and I went to Holland today."

"You're fortunate that he has time," Rosemary said, while gathering pots and pans.

Jacob sat quietly hoping that something the women said would trigger his memory.

Morgan caught him staring and smiled. "You don't recognize me, do you?" she asked.

Just then, Rosemary placed a step stool in front of the sink.

"Ma, what are you doing?" he asked. She pointed towards a large cast iron pot. "All you had to do was ask," he said, while effortlessly retrieving the item.

"You should take your own advice and stop gawking at the poor girl," Rosemary said.

Jacob grinned boyishly.

Rosemary rolled her eyes. "Child, forgive him for not recognizing you."

Morgan chuckled. "I don't believe that I've changed that much." She laughed heartedly while holding out her hand to Jacob. When they shook, confidence collided with strength. "I'm Grace Harding's granddaughter. I own the cottage that Petra broke into."

Jacob stared in disbelief. The woman standing before him was formidable, but her appearance was inconsistent with what he knew of her lineage. He continued staring and tried collecting his thoughts.

"Daddy, you are so embarrassing," Petra moaned.

Jacob ignored his daughter's outburst.

"So you're Momma Harding's daughter," he said.

Rosemary looked sharply at her son.

Spattering grease landed on Petra's exposed arm. She yelped in pain.

"Reduce the heat and place a lid on the pan," Rosemary said instructively.

"She doesn't have to cook tonight," Jacob said, trying to regain control of the situation and his warring emotions.

Rosemary ignored his comment and addressed her granddaughter. "Go wash and cube the sweet potatoes, I'll finish the meat."

Jacob frowned. "How long will dinner take?" he asked, now thoroughly perturbed.

"If you stop asking questions and let us get back to work, it shouldn't take long at all," Rosemary snapped.

Morgan grabbed her bag. "Rosemary, I'll call you tomorrow."

Rosemary shook her head. "Be a dear and take Jacob into the living room. Please keep him company until we're done."

Jacob exhaled.

Morgan calmly hung her purse on the back of a kitchen chair. Then she led him down the hallway and back into the living room. Jacob wasn't immune to her charms, but she wasn't his type. He plopped in his father's old recliner. Morgan sat on the couch.

"So, which daughter are you?" he asked.

Guarded eyes stared back. "The oldest, I graduated with Neville."

"Ah, that's why I couldn't place your face."

"Have I ever done anything to offend you?" she asked.

Her candor caught Jacob off guard. "Why do you ask?"

"Let's just say, you've been a bit abrupt."

He blushed. "Then let me apologize for my bad manners."

Morgan theatrically waved her hand. "There's really no need, but I'll accept it anyway."

"I'm sorry that my daughter broke into your cottage."

"Her trespassing only added to its colorful history."

Jacob understood the implication. His blush deepened. "So tell me, how did my mother rope you into spending the day with my daughter?" he asked.

Morgan leaned forward, grinning naughtily. "I'm surprised, you don't know. I'm Petra's companion for the summer, unless you object." Morgan waited patiently for Jacob's response.

He threw up his hands in surrender.

Morgan leaned forward. "You're okay with your mother's choice?" she asked. Her perceptiveness was discomforting.

"I have to be, now let's get out of here." Jacob stood.

"Are we going somewhere in particular?" she asked.

"Where would you like to go?" he asked, while leading her back down the hallway.

"How about Hardeman's, I still need to pick out appliances."

Rosemary looked up when the duo entered the kitchen. Morgan grabbed her purse and stood quietly by the back door.

"Ma, we're leaving. What time should we be back?" he asked.

"In about an hour, why?"

"I'm taking Morgan to Hardeman's. The store carries a fairly good selection of appliances."

Rosemary faced Morgan. "You'll find everything you need, including a hefty price tag over there."

"Grandma, the meat looks done."

"You two better leave, before Petra burns up my best skillet."

"I should probably drive. That fancy sport's car of yours might have people talking and we wouldn't want that, now would we?" Morgan said.

Jacob's temper darkened. "I'll drive, you should be used to people talking about you by now?"

Morgan's eyes frosted over.

Rosemary inhaled.

Petra frowned.

Frustrated with his family's censure, Jacob motioned for Morgan to follow. "Are you sure that the store is still open?" Morgan asked, as they left through the back door.

"No, but I needed some fresh air," Jacob said, walking briskly across the lawn.

Minute's later, expensive tires spewed rock and gravel across the yard as Jacob veered his BMW onto a lonely country road.

CHAPTER 23

†

"PETRA, TURN THE FLAME DOWN," GRANDMA ROSEMARY BARKED.

Hot water bubbled and splashed against the teen's exposed arm. This was her second burn in less than one hour. "Grandma, I don't want to do this anymore," Petra moaned.

Grandma Rosemary calmly reduced the heat. Then she peered closely at the angry red marks on her granddaughter's hand and arm. "Grab the ice tray from the freezer," she said. Untroubled by Petra's injury, she placed a lid on the pot of boiling potatoes. "Next time, cover the pot or reduce the heat so that you don't get scalded."

Petra groaned. "Can I go upstairs?" she asked.

Grandma Rosemary placed a hand on Petra's forehead. "You aren't running a fever and you definitely don't look ill. What's going on?" she asked her granddaughter.

"I just don't feel right."

"I think I understand," the older woman said, handing Petra a plastic bag filled with ice. "You've apologized for drinking, but have you asked for God's forgiveness?" she asked.

Petra shook her head.

Grandma Rosemary took her granddaughter's hands into her own. "Repentance shows humility."

"What's repentance?" Petra asked.

Grandma Rosemary smiled. "It's an apology to God."

"Will you show me?" the teen asked.

70

Grandma Rosemary nodded. "I'd be honored."

Then Petra repeated every word that her grandmother said, more than willing to rid herself of shame. Petra held onto her grandmother as they prayed.

"Now let's get back to work," Grandma Rosemary said, when she finished.

Her grandmother went to the refrigerator and gathered eggs and milk.

"What are we making next?" she asked.

Grandma Rosemary grinned. "Cornbread."

Petra's eyes lit up. Her grandmother's cornbread was the best. "You never share your recipe."

"I'm making an exception today." The older woman winked.

Excitedly, Petra leaned over the counter. "So what do I do first?"

Grandma Rosemary laughed loudly. "Grab the measuring spoons and cups, while I get the baking soda, cornmeal, and flour. Then we'll begin."

Petra grabbed the utensils and then watched her grandmother measure out the following items: one egg, a half teaspoon of baking soda, one and a half cups of buttermilk, a half cup of flour, two teaspoons of baking powder, one teaspoon of salt, and one cup of cornmeal. Next her grandmother combined everything except the flour and cornmeal into one bowl. Then she slowly added the dry ingredients and stirred. Lastly, Grandma Rosemary placed a cast iron skillet of yellow batter into the four hundred degree oven.

"Grandma, how tall will the batter rise?" she asked.

Grandma Rosemary chuckled. "As tall as cake, now grab a knife. We've got more vegetables to chop."

Petra followed her grandmother's lead. The pair worked side by side until a large pot of vegetables and thick chunks of browned beef simmered on the stove.

"Are your burns still stinging?" Grandma Rosemary asked.

Petra glanced at the red whelps on her hand and arm. They were throbbing badly.

"Yes, but I'll live."

Grandma Rosemary smiled. "I had no doubt, burns are an occasional kitchen hazard and the pain that results helps us learn," Grandma Rosemary said.

Petra looked doubtful. "How so?" she asked.

Grandma Rosemary chuckled. "You won't forget to reduce the heat or cover a boiling pot again, now will you," she asked.

Petra giggled.

"Then knowledge gained from receiving those burns was worth the pain that they caused," Grandma Rosemary said, as she hugged her granddaughter snugly.

CHAPTER 24

✝

WAYWARD STRANDS OF HAIR SLAPPED MORGAN'S FACE. THE MOTOR REVVED AS JACOB switched gears. Music thumped rhythmically through the car's expensive sound system as it careened around curves.

"Am I scaring you?" he asked.

Morgan shook her head. "No, I'm a risk taker by nature." Then she began singing the lyrics of the song that was playing.

Jacob glanced sideways. "Very few people know about this artist."

Morgan closed her eyes and sang louder. "My tastes are eclectic. So tell me about yourself."

Jacob's jaw tightened. "There isn't much to share. I graduated from college, finished graduate school, and married young. My wife died a few years back and now I'm a single parent."

"It sounds daunting," she said.

"It is at times, but single parenting can be rewarding."

Morgan found his comment amusing, but she remained respectfully quiet.

"What about you?" he asked.

She paused before speaking. "I've lived in Europe for the past five years."

"I wondered about the accent. So, what brought you home?" he asked.

Morgan became pensive. "My grandmother's estate for one and I needed to handle a few personal matters."

"How long will you be staying?" he asked.

Morgan's face clouded. "As long as it takes, how about you?"

"A few weeks if all goes as planned."

Morgan nodded.

"What did Petra tell you about me?" Jacob asked.

"That you don't date much," she said. Morgan's grin was sly and intentional.

"But it's not for lack of trying. You sistas want a brotha's time, money, and commitment. I lack two of the three right now," Jacob said light heartedly.

"You'd make it happen, for the right woman."

"You think so?" he asked, amused by her response.

"Yes, I know your type." Morgan said, baiting him.

Jacob glanced sideways. "What type am I?"

This time, Morgan didn't hold back. "You're brilliant, focused, and determined. You're also arrogant and used to getting your way."

"So you think you know me."

Morgan shrugged. "I don't have to know your story to understand you. Harding women know men."

Jacob's jaw tightened.

"Did I offend you again?" she asked innocently.

They pulled into the store's parking lot. "Let's see how much damage you can do in thirty minutes," he said, ignoring her last comment.

"I'll know whether they have what I want in about five minutes."

"I'll believe it when I see it," Jacob said, opening the passenger door for Morgan.

"Will you help?"

"No, I'm going to watch and learn," Jacob said, as they walked into the shop.

Morgan walked towards the counter. No one was present, so while she waited for a sales clerk, she thumbed through a catalogue.

"I'll be with you shortly," a woman hollered from the back of the room. She was assisting another customer.

Morgan nodded. Then she felt Jacob staring.

"Do you see anything that you like?" he asked.

Morgan smiled. "Yes, I do."

Jacob appeared surprised.

The sales associate returned to the counter. "Thank you for your patience. We always seem to get busy, right before closing." The woman's comments were said congenially. "How can I help?" she asked, glancing between Jacob and Morgan.

"I'm interested in purchasing a gas stove with a grill," Morgan said.

"Stainless steel?" the woman asked.

"Yes."

The woman motioned for them to follow. "Do you have a budget?"

"Not really, I usually buy what I like," Morgan said matter-of-factly.

The woman turned and smiled. "Then, let me show you our top seller."

But as the pair followed the woman, Morgan saw the brand that she wanted. "Does this stove come any smaller?"

"Yes it does, but it's quite expensive."

Morgan scoffed at the sale associate's remark. "I'm aware, I had a larger model of this brand installed in my last home. It's just what I'm looking for."

Jacob glanced at the price tag and whistled.

Morgan turned towards the clerk. "I'll take it. I also want to order the matching fridge and dishwasher, and I'll need delivery in about three weeks, if not sooner."

The woman stared opened mouthed. "Is there anything else that I can do for you?" she squeaked.

Morgan shook her head. "No, that will be all for now." She followed the clerk to the counter. Then she placed her credit card on top. Morgan's eyes twinkled when she caught Jacob staring at its color, which indicated limitless spending. "How are we doing for time?" she asked.

Jacob glanced at his watch. "We've only been here twenty minutes."

The sales associate handed Morgan her receipt.

"I look forward to working with you again," Morgan said to the woman, before sauntering towards the door."

Jacob held it open.

Morgan exited and walked across the parking lot. Once the pair was comfortably seated, Jacob gunned the engine. Morgan fastened her seatbelt.

"I've never experienced that level of power shopping before," he said.

"You've never shopped with me," Morgan bantered.

Jacob chuckled. "Nor with anyone like you," he said.

Morgan contemplated his last remark. She was used to intimidating men and Jacob was no exception. As they traveled back to Rosemary's house, Morgan's mood darkened.

"Have I upset you?" Jacob asked.

"Not at all, thank you for taking me to Hardeman's."

"I should be thanking you," he said, sounding calmer.

"I'm glad that I was able to help."

"You'll be doing a lot of that this summer. My daughter is a handful."

"I want to bless her."

"That's an interesting choice of words," Jacob said.

Morgan didn't take offense. "Years ago, a dear friend explained that I had an obligation to help others, because I'd been given so much. I'm honoring her right now."

"That was good advice."

"She was the wisest woman that I've ever known," Morgan said.

The pair arrived at Rosemary's house. Deeply pensive, Morgan walked across the grass. Jacob was prideful, opinionated, and selfishly irritating. His unpredictability made him dangerous and attractive. He and Petra had similar temperaments, which explained why they clashed so often. Morgan also knew that she could help. She just wasn't sure how Jacob would handle her intervention.

CHAPTER 25

✚

PETRA FIDGETED WHILE HER GRANDMOTHER CALMLY SIPPED TEA AND READ SCRIPTURES AT THE dining room table. The stew simmered on the stove, while they waited for Jacob and Morgan's return. Petra munched loudly on a carrot. Grandma Rosemary looked up, scowling. The teen glowered. "Grandma, what are you doing?"

"Reading God's Word," her grandmother said.

Petra sighed. Old people were so hard to understand. "What does that mean?" she asked, crunching louder.

Grandma Rosemary chuckled. "Reading God's Word strengthens my faith. Daily devotion is important for spiritual growth."

"Is that the only reason for reading scriptures?"

Grandma Rosemary shook her head "No child, it helps me make better decisions."

"How?" Petra asked.

"Well, God's Word gives me peace when I'm feeling lonely, need direction, or when I mess up."

Petra had never heard her grandmother discuss personal failure.

"You never make mistakes," she said.

Grandma Rosemary smiled and then pushed her Bible aside. "I make them all of the time."

"Name one," Petra said.

"Okay, I regret not telling your father about your mother's drug usage or that you started drinking heavily last year."

Petra looked wide-eyed. "You knew," she squeaked.

Grandma Rosemary's eyes narrowed. "Yes, just like I know about that silly little boy you've been sneaking around with, back home."

Petra lowered her head. "But how?"

Grandma Rosemary shrugged. "Discernment, but knowing when to use it is tricky."

"Grandma, did I cause my mom's death?"

Grandma Rosemary's forehead furrowed. "Good Lord No!" she exclaimed.

Petra's eyes moistened. "Momma and Daddy argued horribly that day and I suggested that she leave the house."

Rosemary leaned forward and hugged her granddaughter. "Sweetheart, the accident wasn't your fault."

Petra shook her head. "That's not true. My parents hated each other. They only stayed married because of me." Petra's eyes welled.

Rosemary patted her hand. "Honey, your birth was a blessing from God." She handed Petra a napkin to wipe her eyes.

"Are you sure?" the teen asked.

"Yes, so put that nonsense out of your head. Your parents created a bad marriage. And your mother drove drunk. Neither decision was your fault."

"Grandma, you're the best," Petra exclaimed.

"Thank you, but I don't feel it at times. Watching you stumble through prayer today was sobering. I've still got a lot of work to do."

"Grandma, does God always answer prayer?"

"When it lines up with His Word."

"Good, because I'm going to pray for you right now," Petra said happily. She watched her grandmother bow her head.

"Lord God, thank you for my grandmother and give her boldness, Amen." Petra looked at Grandma Rosemary expectantly.

Her grandmother clasped her hands. "That was much better."

Petra's eyes sparkled. "I'm a fast learner," the teen joked. Petra felt her grandmother's deep and unconditional love. More importantly, she felt hope, which was better than the icky feeling of shame that she'd been experiencing. Once her grandmother resumed reading, Petra grabbed another carrot. This time, she munched more quietly.

CHAPTER 26

✝

PETRA DUMPED A GREASY POT INTO THE SINK OF SOAPY WATER. GRANDMA ROSEMARY'S BEEF stew recipe and her homemade cornbread had turned out beautifully. Sweet like cake, the corn bread's texture was almost as velvety. During dinner, Morgan had regaled them with tales of her travels abroad. All too soon, the meal was over. Then Morgan was gone.

Jacob's voice interrupted Petra's thoughts.

"How much longer?" he asked.

She shrugged. Dirty dishes were stacked high on the counter. She would be washing for quite some time.

"If you helped, she might get done quicker," Grandma Rosemary said, before leaving the room.

Jacob glowered at his mother. "What do you want me to do?" he asked his daughter.

She flung suds at his face.

"Hey, cut it out!" he cried. Then he reached into the soapy water and grabbed a handful of soapsuds and smeared them across Petra's forehead.

Giggling, she screamed. "Grandmaaa, Daddy is bothering me."

"You're actually snitching on me?" he said.

Petra's eyes glistened.

"Jacob, leave that girl alone. You're trying my patience," Grandma Rosemary hollered from the dining room.

Spasms of uncontrollable giggles had Petra doubled over. "The dish towel is over there." Petra pointed.

Jacob grabbed the rag from the rack and began drying. The pair worked silently until the kitchen was neat and clean.

"What are you doing tomorrow?" Petra asked.

Jacob turned off the light before they left the room. "I have an appointment at ten o'clock. Then I'll be free. Why?"

Petra felt disappointment. "I thought we might be able to spend the day together," she said.

Her father smoothed her hair. "No pumpkin, tomorrow won't work. Besides, you're going to be with Morgan?"

"I'd much prefer spending the day with you."

"We have three whole weeks of vacation to enjoy."

"Something will come up like it always does and our plans will change," she said.

"This time will be different."

"You've said that before," Petra said.

"When?" he demanded.

Emotions raw, Petra ticked off each and every disappointment and every wound that was still open.

Her father's pale brown eyes turned remorseful. His voice was low and emotional when he said, "I'm sorry."

Simple words propelled Petra back into his arms. "You can let me go," she whispered.

Jacob tightened his hold.

"Uh, you can let me go, for real," she said, hitting his back. Petra felt his laughter long before she heard it. "Grandmaaa, Daddy won't let me go!" she hollered.

"Jacob, don't make me come in there!" Grandma Rosemary yelled.

"I'm going to remember this," he whispered into his daughter's ear.

She continued laughing. "Remember what?"

"Your total and absolute disloyalty," her father said.

Petra burst into spasms of giggles, as she ducked under his arm. The teen ran past her grandmother and bounded up the stairs with her dad in close pursuit. Then she quickly entered her bedroom and slammed the door. She turned the lock just before he reached it. Jacob began pounding.

"Go away," she yelled excitedly.

Her father kept banging.

"Grandmaaa, Daddy is bothering me again," the teen screeched.

"Jacob, leave that girl alone," Grandma Rosemary hollered up the stairs. Eventually, her dad retreated. Then she heard his bedroom door close.

Petra sprawled happily across her bed, wondering just how long their vacation would really last.

CHAPTER 27
⊷ † ⊶

JACOB HAD BEEN UP FOR HOURS AND WAS LOUNGING AGAINST THE TWIN-SIZED HEADBOARD IN his old bedroom. He'd awakened rested, if not a little sore from his legs hanging over the mattress. He massaged his aching calves before he stood.

Jacob put his laptop away and made the bed before padding towards the bathroom down the hall. The smell of sausage wafted upstairs. Obviously, his mother was up. He stood on the bathroom's faded linoleum and shaved. Jacob peered into a dated mirror, while running water flowed into a chipped porcelain sink. He shook his head. He just didn't understand why his mother hadn't remodeled this room when she'd completely renovated the first floor. He'd come far from his humble beginnings. After completing his morning routine, Jacob stepped into the shower. Then he heard a knock.

"Daddy, did you leave any hot water?" Petra yelled through the door.

"Some, but you know the rules. The last person in the bathroom, takes his chances," he said, unapologetically.

"I hate my life," Petra hollered.

Jacob chuckled, as his daughter stomped back towards her room. Once his ablution was completed, he knocked on her door. "The bathroom is empty," he said.

"I swear I hate my life," Petra yelled. Jacob laughed open mouthed. Then he walked across the hallway and entered his bedroom. After dressing, he went downstairs.

His mother looked up when he entered the kitchen. "You're up early?" she said.

82

Jacob heaped eggs, sausage, and toast on his plate.

"Juice?" Rosemary asked.

"No, coffee will be fine."

Rosemary poured the steaming liquid into his mug. "What are your plans for today?" she asked.

Jacob slathered butter on his toast. "I have a few errands to run," he said, avoiding her stare. Her perceptive smile told him that she already knew about his meeting with Pastor Deon. He chewed on a sausage link, wondering how his mother always seemed to know things that she shouldn't.

"I'll see Petra off at eleven. Then I'm going to my dentist appointment."

Jacob nodded. "Where do you suggest that I take Petra when she gets home today?" he asked.

Rosemary appeared thoughtful. "Why don't you take her to Indigo Beach."

"That's an excellent idea. We haven't been there since last summer."

"And then stop by the dairy," Rosemary added.

Jacob smiled. Visiting the dairy had always been a favorite excursion for the McDonald children.

His mother pushed the morning paper towards him.

He opened it and began reading while Rosemary washed dishes.

She refilled his mug and then left the room. Hearing his mother pray in her heavenly language reminded him of happier times. His father had been a mighty prayer warrior too. Sadly, Jacob hadn't continued the legacy.

He added sugar to his mug and stirred. Had he allowed distractions to dilute his character like the dissolving sugar crystals in his drink? He gulped the remaining coffee and then quickly washed his tableware. Then he left the items to dry in the drainer. Jacob glanced at his watch. There was ample time to continue studying scriptures before his appointment. He climbed the stairs two by two.

Petra's comments from last night niggled his conscience. Her list of broken promises had been unsettling. He closed his door, lay across the bed, and reflected. He'd given himself far too much credit for intent. His daughter was justified in her refusal to accept his double standard.

His child had only been in Indigo Beach for a short time, but her perspective on life was already changing. He wasn't sure that he liked the transformation. Morgan had encouraged debate at dinner. He'd been surprised by his daughter's passion and was very uncomfortable with some of her opinions.

The Holy Spirit nudged him to read the book of Galatians. His father had made him study scriptures from this text many times. His mother had told him on more than one occasion that he was prideful and maybe he was, since he didn't want his daughter to be right.

CHAPTER 28

✝

DEON WAITED PATIENTLY FOR MAMIE TO ARRIVE. RARELY LATE, SHE WAS TODAY. FROM THE outer office window, he watched her hustle across the parking lot. Deon walked to the back door and held it open for his dear friend.

"Good morning Mamie," he said.

"Is it a good morning?" she asked testily.

Her forehead was deeply creased. Deon led her into his office, but left the door open. He seldom counseled women without Rosemary being present. Since Mamie's reputation wasn't the greatest and because in a small town, perception often became fact, Deon had notified his wife about the unscheduled counseling session. Summer had appreciated the call. "As I told you on the phone, my calendar is full, so let's get started," Deon said, while motioning for her to sit.

"Thank you for fitting me in."

"Well, what's got your hair all mussed up?" he said, while plopping into his seat.

Mamie patted her blond tracks. "My daughter hates me."

"What brought this on? Have you argued?" Deon asked. He grew concerned when he saw her eyes moisten.

"Deon, Morgan still hasn't called or stopped by."

He sighed. Then he proceeded cautiously. "Mamie, you've refused to discuss Morgan or Sara in previous counseling sessions. So, I don't know where to begin or what to say."

She quickly looked away.

"Why haven't you told Morgan about her father?"

Mamie squirmed. Then she looked down. "It isn't my story to tell. Well, not entirely," she said, making an excuse.

Deon shook his head. "On the contrary. It's always been your responsibility. That child should have been told about her father years ago." Deon watched tears trickle down her cheeks.

"I didn't come here for this," she said angrily.

"Yes you did."

"Deon!" Mamie snapped.

"Woman, you have to trust in God!" He handed his friend a box of tissue and waited until she finished blowing her nose.

"She's going to hate me."

"You just said that she already does. It's been almost thirty-five years." Deon took a deep calming breath before proceeding. "We've known each other since we were kids. You were young and foolish when your oldest children were born. Can I be honest? You didn't get any sense until Tonya got here. Older and wiser, you parented the younger girls differently, more responsibly and it shows." Deon tapped his fingers on his desk.

Mamie sat stunned. Her eyes widened.

"But you lied to Morgan and Sara." His truthful words were compassionately spoken.

"How dare you," she said, with fire in her eyes.

Deon sighed. "Woman, you're in my office, not the other way around."

"I did the best that I could," she said defensively.

Deon frowned. "No you didn't. You did what you wanted, not what was right? You chose sin and the girls suffered."

Mamie's eyes blazed. "You can't judge me."

Deon responded calmly. "I never have and won't begin now. That's God's job not mine, but it's time that you took responsibility for your actions."

"Don't you think I have?" she asked. Tears continued streaming.

"You've repented, but your daughters need an apology. It is asinine to expect them to fix a problem that you created," Deon said, hoping that she understood.

"So this is all my fault," Mamie said.

Deon's eyes narrowed. "No, you and Morgan's father created this situation together. She's a victim, the consequence of your disobedience."

Mamie gasped. "Deon, you've gone too far." She threw the box of tissue across his desk. Then she heatedly stormed out of his office.

Deon hung his head and rubbed his throbbing temples. God expected results and getting them wasn't always easy. Mamie was deceived if she thought that Morgan, alone was responsible for their impasse.

Deon began praying. He petitioned God for a break through. Sin produced consequences, and from his experience, others often paid the price.

CHAPTER 29

✝

MORGAN FELT UNCOMFORTABLY STICKY AND WASN'T SURE WHETHER SHE WAS SWEATING because of nerves or the humidity. She was parked in front of her mother's home. The house had been a very generous gift, just like everything else her mother owned. Morgan couldn't remember his name, but she would never forget the smell of the man's cologne. At one time, its aroma had been deeply infused in the expensive furniture that he'd also purchased. Men, not a husband had controlled her family's fate. Her mother had taught her oldest daughters to choose their lovers wisely. It had taken Mona years to get Morgan to view life differently.

After taking a cleansing breath, Morgan exited the car. Because of the intense summer heat, her natural hair was pinned into a sophisticated chignon. Still, sweat dripped down her neck and back. As she approached the house, she heard children's laughter. It was funny that Mamie hadn't raised her own kids, but now happily babysat her grandchildren.

Morgan approached the front door and knocked. Then a passing car caught her attention. It was always odd seeing vehicles this far out in the township. She turned around when she heard the front door open. Apprehension had her pulse racing.

"Well it's about time," her mother said. Mamie opened the door wider.

Soon, Morgan luxuriated in her mother's arms. "Hi Momma," she said, holding on tightly.

Mamie disengaged and smoothed her dress. She appeared slightly embarrassed by the display of affection. "Girl, close the door. You're letting all my cool air out."

Morgan smiled at her mother's frugality.

"Let me look at you?" her mother said.

Morgan felt naked and exposed. Then she realized that three sets of eyes were also watching the melodrama from behind a chair. She knelt and smiled at her nieces.

"Come greet your auntie," Mamie said, motioning for the kids to come out. Morgan recognized Kimmie, Destiny's daughter immediately. The tyke now hid between her grandmother's leg. The older girls belonged to Tonya. Both looked just like their father.

"Where is Myles?" Morgan wondered aloud.

"He's in my bedroom, playing video games with Sara's kids.

Morgan nodded and then followed her mother down the hallway. The children resumed playing. Not much had changed. Even with youngsters about, the house was uncluttered and clean. Her mother had always maintained a beautiful home.

"Momma."

Mamie stopped and turned.

"The house looks nice," Morgan said.

Her mother smiled. The gap between her mother's top front teeth appeared more pronounced then she remembered. Morgan had always loved her mother's smile. It mirrored her own.

"Thank you baby, your sisters pay me well," she said.

Morgan followed her mother into the kitchen. The hum of the blaring television overrode embarrassing silence.

"Are you hungry?"

Morgan nodded.

"Good, I'll make your favorite breakfast."

Morgan had been hopeful. "You don't have to."

"I want to," her mother said.

"I'll help."

"That would be nice," Mamie's smile was sweet and friendly.

Morgan washed her hands at the kitchen sink. Then she gathered flour and sugar from the pantry. Mamie reached into the refrigerator and retrieved eggs, milk, butter, and bacon. The women worked quietly and harmoniously, as batter was prepared. Morgan pulled off strips of thick slab bacon and placed them on a cast iron griddle. Grease spit and sizzled as the meat cooked.

Curiously, Morgan's nieces and nephews gathered around the table.

Mamie shooed them out while she and Morgan worked. "A penny for your thoughts," she said, peering into Morgan's shuttered eyes.

Not wanting to dampen the mood, Morgan coughed and cleared her windpipe of sentiment. "Not much has changed in town," she said.

"A new grocery store opened two years ago," Mamie said.

"I shopped there last week. Although, I still like the butcher's meat better," Morgan said, making small talk. Their movements were fluid, but communication felt unnatural.

"I hear that you're fixing up the cottage," Mamie chattered, as she placed plates on the table.

Morgan beamed. "Yes I am." She watched her mother pour juice into glasses.

"I can't wait to see what you're going to do with the old place," Mamie said, right before she summoned her grandchildren.

Soon Morgan was pouring syrup over stacks of pancakes as her mother doled out bacon strips to the greedy tykes. Fascinated with their boundless energy, she leaned against the kitchen sink and watched them eat.

"What's on your mind?" her mother asked.

"Nothing much."

Mamie appeared happy.

"You're a good grandma," Morgan said.

Her mother smiled. "Thanks, I try," she said, as she gave the older kids more bacon. "I don't take this opportunity lightly."

"Me neither," Morgan said. She waited patiently for her turn. As soon as the children finished eating and the tabletop was cleared, she and her mother would dine alone. She'd been waiting her whole life for answers. So another delay was nothing to get concerned about.

CHAPTER 30

✝

DEEP IN THOUGHT, DEON PEERED OUT HIS OFFICE WINDOW. SUNLIGHT WASHED THE ROOM'S DARK shadows away. From his window, Deon observed rolling waves crash ashore.

Many years before, Great Grandma Bradford had inherited three lots from her employer. The deathbed gift had caused uproar in the tiny beachside community. The will's validity was eventually upheld. Fortunately, Deon's great grandfather's employer was the judge who presided over the court proceedings. The church was built on prime real estate, more than seventy-five years ago. Deon didn't take his legacy lightly.

Now, he waited for his next appointment to arrive. The doorbell buzzed. Deon advanced down the back hallway. Guarded eyes peered at him through the glass door. Deon pushed it open.

"Morning Pastor," the visitor said.

Deon shook the guest's hand firmly. "It's been a long time."

Jacob looked away.

"Son, I didn't mean it like that," Deon said. This meeting wasn't beginning any better than his previous appointment had ended. "Follow me," he said, before leading Rosemary's second born back towards his office. Deon waited until Jacob was seated, before he closed his office door. Then he sat on the couch, facing the young man. "Can I offer you something to drink?" he asked. "Your mother and Summer keep my fridge stocked with water and juice."

"No, I'm fine."

"So what's troubling you?" Deon asked.

Jacob's face flushed.

Deon massaged his temples again. "I'll word my question differently. Why are you here?" he asked. He waited for Jacob to compose himself.

Finally, he spoke. "I grew up in this very church. My dad was a deacon and my mom was and still is an employee. I attended children's church, memorized scriptures for annual pageants, and honored my parents, as instructed. Parents shouldn't provoke their children and deacons must live exemplary lives. That's what I was taught, but I didn't see any of it in my home," he said.

Knowing there was more, Deon remained quiet.

"My dad was selfish and judgmental when he was alive," Jacob said passionately, before pausing.

Deon sighed. He was well aware of Deacon McDonald's hypocrisy. "I understand things more clearly now." He grabbed his Bible from the top of his desk. "The scriptures that you're referring to are a wonderful place to begin," he said, following the Holy Spirit's lead.

"I didn't come here to discuss scriptures," Jacob said.

"Well, that's what we're going to do. Where's your notebook?" Deon asked.

Jacob held up his smart phone. "Good, you can record our session. Let's begin in Proverbs." Deon ignored the young man's annoyance. "Then we'll study 1 Timothy 3."

Jacob sighed.

Deon grinned.

CHAPTER 31

✝

MAMIE WASHED DISHES, WHILE MORGAN DRIED. SURPRISINGLY, SHE'D ENJOYED EVERYTHING about the morning thus far. Being with her family had actually stirred longing. Now the younger children were taking a well-needed nap.

"Tell me about your job?" Mamie asked. Morgan placed a stack of clean dishes on a shelf and faced her mom.

"I haven't worked full time in almost five years."

Mamie stopped washing, but her arms and hands remained in the soapy water. "How have you been supporting yourself?"

"A wealthy man," Morgan said matter-of-factly.

Mamie scrubbed another plate. "Did he take good care of you?" she asked. Morgan nodded again.

"I take it, the relationship is over."

"Yes, I walked away before he threw me out," Morgan said.

"Good, that's the best way to leave," Mamie whispered. The timbre of her voice deepened. Then a lone tear trickled down her cheek.

"Momma, I'm fine. He treated me well and I'm financially secure," Morgan said, far too quickly. Her mother's tears were confusing. Morgan became alarmed when soulful moaning wracked her mom's body. "I thought that you'd be proud," she said, baffled by her mother's response.

Mamie gripped the edge of the counter for support. She wiped her eyes with the corner of an apron and then she slumped into a kitchen chair. Morgan pulled up another chair and peered questioningly into her mother's eyes. "Momma, you're scaring me. What's the matter?" she asked.

Mamie's voice was low when she finally spoke. "I taught you things that a mother shouldn't."

Anxiety had Morgan's stomach knotted. "You taught me survival skills."

Mamie shook her head. "Not everything was right," she explained.

Morgan hadn't counted on this response. Her mother appeared embarrassed and uncertain.

"What I taught you goes against God's laws," she said.

Shame crashed over Morgan like waves rolling towards shore.

Brazenly, Morgan argued. "I worked hard." Morgan saw remorse in her mother's eyes. A tidal wave of emotion threatened to overflow. "Why are you crying?" she asked her mother.

"All of your failed relationships have really been my fault," Mamie said. Her voice was barely audible.

Morgan stood and pushed her chair aside. Dammed up emotions threatened to overflow.

"Morgan wait!" Mamie cried.

She strode into the living room and grabbed her purse. Then she sprinted out the front door. Fresh tears streamed down Morgan's face. Ignoring Mamie's yelling, Morgan jumped into her car and backed out of the driveway. Gravel crunched loudly under the vehicle's weight. From the rear view mirror, she saw that her mother was standing on the porch steps. More tears blurred her vision. She looked back, one last time and saw that her mother's arms were stretched towards heaven. Morgan's anguished wail rumbled deeply from her battered soul, as she drove erratically towards town.

CHAPTER 32

✝

"TIRED?" DEON ASKED.

Looking up from his borrowed Bible, Jacob rubbed his chin. Then he scratched his jaw. Today, he'd learned that an angry teenager had grown into an equally bitter man. Jacob didn't like who he'd become, or what God had revealed. For over two hours, the men had discussed a wide range of topics, but more specifically, about how sin blinded believers from seeing God. Truthfully, he didn't want the visit to end. "Are your sessions usually this intense?" Jacob asked.

"Sometimes," Deon said, stifling a yawn. "Most folks understand that God's Word is the same yesterday, today and forever and it isn't up for debate."

Jacob looked away. "I appreciate all the time that you've given me today," he said.

"You need to find a church home in Chicago. It will provide fellowship and instruction. Your walk will become easier if you surround yourself with like-minded believers."

"You've given me something to think about," Jacob said, before standing.

Deon shook the young man's outstretched hand. "I look forward to seeing you on Sunday," he said. Jacob threw his head back and laughed.

"When did I agree to attend church?" he asked.

Deon shrugged." You didn't."

Jacob laughed riotously. Then he followed Deon back down the hallway.

"For your information, I'd already planned on escorting my mother and daughter to church. So, I will see you on Sunday," Jacob said grinning. He pushed the door open and walked across the lot.

Deon beamed like a Cheshire cat as he watched Jacob advance towards his car. Their meeting had been most insightful. Jacob was deceived about a lot of things, but Deon knew that God was in control. He glanced at the wall clock. Rosemary would arrive soon. Tired from the intensity of his morning appointments, Deon reclined on his couch and placed a pillow beneath his head. Then he stared out his picture window again. Billowy white clouds dotted the azure colored sky. This room was and had always been his safe harbor.

Deon thought about Rosemary and the road that she'd traveled. His administrative assistant was tough, a strong woman of God who had danced in the fiery furnace of life, and survived. Just like the three Hebrew boys, God had lovingly held her hand through every adversity. Unfortunately, Jacob was his father's mirror image. Chauvinism masked personal insecurities and inadequacies. His gifts and talents had opened professional doors in Latin America, where machismo ruled. However, heavy handedness at home had forced Lillian to surrender her dreams. Now, he was earning professional recognition at his daughter's expense. Petra deserved better and change had to occur before it was too late.

Deon's eyes grew heavier. He'd poured loving truth into both Mamie and Jacob this morning and he was emotionally spent. Now he needed recharging. He slept soundly, until Rosemary arrived.

CHAPTER 33

✝

BLINDING TEARS FORCED MORGAN TO PULL OFF THE ROADWAY. UTTERLY DISTRAUGHT, SHE dialed the one person who knew her well.

"I take it that you've spoken with your mother," Jeffery asked.

"I wish you were here," Morgan cried.

"What did you talk about?" he asked.

Morgan blew her nose. "I told her about Edward," she said.

Jeffery sighed. "I see."

"No you don't, Momma finally admitted to being wrong." Morgan knew that she sounded hysterical. "But it's at my expense," she said, between sobs.

"I'm so sorry." His response was heartfelt. "Why don't you go to the cottage and rest?"

"I can't, I'm supposed to spend the afternoon with Petra," Morgan said. She started the engine again.

"I wish I could be there for you."

"I wish you were here too. Will this nightmare ever end?" she asked.

"Yes, when you walk in forgiveness."

Jeffery's words caused more anger.

Morgan exploded. "Why do I have to accept her half-truths and forgive? It's all so unfair," she complained.

"Because you want to live a long and prosperous life and you can't honor a person that you hate."

Morgan was well acquainted with the scripture that Jeffery had just paraphrased. "I don't even know why I dialed your number," she said.

He chuckled. "Yes you do, you called for sane advice."

"I'm hanging up," Morgan said.

"As you wish," Jeffery said, still laughing.

"Minutes later Morgan parked in front of Rosemary's well-manicured lawn.

"Morgan, what took you so long?" Petra yelled from the porch. Earphones from the teen's MP3 player dangled from her ears.

Morgan quickly masked her emotions as she walked up the sidewalk. She hoped Rosemary didn't notice her puffy eyes through her sunglasses.

"If today isn't good, I can take Petra to work with me," the older woman said, having obviously realized that she'd been crying.

Rosemary's discernment was unsettling. "I'm fine," Morgan said.

Petra rolled her eyes as she ran to the car, oblivious to Morgan's dismay. She slammed the passenger door shut.

Rosemary sat beside Morgan on the top step. "I'm a very good listener."

Morgan shrugged. "I wouldn't know where to begin," she said, as tears welled again.

Petra opened the passenger door. "Can we go now?" she yelled.

Rosemary rolled her eyes and hollered across the yard, "Close the car door now!"

The youngster moaned melodramatically, before slamming the door shut again.

Rosemary looked at Morgan. "Take all the time that you need," she said.

Morgan gathered her thoughts. Then she told Rosemary the sad truths of her life.

CHAPTER 34

✠

ROSEMARY'S CAR WAS IDLING IN THE DRIVEWAY WHEN JACOB ARRIVED HOME. HE WALKED towards his mother's vehicle. Jacob leaned in and kissed the top of her head.

"I hate it when you do that," she said.

He kissed her cheek. "Is that better?"

"Much," she said.

"When did the girls leave?" Jacob asked, squelching unease. Although Morgan was educated and well traveled, he still felt that her background was troubling.

"They just left."

"Where to?"

"Kalamazoo, they'll be home in a few hours," Rosemary said.

"Will I still have time to take Petra to the beach," he asked.

Rosemary looked crossly at her son. "They won't be gone that long."

Not wanting an argument, he refrained from questioning her decision. Jacob glanced at his watch. "You better leave, or you'll be late for your dentist appointment," he said.

Rosemary looked at the clock in her dashboard. "You're right. Enjoy your afternoon. I'll be home around five o'clock," she said, as she backed out of the driveway.

Jacob stepped back from the moving car. He hadn't counted on Deon Bradford's perceptiveness or astute intellect. He'd sniped and berated the pastor unmercifully. Usually the negotiation tactic worked, but it hadn't today. Using the Word of God, Pastor Deon had calmly defused Jacob's wrath. Eventually, he'd shut his mouth and began listening, which was a humbling and instructive experience.

The minister had then been able to explain pride's deceptiveness. He and his late father were more alike than he cared to admit. Pastor Deon had also pointed out other similarities in character between the men. Apparently, pig headedness also ran in the family.

Jacob entered his bedroom and lay across the bed. With his eyes closed, he processed what he'd learned today. Eventually, he fell asleep. Jacob slept fitfully, while angels toiled in the heavenly realm on his behalf.

CHAPTER 35

✝

DEON AWOKE FROM HIS NAP AND PATTED HIS GROWLING STOMACH. HE HEARD ROSEMARY moving about in the outer office, but he wasn't ready to go back to work just yet, so he dialed his wife.

"Hi Honey, what's up?" she asked cheerfully.

Deon's chest expanded. Summer's love kept him grounded.

"I'm hungry. Have you eaten lunch yet?" he asked.

"Yes, but I can bring you something."

"You'd do that for me?"

"Absolutely, your wish is my command," she said.

"Well, I have a taste for ribs and potato salad."

"I'm sure you do, but I'm going to stop by Meriwether's Convenience Store and pick you up a salad."

Deon laughed. "Add a couple of chocolate covered donuts and you've got a deal."

"Deon, I am not buying donuts."

"Please."

"No Deon, no donuts." Summer said flatly.

"I've been treated better."

"Well then, you should have married one of those other women. Now get off the phone," she said good-naturedly.

"I love you."

"I love you too."

After ending the call, Deon walked into his private bathroom. He washed his face. Then he ran a comb through his dark, thick curls. Feeling somewhat refreshed from his nap, he stepped into the outer office. Rosemary looked up from her desk.

"How's your tooth?" he asked.

"I need a crown."

Deon hated dentists. So, the thought of having any kind of dental work was unsettling.

"Will it hurt?"

Rosemary shrugged. "Probably, but what choice do I have?"

Deon sat and faced his administrative assistant.

"Are you worried?" he asked, noticing her strained expression.

She shook her head. "No, I was just thinking about a conversation that Morgan and I had this morning."

Deon leaned forward. "What did you talk about?"

"Morgan visited her mother today and Mamie tried apologizing."

"That's encouraging," Deon said.

Rosemary shook her head. "The poor child couldn't accept the apology. She's been terribly hurt by her mother and men."

"Is that why she came home?"

"Yes, she just ended a very unhealthy relationship."

"I figured as much, how's she doing?" he asked.

"She's confused."

"I would be too, if her parents were mine."

"I wanted to tell her the truth so badly."

Deon leaned forward. "Are you having any doubts about her character?"

Rosemary shook her head. "Not at all, she's going to be the perfect companion for my granddaughter."

"Jacob doesn't like it."

Rosemary smiled. "I know."

"You just put the devil on notice," Deon said. Then he stood and walked towards his office door.

"I don't scare easily."

Deon laughed loudly, as he sat at his desk. He opened his laptop and got back to work.

CHAPTER 36

✝

SPENDING THE AFTERNOON IN KALAMAZOO HAD BEEN FUN. NOW, MORGAN AND PETRA WERE munching on hamburgers and salty fries as they drove home. Because of her father's plans for the evening, her grandmother had cancelled her kitchen duties. Petra observed Morgan's strained expression. "What are you thinkin' about?" the teen asked, between sips of pop.

Morgan took another swig of her beverage before answering, "Nothing."

"I'm not stupid. You were crying earlier," Petra said.

"I usually have better control of my emotions."

"So, who pissed you off?" the teen asked.

Morgan chuckled. "That's an interesting question."

Petra turned and faced the adult. "You don't look like someone who gets her feelings hurt often." Her ponytail bounced as she talked.

Morgan grinned. "So you think you've got me pegged."

Petra smiled.

"Usually I'm not so emotional, but today was different."

"Well, if there's anything that you want to talk about, I'm here. All of my friends call me for advice," Petra said.

"Thank you," Morgan said. Her smile was warm and sincere.

"And thanks for taking me shopping," Petra said, feeling very mature.

"You're welcome." Morgan's smile widened.

"Morgan?" Petra said tentatively.

"Yes."

"Did you have someone to talk to, when you were my age?"

Morgan kept her eyes on the road. "No, but I'm sure that my life would have been different, if I'd had someone to look up to and give me advice."

Scenery blurred as the SUV traveled fast. In summer, M-43 was beautifully scenic, but its curves were still treacherously dangerous. The ride was both exhilarating and enjoyable.

"How much longer?" the teen asked.

"We'll be at your grandmother's house in less than twenty minutes," Morgan answered.

Petra glanced back out the window. "Chicago doesn't look like this," she said.

"Rome doesn't either."

Petra faced Morgan again. Her eyes were bright. "You've visited Rome?" she asked.

"Many times."

"Where else have you traveled?" the teen asked excitedly.

"New York, London, and Switzerland."

"Anyplace else?" Petra asked.

Caught up in frivolity, Morgan said, "Paris."

"Wow, what did you do there?" Petra asked breathlessly.

Morgan looked uncomfortable. Then she squared her shoulders. "I promised your grandmother that I wouldn't lie about my past. So I'm not going to."

Petra sensed that the mood had changed. She looked Morgan straight in the eye.

"If you really knew me, you'd know that I'm not shocked by much."

Morgan's grin was slight. "I've made a few decisions in my life that I regret." Her eyes remained low.

"Does it involve a boyfriend?" the teen asked maturely.

Morgan's eyes widened. "Why yes, it does."

Petra brushed her comment aside and added, "My mom used to talk to me about men all of the time," she explained.

Then Morgan told Petra about Edward.

Petra listened without comment. Right before they pulled onto her grandmother's street, the teen finally spoke. "Were you happy in Europe?" she asked.

"Sometimes, but mostly I felt alone," Morgan said honestly.

"I know the feeling."

Morgan's eyes moistened. "We have a lot in common, my friend. I won't make anymore bad decisions, if you don't." The girls playfully pressed their thumbs together and then began laughing.

"Morgan?"

"Yes, Petra?"

"Thanks for telling me the truth."

"I had too. I made a promise to your grandmother." Morgan parked in front of Rosemary's house and faced Petra. She was smiling.

"What's so funny?" the teen asked.

"Petra McDonald, you are wise beyond your years."

Petra smiled back. Then she opened the passenger door, ran across the grass, and up the front steps. Petra was pleased with how her day had gone. The evening could only get better.

CHAPTER 37

✝

"HONEY, I NEED TO TAKE A SHOWER," JACOB YELLED.

The bathroom door finally opened. "Geez Dad, you should have gotten up earlier. When you snooze, you lose," Petra said.

Petra darted through the open door, just before Jacob snapped his towel, missing her by inches. Father and daughter laughed.

"Uh-huh, I'll remember this," he said, as Petra slammed her bedroom door shut.

Rosemary frowned. "I'll expect to see you downstairs in fifteen minutes," she said.

Jacob felt twelve again. "Yes Ma," he said, before closing the bathroom door. He never saw his mother's sly smile. Twenty-five minutes later, Jacob, Petra, and Rosemary left for church. The routineness of the morning rekindled feelings that he'd long since forgotten.

In childhood, Jacob had eagerly anticipated Sunday morning service. New Life Full Gospel Church had been his second most favorite place in the world. All of the McDonald children relied on their mother's pragmatism and unconditional love, but his father's irregular work hours and frequent church obligations had frequently kept him away from home. Deon had explained that middle children often felt neglected. He'd never considered himself a middle child until their discussion. Jacob glanced towards the bluff. Lake Michigan's blue waters sparkled and shimmered below. After exiting his mother's car, he jogged around the vehicle and opened her door.

Rosemary used his arm for leverage before she exited. "It's been a pleasure escorting mi' lady to church," he said teasingly.

His mother brushed his hand away. "Jacob, stop playing."

Petra giggled from the backseat.

He closed his daughter's door. Then the threesome entered the building. Much had changed over the years. Deep purple carpet accentuated dark mahogany pews. The alter was awash in lighting. "When was the sanctuary remodeled?" he asked.

Rosemary nodded. "A few years ago."

"It looks nice." It had been years since he'd last visited this building. Jacob glanced at his watch. It was still early. People were scuttling about, preparing for morning service. In one corner, deacons and deaconesses were praying. In another section, choir members languidly talked while putting on their robes. The calm busyness was comforting and familiar.

"What's on your mind?" Rosemary asked, as they approached the McDonald pew.

Jacob remembered how happy his father had been when the pew pledge was finally paid off. "I was just thinking about Dad," he said wistfully.

His mother nodded. "I think about him often."

Jacob stared at his mother. In all these years, he'd never contemplated his mother's singleness, her loneliness. Never complaining, she'd raised her children and even a few of her grandchildren alone.

"Ma, why didn't you ever remarry?" he asked impulsively.

Her eyes shuttered. "Five kids kept suitors away. Then, I got comfortable. Now it doesn't matter."

"Don't you get lonely?" Jacob asked, struggling with the ever-present emotion, himself.

"Absolutely, nights are the worst," she said.

"Still after all of these years?" he asked, truly surprised by her answer.

His mother chuckled. "I'm not dead."

Jacob blushed. His father's death had altered God's plan. Lillian's death had altered his life. His mother had always relied on Godly support. He was freefalling, with no land in sight. Jacob grabbed his mother's hand. "I didn't mean to rekindle unpleasant emotions," he said.

Rosemary glanced sideways. "You didn't, your father and I had eighteen good years together."

Jacob cringed. He couldn't say the same about his marriage. He sat and stared.

"Forgiving ourselves is often harder than forgiving others," Rosemary said.

Jacob exhaled. Then he looked up. The room was now half full. Time had passed in the blink of an eye. A short time later, service commenced. Then, the choir began singing. Jacob sang loudly, hoping to drown out voices in his head, but try as he might, the ploy didn't work.

CHAPTER 38

✝

MORGAN FINISHED BRUSHING HER TEETH AT THE KITCHEN SINK. SHE'D SHOWERED AT HER SISTER'S house the previous night since the bathroom was still gutted. At least, Leroy had installed her new toilet.

Morgan walked back into the bedroom. Already dressed, she sat on the end of the bed and buckled her strappy sandals. Then she stood in front of the dresser mirror and critiqued her attire. The expensive fabric of her summer dress flattered her ample curves. Morgan placed diamond drop earrings in her ears and applied lip color to her full pouty lips. When she smiled, a carbon copy of her mother, smiled back.

Morgan's stomach was tightly knotted. Dread had turned into panic that morning. She wasn't ready to speak with her mother again. So, she'd decided to sit with the McDonald family this morning. Destiny was well aware of her plans. She'd stayed with her sister the past two nights and they'd spent long hours, just talking and getting to know each other. Morgan had greedily consumed any and all information about their family.

The two sisters had also explored their similarities. Like Morgan, Destiny didn't know her biological father and paternal abandonment had caused low self-esteem and feelings of unworthiness. Destiny had two adorable children, fathered by two equally dangerous men. She'd finally made peace with her children's fathers and their mom. Christ centered decisions appeared to be working for the young single mother.

Morgan was happy for her sister and she desperately wanted the same kind of peace that Destiny exhibited. She'd mistakenly assumed that the younger siblings had received better treatment from their mother. She and Sara had grown up feeling jealous and alienated from the younger girls. Now, the two older siblings were estranged. At one time, secrets had bonded them closely. Now, those same secrets kept them apart. Destiny had given Morgan a lot to think about.

As she drove towards the church, Morgan enjoyed the lush foliage that lined Blue Star Memorial Highway. She saw deer on the side of the road and slowed her vehicle. The animals darted in front of her car, forcing her to stop entirely. Morgan gazed in wonderment at their beauty before she resumed driving. Soon, the church came into sight.

The lot was full, so Morgan parked on the side of the road. She put on sunglasses, grabbed her purse, and gingerly tip toed along a rock-lined ditch. Head held high, she strode into the building alone. The lobby was fairly empty when she arrived. The sanctuary doors were closed, so she patiently waited with a small group of latecomers until the doors were opened again. Morgan was the last to enter the sanctuary. She stood in the entrance and looked out over the congregation. Heads turned and eyes gawked as she walked down the center aisle. She desperately searched for Rosemary. Her stomach cramped and churned. Then she saw Petra waving. Anxiety became relief. Now all she had to do was maneuver to the far right aisle without making eye contact with anyone. An usher gave assistance. Morgan reached the McDonald pew and relaxed. Jacob's expression was unreadable, but Petra grinned joyfully.

Morgan exhaled. Her family was seemingly unaware of her presence. Then she noticed that the McGregor clan was seated to the left. She waved at Stewart McGregor and his wife. She owed Stewart so much, having learned about property acquisition while working for Property Management Inc., during high school and college. His mentorship had ignited her passion for business. Then movement caught her eye. Chandra O'Neal, an old classmate was waving. Morgan grinned and waved back excitedly at her old high school friend.

She removed her sunglasses, since they weren't hiding her identity and placed them in her purse. Rosemary patted her hand. She relished the older woman's kindheartedness. Morgan continued scanning the room. So many faces looked familiar even if she couldn't recall any names. She wondered how many other parishioners were struggling with shame.

Then the choir stood for its final selection. Morgan closed her eyes and allowed the song's words to sooth her spirit. A single tear fell. Then another. She wiped her eyes with the back of her hand. A box of tissue was passed. More tears fell. Morgan felt out of control. Then she felt Petra lean closer. The teen grabbed her hand and held it tightly. Morgan not only mourned another failed relationship, but her father's abandonment and her mother's deception. Applying pressure to her eyelids didn't stop the tears from flowing.

Soon Pastor Deon stood behind the podium. He delivered a fiery message on hope. Morgan held on to every word. She needed a do over. She really needed God's forgiveness and a fresh start. As Pastor Deon preached, she recalled Mona's unwavering faith and her commitment to family. She'd loved Morgan unconditionally. So, there was no reason to believe that God couldn't love her.

Before the service ended, Morgan stood with the entire congregation and repeated *The Sinner's Prayer.*

"Are you okay?" Petra whispered.

Morgan nodded. Pews began emptying. Once again, Morgan pushed her sunglasses high on the bridge of her nose. This time, they covered swollen eyelids, not shame. She followed Rosemary through a side door. A small group of parishioners merged with a larger crowd that was walking down a long corridor. The foursome eventually reached the foyer.

"I'm so glad that you came," Rosemary said.

"Did I have a choice?" Morgan asked.

Rosemary cradled her hand. "Always, choice is a gift from God."

From the corner of her eye, Morgan watched Jacob hug Verna McGregor. The elder McGregor's were snowbirds that spent the summer months in Indigo Beach and wintered in Arizona. Stuart, her husband shook Jacob's hand. Apparently, she and Jacob's lives were intertwined as well.

"What are your plans for the rest of the day?" Rosemary asked.

Morgan shrugged. "I don't have any."

"We're going on a picnic. You're welcome to join us."

Morgan smiled. Spending the afternoon with Rosemary's family sounded wonderful, almost normal. "Thank you, it sounds like fun."

Rosemary smiled. "You and Petra wait here while I grab a few items from the office."

The teen rolled her eyes.

"We'll be out on the bluff," Morgan said, humored by Petra's response.

The new friends strolled from the building and walked across the parking lot. They stood on the bluff and watched waves crash against the jagged rocks below. The water was three shades of blue, mimicking the Caribbean Ocean, a slice of heaven few Midwesterners ever had the chance to view or enjoy.

"Wow," Petra said, in awe.

Morgan understood the child's reaction. Her admiration was equally intense. "I've traveled all over the world and there's no place more beautiful than Lake Michigan."

"The view is prettier on this side of the lake," Petra said, quite confidently.

"Oh, I'm sure it's similar," Morgan said, baiting the teen.

Petra's forehead furrowed. Then tears shimmered in the child's pale brown orbs.

"What's on your mind?" Morgan asked.

Petra wiped her eyes with a shirtsleeve. "I miss my mom."

Morgan gave the teen a side hug while they continued staring at the shoreline. Right there on the bluff, Morgan prayed for the kind of peace that only God could provide. Then she prayed for Petra. The child had experienced so much loss. It wasn't fair that children paid for their parent's mistakes, but from personal experience, she knew that they did.

CHAPTER 39

✠

EDWARD STARED AT THE PAPERS ON HIS DESK. THEN HE RECALCULATED THE NUMBERS AGAIN. The results didn't change. Something was off. He dialed his assistant.

"Jacque, what's the name of the employee that Jeffery uses for trouble shooting in Mexico?" Edward's memory was failing him again.

"I'm not sure, Sir, but I'll get the information for you."

"Do it now!" Edward slammed the phone down. Nothing was going right. The spot that he was in was Cherie's fault, so a visit to the penthouse was out of the question. Besides, the office rumor mill was in overdrive and he was tired of being talked about. The situation was intolerable. His phone rang again.

"Sir, his name is McDonald, Jacob McDonald, and he's on vacation."

Edward cursed. "For how long?" he asked.

"Two more weeks, Sir."

Edward cursed louder. Jeffery would never forgive him for meddling in Mexico. But he'd been so sure of this new project's potential. Jeffery would be displeased, but he'd never abandon Edward or allow the company to be jeopardized.

"Set up a conference call with Jeffery for Friday," Edward screamed, at his employee.

"Yes sir."

Edward paced back and forth. The walls of his expertly designed office reeked of money, but his wealth meant nothing, compared to his failing health. Then his phone rang. "Yes Jacque."

"The Naples office is on line two. Another contract was improperly signed." Edward's frustration bubbled over.

"What do they want me to do about it?" he yelled.

"Fix the problem, Sir, that's your job," the man said dully.

Edward sighed. He knew that his behavior was both irrational and irresponsible, but he didn't care.

"So, what do you want me to tell them?" his employee asked. Edward rubbed his temples. "I don't care, tell them anything that you want. Just leave me alone," he growled. Then he threw the phone against the wall.

Edward stormed from his office and strode towards the elevator. The passageway felt hot and stifling. He needed fresh air. His breathing soon became labored. Beads of sweat slowly trickled down the sides of his face. While he waited for the elevator, he leaned against the wall. When it arrived, he quickly entered. Then he slowly collapsed to the floor. His medication was wearing off. Edward glanced wildly around the empty cab. When the elevator's doors finally opened, he kept his eyes tightly closed and tried not to focus on the gasps and yells of his employees. He was embarrassed, but the feeling soon left as consciousness faded to unconsciousness, then to blackness.

CHAPTER 40

✞

JACOB DROVE FAST. FORTUNATELY, TRAFFIC WAS LIGHT. HE'D LEFT MICHIGAN AT THE CRACK OF dawn after he'd received the emergency call from the Rousseau office. His mother had voiced her displeasure, but Petra had responded with stony silence. After placing MP3 earphones in her ears, she'd stomped up the stairs and slammed her bedroom door. He'd apologized, but not surprisingly, she hadn't accepted.

Jacob revved his motor. The car's engine purred on the open highway. Then he called his administrative assistant. "Evan, what's your take on the Rousseau problem?" he asked.

"Puzzling," the man said.

He'd stated precisely what Jacob was feeling. The coworkers discussed the matter until Jacob reached the city limits. Chicago's famous skyline was picturesque against a brilliant blue sky. After parking in the underground garage, Jacob rode the elevator to his floor. When he entered, the condominium felt sterile and cold, which contrasted greatly with the comfortableness of his childhood home.

Lillian had yearned to express her bohemian and eclectic decorating style in their home, but he'd staunchly rejected her decorating ideas. His world was orderly. Her panache was impractical and unsophisticated. He'd forced her to accept white walls. She'd lived miserably. He'd made her live a lie.

Out of habit, Jacob gazed into Petra's bedroom. Her diverse taste and bold color choices made him smile. The room was the only space in the house that radiated personality. The rest of the living space was colorless and devoid of character. Jacob was starting to see how domineering he'd been. The revelation saddened him. He quickly changed his clothes and left, hoping for light traffic.

As he drove to the office, Jacob mourned another broken promise. Once again, work was taking precedence over his family, but this time, he felt terrible. Jacob knew that he'd blown it with his daughter. He'd disappointed Petra again. She was also right about his character, although, he hated to admit it. Her assessment of him was correct. He was a liar, a very bad liar.

CHAPTER 41

✝

MORGAN DROVE TOWARDS THE COTTAGE. ROSEMARY HAD CALLED EARLIER, SO SHE KNEW THAT Jacob had left that morning. Sympathetic to the young girl's feelings, she was ignoring the teen's hostility. "I want to show you how much work Leroy has completed," she said brightly.

Petra continued moping.

Morgan used humor to get the young girl's attention. "Earth to Petra, Earth to Petra."

Petra cut her eyes.

"I know that you're upset, but I will not let your father's unexpected departure ruin our day."

Petra glowered.

"Do you remember what Pastor Deon said yesterday?" Although the teen was scowling, Morgan knew that she had her attention. "He said that we should place our hope in God, not man. People make mistakes. We both have. Your father promised to spend three weeks of vacation with you and he will. It just won't be three consecutive weeks."

"He's such a liar," the teen growled.

"You have every right to be angry."

Petra's eyes moistened. "I hate him. Is that wrong?"

Morgan thought for a moment, desperately hoping that she answered the question correctly. "Anger is a natural response to disappointment, but acting on it, is sinful."

"What do you mean?" the teen asked.

Morgan parked and then turned sideways. "Your dad has to answer to God for breaking his promise, but you shouldn't judge him."

"So I can't give him the silent treatment?"

Morgan smiled. "You can, but you still have to forgive him and move on. I'm not saying that it's going to be easy, but it's what God expects. Now let's go inside. I want to show you my new bathroom."

Petra moaned melodramatically and slammed the passenger door. Then she followed Morgan into the house. The duo sidestepped equipment that had been left on the kitchen floor and wound their way into the bathroom. "It's beautiful," she exclaimed, as she glanced wide-eyed at the new walls, flooring, and tile work. Petra ran her hands across the porcelain sink.

"I couldn't have done it without you," Morgan said.

"You know, coral colored towels would look great against those taupe walls."

Morgan grinned. "I'm not so sure about that."

"Either that or purple," the teen said animatedly.

Morgan seriously contemplated the last suggestion. "I could live with purple."

Petra's smile grew wider.

"Now come on, we've got some shopping to do," Morgan said, as she led Petra from the room. Once they were back in the car, Morgan hoped that the teen's mood improved.

Petra glanced sideways. "Morgan, have you forgiven your mother?"

Morgan was shocked that the teen had unearthed her hypocrisy. "No," she said.

"Will you?" Petra asked.

Morgan knew that her answer was critically important. "Even though, I don't want to, I will."

Petra thought about Morgan's answer before responding, "If you can do it, then I can too."

Morgan smiled.

"And Morgan," Petra said.

Morgan peered at the teen.

"Thanks for being truthful."

Petra deserved nothing less. As Morgan continued driving, she reflected on another truism that Mona had shared. Lies, no matter how small, didn't stay that way for long. She wondered whether her life would have turned out differently, if her mother had told the truth.

CHAPTER 42

†

DEON'S MIND WANDERED AS HE GAZED OUT OF HIS OFFICE WINDOW. RURAL PARISHIONERS OFTEN sought pastoral counsel because of groundless bias against mental health advocacy. Untrained clergy often lumbered under the weight of this additional responsibility. Deon held confidences close and honored trust above all else, but keeping his mouth shut wasn't always easy. Mamie's secrets needed exposing, but doing so would violate the privacy of others. He was caught in the middle.

His friend had just left his office. She was furious with Morgan's snub and with Destiny's apparent complicity. Considering Morgan's delicate emotional state, Deon was just thankful that the child had come to church at all. He'd been unsuccessful in getting Mamie to take responsibility for the chaos that she'd created. Her response hadn't been surprising. From his experience, folks usually wanted God's unequivocal forgiveness, but weren't willing to give it to others. During their heated debate, she'd even attacked his character. Deon had quickly rebuked Satan, the author of lies who was causing so much havoc.

Deon's thoughts shifted towards Morgan. God had brought her home for more than reconciliation with her mother. As He often did, the Father was weaving a tapestry, connecting people for a specific reason and a predetermined season. He couldn't wait to see where the Holy Spirit was leading this family.

Sea Gulls frolicked above the calm blue water. From the bluff's height, the lake shimmered silver below, which complemented the pale azure sky, marred only by soft fluffy clouds. Deon walked over to his desk and glanced at his calendar. Morgan's younger sister was visiting later that day. Destiny wanted to talk about her budding relationship with Mack McGregor. The bad boy was smitten with his childhood friend and Deon was pleased. It was time that the young man settled down and Destiny's calming spirit was the perfect counterbalance.

Deon sat and leaned back in his chair. He called out to Rosemary. "Did Bishop Josten return your message?"

Seconds later, Rosemary hollered back, "Yes, you have a four o'clock call with him."

"Excellent." Deon checked off another item on his to-do list. With two more scheduled appointments before Destiny arrived, he opened his Bible and began researching the topic of his next sermon.

CHAPTER 43

✝

JACOB'S ANALYTICAL MIND WORKED HARD TO MAKE SENSE OF WHAT HE'D JUST HEARD DURING the conference call. If not handled properly, Edward Rousseau's problem could negatively affect The Kennedy Group, his boss's privately owned interests. This wasn't his first interaction with the Rousseau organization, but he'd never been asked to trouble shoot for them before. It was quite disconcerting that Edward had signed a governmental contract without first consulting Jeffery, who had varied business interests in Mexico. Something didn't feel right and his instincts were rarely wrong. He dialed his boss.

"McDonald, what can I do for you?" Jeffery asked.

"What's really going on?"

Jeffery exhaled. "I don't know all of the details, but I really need your help. I'll reassign your other projects."

"You know that I'm supposed to be spending time with my daughter. She's having a few problems," Jacob said.

"You'll be well compensated for any inconvenience."

"It's going to take more than money to nullify that contract and sooth bruised egos. I need time, that I really don't have right now."

"Son, we've worked too hard in Mexico. We have too many investments…"

Jacob's temples throbbed from mounting pressure. "I thought that Edward used an outside consultant to evaluate deals. What happened?"

"That partnership dissolved a few weeks ago."

Jacob pondered his boss's response. Then he acquiesced. "Consider it done."

"I already have."

After their call ended, Jacob dialed another number.

"McDonald, it's been awhile." The tenor of the man's voice was low.

"I've got a job for you."

"I don't normally hear from you unless you do."

"Find out everything you can on Edward Rousseau."

"Checking up on your boss's business partner, huh?" the voice asked.

"Unfortunately, yes."

"Same compensation plan as before?"

"Yes."

"I'll be in touch," the voice said, before disconnecting.

There were costs associated with breaking any contract. Jacob's job had always been to minimize the collateral damage that often resulted. Then it hit him. He'd broken many promises to Lillian. Petra's rebellion was nothing more than collateral damage. Grief weighted his shoulders.

In spite of work and ministry obligations, his father had always provided spiritual guidance. Jacob had viewed his father's prayerful wailings as theatrical performances, never truly understanding its true value, but now he did. What he'd viewed as weakness, God only saw as strength.

After turning off the lights and locking his office door, Jacob walked down a brightly lit hallway. Only a few employees remained. Most had left hours before. He stepped into the empty elevator. The cab descended to the underground parking lot, located below. Jacob exited and then treaded across stark gray concrete. *Swish, tap, swish tap.* His footsteps echoed distinctively as he walked. He entered his car and fastened his seat belt. Jacob pulled out from his assigned parking space, acknowledging the structure's unnatural silence. Then he turned on his stereo. God's Word instead of music blasted from its speakers. Dusk had finally descended in the city. Downtown Chicago pulsed with excitement and energy, but his drive home was short and bittersweet.

Once, owning a large condo, in an urban high-rise had meant everything. It didn't now. Jacob rode the elevator up to his floor and entered his home. He set his briefcase down by the door and immediately ordered dinner from the concierge. Then he walked into his bedroom and undressed. A quick shower later, he was lounging in pajama pants, while he waited for his meal to arrive. Then the living room walls began constricting. The air thinned and his breathing became short and erratic. He gasped and then a moan caught him off guard. Memories flooded, making him emotional. Soon, he was sobbing for a father that he'd never respected. More tears fell. Jacob brushed them away in shame, but an emotional dam had been breached and now overflowed. When his meal arrived, he pulled himself together long enough to accept the expensive steak that now set uneaten on the kitchen counter.

Overwhelmed with grief and regret, Jacob lay prostrate on the room's plush white carpeting. He cried repentantly, for acknowledged and unintentional sin. His mother had been right about so many things and it was a hard pill to swallow.

CHAPTER 44

✝

DEON SAW HIS WIFE AS SOON AS HE ENTERED THE CHURCH VESTIBULE. SUMMER AND MAMIE were talking by the main entrance. Bible study had just ended. Parishioners were still milling about.

"Bishop Bailey taught a wonderful lesson tonight. Deon, don't you agree?" Summer asked.

Mamie stifled a giggle.

Deon sighed. At almost ninety, the deacon's best teaching days were probably behind him. He cleared his throat. "I'll speak with the deacon tomorrow."

"I know that you'll do what's best," Summer said. Her eyes danced in merriment.

"Pastor, I was just congratulating your wife on the sweet corn I purchased at your farm stand. It's been some of the best that I've eaten in years."

"Why, thank you?"

"I fried the last of it today."

"Mamie, you babysit all day and cook too. I don't know where you find the time," Summer said, in amazement.

Mamie smiled proudly.

Frustrated that their counseling sessions were yielding so little progress, Deon muttered under his breath.

Summer glared.

"What have I done now?" he demanded. Then he scowled at his

childhood friend. "Have you studied any of the scriptures that I've given you?" he asked, deliberately needling her.

"When have I had time? I watch kids and cook all day," she snapped.

Deon glared.

Just then, Destiny's daughter ran across the lobby. "Grandma, Grandma," the child chanted, before she hid between her grandmother's bare legs.

"Give your grandma some suga'." Mamie hunched down and accepted Kimmie's sloppy kiss. "Umm, that was good," she said, as she affectionately swatted the youngster's chubby thighs.

"Sorry for the interruption," Destiny said, as she approached the group. "Evening, Pastor." The young woman hugged Deon paternally.

"Are you on your way home?" Mamie asked her daughter.

She nodded. "Do you need anything before I leave?"

Mamie shook her head. "No, but drive safely. I worry about you girls traveling these country roads alone."

Destiny smiled. "I'll call when I get home," she said, as she ushered her kids out the door.

"'That child didn't turn out too badly?" Mamie said, watching Destiny depart.

"Not bad at all, are you ready to leave?" Deon asked his wife.

Summer nodded.

"Don't forget that I want another bushel of corn," Mamie said.

"We'll have it ready. Enjoy the rest of your evening," Summer said, before the couple exited the building.

Deon remained somberly quiet as he escorted his wife to their vehicle.

"What's on your mind?" she asked.

"I'm sick of generational sin." He held the passenger door open.

"Most folks don't recognize its affects until it's too late," Summer said.

Deon thought about his wife's insightful observation. Sin ruined lives and aborted dreams. What most folks didn't realize was that deeds done in darkness always came to light. Deon made sure that Summer was comfortably seated and then he sat behind the steering wheel of their car. The couple was reflectively quiet as they traveled towards their farm.

CHAPTER 45

✝

"PETRA, IT'S TIME TO START DINNER."

Petra ignored her grandmother's directive.

"Petra, get down here right now," Grandma Rosemary hollered again.

The teen turned off the music and scooted off of her bed.

"Petra!"

This time, her grandmother sounded serious. Petra raced down the stairs. Grandma Rosemary stood at the base of the staircase with her arms folded tightly across her heaving chest. She was irritated.

"Sorry, I didn't hear you," Petra said, making an excuse.

Her grandmother scowled.

Petra kept quiet. Then she asked, "What are we fixing for dinner tonight?"

"Meatloaf."

Petra followed her grandmother into the kitchen. Then she saw a package of ground beef on the counter. "I hate touching raw meat."

"I'm well aware, now wash your hands and dump the meat into that bowl."

Petra gagged.

Grandma Rosemary placed a knife and an onion on the counter. "When that's done, then start dicing."

Grandma Rosemary was short tempered and cranky. "Are you making dump cake or a cobbler?" the teen asked. Two cans of peaches were on the counter.

"Cobbler."

One-word answers weren't characteristic of her grandmother at all. Petra started chopping. When she finished, she set the onions aside.

"Grandma, I'm done."

Startled, Rosemary looked up from kneading dough. "What did you say?" she asked.

Petra sucked her teeth. "I said I'm done."

"Don't get fresh with me young lady. You're not done. Add those breadcrumbs, eggs and seasonings to the meat."

"With what?" Petra asked, not seeing a spoon.

Grandma Rosemary lost all patience. "With your hands, the quicker you work, the faster you'll finish."

While her grandmother watched. Petra plunged her hands into the bowl of raw meat. The mixture squished between her fingers. She fought waves of nausea and then quickly dumped the contents into two loaf pans. Gasping for air, Petra raced to the sink and washed her hands.

Ignoring her histrionics, Grandma Rosemary placed the pans into the preheated oven.

"'This is so nasty," the adolescent yelled.

"Hush up and sanitize the counter," Grandma Rosemary said, without looking up. Then she handed Petra a spray bottle of cleaner.

Petra's eyes narrowed suspiciously. "Grandma, are you okay?" she asked.

"Why do you keep asking questions?"

Petra shrugged. "Because you're acting funny."

"Everything is fine. I just have a few things on my mind. It's nothing for you to worry about."

Petra wasn't convinced.

"Set the timer. Then peel these potatoes," Grandma Rosemary said, pushing a five-pound bag of organically grown white potatoes across the table.

Petra picked up a paring knife.

"Let me know when you're finished," Grandma Rosemary said. Then she took off her apron.

Stunned, Petra stared after the retreating figure. "You're leaving."

"Yes."

Petra's eyes narrowed. Grandma Rosemary never let anyone work in her kitchen alone.

"I'm confident that you have everything under control," her grandmother said. Then she walked out the back door.

Petra grew increasingly alarmed as she thought about her grandmother's odd behavior. She thought about calling Morgan and then she decided to pray.

CHAPTER 46

✝

RARELY PRONE TO EMOTIONALISM, ROSEMARY PLOPPED DOWN ON A GLIDER HIDDEN UNDER THE gigantic willow tree in her backyard. Even when her husband had been alive, she'd found comfort beneath the tree's massive branches. The metal chair creaked as it teetered back and forth while she swung. She couldn't believe that Jacob had left again, especially after promising his daughter that he wouldn't.

Within minutes of taking his administrative assistant's call, he'd begun packing for his trip back to Chicago. Rosemary knew that he was paid handsomely for troubleshooting. He'd jetted across the globe for years, but reneging on a promise was horribly irresponsible. God could turn their situation around, but Petra was still left hurting.

Rosemary rocked angrily. Her husband had died, leaving her with children to raise, bills to pay, and limited resources. Years later, she was still cleaning up problems his self-centeredness had created. Not for the first time did she curse his stubborn pride. Tears of frustration pooled in her eyes. She was tired of parenting hardheaded children and their insolent offspring. She'd once dreamed of retiring young and traveling abroad, but life had gotten in the way. Or more accurately, she'd allowed the enemy to highjack her plans.

She rocked harder, overwhelmingly frustrated at her son and with life. Petra was paying a tremendous price for her parents' sins. Rosemary cried out to the Father and thanked him for His sustaining love. She'd never taken His blessings for granted. She also shared her heartache and frustration with him. God desired transparency, real dialogue concerning real issues.

That morning, she'd stood in the doorway and watched her second born drive off, knowing full well that a storm was gaining momentum. Self centered, stubborn, and argumentative, he'd gotten into his car without a care in the world, focused on the bonus that he'd earn once this new project was completed. He'd happily explained the compensation plan and then made another promise to Petra, one he would never keep.

Petra thought the worst of her father. Truthfully, so did Rosemary, which was why she was shamefully hiding under the swaying limbs of a weeping willow tree. Her faith in God was high, but there was little left for Jacob. She continued rocking. Petra had been correct about one thing. She was acting differently. She felt waspish.

The girl probably deserved an apology, but on second thought, her conduct just might get the teen's attention. Rosemary slowed her swinging. Handling Petra was easy compared to managing her knuckleheaded son. Jacob needed a swift kick to his backside along with prayer. He misguidedly thought that he was in control, but Rosemary knew better.

Pride caused destruction and her son was at its precipice. Deceived, he couldn't see Satan's destructive forces at work, but Rosemary did. She hoped with all her heart that he didn't take his daughter down with him. The cycle of aborted dreams and death had to stop.

CHAPTER 47

✣

PETRA SPIED ON HER GRANDMOTHER FROM AN UPSTAIRS WINDOW. GRANDMA ROSEMARY WAS partially hidden under the huge willow tree that canopied the backyard. Its swaying limbs not only provided protection from the sun, but also from prying eyes. Petra wondered what her grandmother was doing and decided to find out. Racing down the stairs, she ran out the back door, but stopped when she heard her grandmother praying in her heavenly language. The older woman looked up and motioned for her to sit.

"Is dinner ready?" she asked.

Petra sat next to her grandmother. "I made a side salad and mashed the potatoes. The cobbler will be done in a few minutes."

Grandma Rosemary smiled. "I'm proud of you."

Petra was surprised. "Why?"

"Because, you're really learning your way around a kitchen. You have talent."

Petra warmed from the compliment. "Cooking is easy as long as I don't have to touch any meat."

"You'll outgrow that dislike," her grandmother joked.

"Grandma, why were you praying so loud?"

Grandma Rosemary smiled. "I didn't mean to frighten you."

"You didn't, not really, but your praying sounded different."

"I was interceding."

"What's that?" Petra asked.

"I was praying on behalf of others."

"So someone, other than my dad needs help?" Petra asked.

Grandma Rosemary chuckled. "Yes and deliverance often takes time."

"I think I understand," Petra said.

"I was praying for you, your father, Morgan and her mother, and a whole lot of people from church just now. I'll continue to pray for everyone, until the Lord tells me to stop." Then Grandma Rosemary stopped talking and glanced at her watch. "Hum, the cobbler should be ready."

Petra stood and raced towards the house.

"Set the table after you take the pie out," Grandma Rosemary hollered.

"Okay," Petra shouted. The timer was rhythmically peeping when the teenager entered the kitchen. Petra quickly washed her hands and turned off the oven. Then she removed the deep-dish pie. She set the container on the stovetop to cool.

Minutes later Grandma Rosemary reentered the kitchen. After washing her hands, she reheated left over green beans while Petra placed flatware on their placemats in the dining room.

"Everything looks beautiful," her grandmother said, when she entered the room.

Petra beamed.

"Why don't you bless the food tonight?" Grandma Rosemary asked.

Petra grabbed her grandmother's hand. "Lord, bless the food my grandma and I prepared. I don't know where my dad is or what he's doing, but please keep him safe, Amen."

Grandma Rosemary squeezed Petra's hand affectionately.

After fixing her plate, Petra gingerly took a bite of meatloaf. "This is really good," she said.

Grandma Rosemary chuckled. "Mixing the ingredients by hand makes all the difference in the world. It's part of my secret recipe," she said. She winked at her granddaughter.

After savoring another bite, Petra winked back.

CHAPTER 48

✝

MORGAN STARED AT LEROY'S CRAFTSMANSHIP. THE KITCHEN WAS COMING ALONG NICELY. Freshly painted walls shined brightly. She couldn't wait to see how the new cabinets would look when the doors were hung. Once the project was finished, the cottage would feel homier.

"Miss Morgan, everything should be done by Friday."

Morgan stood in the archway, admiring Leroy's work.

"Pretty fancy stuff for a country cottage," he said.

She smiled, acknowledging his compliment. "I fell in love with travertine when I lived in Paris."

He grunted. "There might be enough left to use on the fireplace."

Morgan's speculative eyes glanced at the hearth. "Do you really think that you'll be done by Friday?" she asked.

"I don't see any reason why I won't."

"Wonderful," Morgan said.

Leroy looked up. "I thought you'd be pleased," he said, focusing back on the job at hand.

Morgan walked into the parlor and sat in her grandmother's over stuffed chair. For days, she'd fought the urge to contact Edward. A habit of constant worry and concern about his health was hard to break. No one knew about his secret, not even his ex-wives.

Years earlier, she'd badgered him into seeing a specialist and had waited until the results of his tests came back. Edward had rebuffed the original diagnosis, gotten a second opinion, and then banned her from ever discussing his prognosis again. She'd honored his request. Morgan suspected that Jeffery knew. He was far too observant to let Edward's failings go unnoticed.

She picked up her phone and stared at Edward's number. Time passed slowly. Temptation almost won. Morgan grabbed an old afghan and draped it across her feet. Morgan closed her eyes while Leroy worked in the kitchen. Soon, drowsiness became sleep. Hours later, she awakened disoriented and disheveled. Shaking off lethargy, she walked into the bathroom and splashed cold water across her face.

"Miss Morgan, I'm done for the day. I sure hope that I didn't wake you." Leroy yelled, preparing to leave.

Morgan dried her face with a bright purple towel that she'd let Petra talk her into buying.

"You didn't bother me at all," she hollered back. She quickly brushed her hair and rinsed her mouth before exiting the room.

"I feel badly that you have to keep eating out," Leroy said, as he stood in the doorway.

"Don't, I've been sampling the best food that Indigo Beach has to offer." Leroy grinned. "Where are you headed tonight?"

"The Diner."

His grin grew wider. "Sounds like you're having chicken and waffles."

Morgan nodded and grabbed her purse.

"It's one of the best meals in town," Leroy said, as he watched Morgan prepare to leave.

Morgan turned the parlor light on before they departed. From her rearview mirror, she watched Leroy follow her out of the Valley. His truck trailed her SUV closely. A mile down the road, she turned right and he veered left. Thoughts of Edward soon faded away. Fifteen minutes later, she parked in the Diner's lot.

"Hey Morgan."

Morgan turned when she heard her name called. An old high school friend waved. The two women hugged in the parking lot.

"Are you eating alone or meeting someone?" the woman asked.

"I'm alone night."

"Me too, let's dine together," the woman said.

Morgan smiled, truly happy that she'd come home. The aroma of home cooked food smelled heavenly. Then she remembered something that her grandmother had told her years before. A good meal could help a woman forget a bad man. She hoped the adage was correct tonight.

CHAPTER 49

✝

EDWARD HAD MIXED EMOTIONS AS HE DRESSED FOR THE GALA. HE WAS BOTH DESPERATE AND scared. Horrible rumors were circulating about him throughout the business community. Shame fleetingly passed through his troubled mind. On top of everything else, his relationship with Morgan had irreparably harmed his bond with Jeffery. He shook off feelings of despair.

Now, Jeffery was justifiably angry with him again because he'd entered into a contractual agreement with the Mexican government. Edward hadn't known it would jeopardize Jeffery's holdings in Mexico or Latin America for that matter. International alliances had been Morgan's area of expertise, not his. Needing affirmation and a kind word, he dialed her number. It took time for the international call to connect. Then she answered.

"Edward! What's wrong?" she asked groggily.

"I'm sorry for awakening you."

"Has something happened?"

"Why do you ask?" Edward wondered whether rumors had reached Morgan in Michigan.

"Just wondering," she said, sounding more awake. Awkward silence ensued.

"Jeffery is in town," he said, making small talk.

"You haven't answered my question. Why are you calling?" she asked again. Edward felt old and replaceable. "I just wanted to hear your voice," he said. "Have you spoken with your mother?"

"Yes."

"How did it go?"

"I talked, she listened, and nothing changed."

"Talking is good, but listening is even better. I believe more talking and listening are needed. Have you met anyone new?" he asked, needing to know.

She chuckled. "No, because my days are spent in the company of a very wise fifteen year old."

" Boy or girl?" he asked.

"Girl."

"Does she remind you of yourself?"

Morgan chuckled again. "Yes."

"Well then, you're time is being well spent."

"Edward, are you well?" Morgan asked.

He contemplated his answer, having never lied to her before. "I really don't know. I've made a few mistakes lately," he said, hearing her gasp.

"How bad?"

"I don't know yet," he said.

"Can Jeffery help?"

Edward hung his head. "That's why he's here. He flew in from Switzerland yesterday."

"If you need me . . ."

Edward cut her off. "Everything will be fine," he said, not knowing whether he was speaking the truth.

"Tell Jeffery, I send my love," she said.

"If I remember, I will, *Au revoir Morgan.*"

"*Au revoir Edward.*"

Overwhelmingly saddened, Edward ended the call.

CHAPTER 50

⊷ † ⊶

CONVERSATION SWIRLED IN A CLOUD OF CONFUSION. EDWARD HELD ONTO THE YOUNG WOMAN who was gracing his arm. Sadly, he couldn't remember her name. She was young, voluptuous, and uninteresting, but because she was being paid generously to attend tonight's function, none of those attributes really mattered. A man standing on the landing, smiled down at Edward. He smiled back. Then the man nodded. Edward stared back in confusion. He didn't recognize the man's face. Nor could he remember his name, but he looked familiar. He reminded Edward of Jeffery, his business partner.

He and Jeffery's friendship had been forged over hours of case study reviews and business meetings. Their relationship had spanned, close to forty years. In life, Edward was wealthy, from old war money. He'd been sent to Harvard to earn a degree that married family name with credentials, promising credibility and prestige. Jeffery on the other hand, lacking title or funds, had used financial aid and keen intellect to complete his degree.

A personal loan from his grandmother had helped launch Jeffery's first business, a coffee distributorship. The Kennedy Group was now one of the top five, privately owned and operated distributorships world wide, employing thousands. One fortuitous phone call had opened the door to a partnership that now spanned the globe and had earned millions. Years later, the two college buddies purchased another small shipping business together and renamed it R. K. International. Edward handled the day-to-day operations from France, while Jeffery managed state side dealings from his home office in Chicago.

Edward glanced up again. The gentleman on the landing was walking down the stairs. Then he realized that the man was walking directly towards him. He grew anxious.

"Edward, you didn't tell me that you were attending this party," the man said, while clasping Edward's hand.

He tensed. Try as he might, he just couldn't connect a name with the man's face. Sweat pooled under his Italian made tuxedo.

Another man approached and addressed the gentleman. "Jeffery, it's good seeing you. How long will you be in Paris?" the stranger asked.

Confusion turned to relief as Edward watched the other man shake hands with his business partner. His brain finally made the connection. These episodes of forgetfulness were occurring far too frequently. Medication was only postponing the inevitable. Reality was slowly slipping away.

"Jeffery," Edward said, hugging his friend. "Are we still meeting tomorrow?"

Jeffery nodded.

"Excellent, but tonight we'll enjoy the celebration," he said, thankful for brief moments of lucidity. "Darling, go get me a refill," he said to his date. She sauntered towards the bar.

"Your new muse?" Jeffery asked.

"No one can ever replace Morgan," he said.

Jeffery nodded. Then his phone rang, interrupting awkward silence.

"Edward, I need to take this call in private. We'll talk tomorrow." Jeffery walked away.

Edward waited for his date to return with a fresh drink. He gulped it quickly. The liquid had a calming affect as it pooled in his stomach. Edward took another sip. Conversations swirled around him and confusion briefly strangled reality again. He stretched out his arm. It was too bad that he couldn't remember the woman's name. She placed a pampered hand on his arm. After gently kissing her upturned cheek, they slowly exited the room.

CHAPTER 51

✞

DEON SAW ROSEMARY STANDING IN HIS DOORWAY. HE HELD UP HIS POINTER FINGER. WHILE SHE waited for his call to end, Rosemary continued staring out of his office window. When his call ended, he motioned for her to enter.

"So what was Sister Laura gossiping about?" she asked.

"Destiny and Mack of course, the kids went out on another date last night."

The co-workers slapped high-fives and giggled like school children.

"I'm truly happy for those two," Rosemary said, as she sat on the couch.

"I love watching how the Holy Spirit brings couples together. So what's on your mind?" he asked, leaning back in his chair.

"I'm concerned about Morgan."

"Me too."

Rosemary talked calmly while her hands lay diminutively across her lap. "God has finally given me permission to intervene."

Deon's forehead furrowed. "What do you have planned?"

"I'm going to offer Mamie some advise."

"Do you think that she'll be receptive?" he asked.

Rosemary smiled. "God's truth will shake things up a bit, but she'll listen."

Deon looked doubtful. "We're talking about Mamie."

Rosemary grinned. "I know, but I'm stepping out in faith. I really need your support."

"You have it, and if prayer isn't enough, I'll begin fasting tomorrow."

"Thanks, Pastor." Rosemary appeared more confident.

"Have you spoken with the girls today?" he asked.

Rosemary stood. "Yes, Petra called after lunch. They are really enjoying their visit to the beach."

Deon grinned. "Please thank your granddaughter for my meatloaf."

"Pastor, you didn't slice any of it, did you?" Rosemary asked.

"That large loaf in the fridge isn't for me?" he asked innocently.

"No it isn't," she chided.

Deon chuckled. "I was just messing with you. Mamie called about it while you were out. She's running a little late."

"I don't know why I fall for your shenanigans," Rosemary said, as she left his office.

A short time later, Deon heard muffled voices. When he opened his office door and peaked out, Mamie was seated in front of Rosemary's desk.

"Good afternoon Pastor," she said.

"How'd you know that it was me?" he asked.

"Your heavy breathing gave you away."

"Miss Harding, it is always a pleasure seeing you."

"I was just telling Rosemary that I'm surprised that you didn't steal my meatloaf."

Rosemary grinned tolerantly while Deon and Mamie bantered.

"It crossed my mind."

"Rosemary, please thank Miss Petra for me. My grandkids really love your meatloaf recipe."

"I will, but Mamie, I asked you to stop by for another reason."

Mamie glanced from Rosemary to Deon questioningly.

Deon shrugged.

"This sounds serious? Mamie joked.

"I'll give you ladies some privacy," Deon said.

Mamie rolled her eyes. "Why bother, when you'll just listen at the door."

Acknowledging the truthfulness of her statement, Deon sat down and crossed his legs.

Rosemary turned serious. "Mamie, we've been friends a long time."

"Yes we have," she said.

"This impasse with Morgan is troubling and I want to help."

Mamie slumped in her chair. "I don't know what you can do. I'm even at my wit's end."

Rosemary breathed deeply. "I need to share something with you."

Deon braced for an explosion.

Mamie peered expectantly.

"I've always known the identity of Morgan's father," Rosemary said.

Deon watched color drain from Mamie's face.

"Wha, what do you mean?" she stammered.

"My husband told me long before he died."

"But you never said anything."

Rosemary shook her head. "It wasn't any of my business."

Mamie peered questioningly at Deon.

"Do you know too?" she asked.

He nodded.

"The two of you must think terribly of me," Mamie cried, as she covered her face with her hands.

"Never," Deon said.

Rosemary nodded. "It's time that you told Morgan the truth. Too many people know it anyway," Rosemary said.

Deon watched Mamie blink back tears.

Then Rosemary walked around her desk and knelt before her friend.

"I'm so embarrassed."

"There's no need to be." Rosemary embraced her friend.

Mamie fanned her hands, attempting to dry her moistened eyes. "It's getting hot in here," she joked.

Deon's eyebrows narrowed. "Not hotter than somewhere else, you could be right now," he said dryly.

Mamie scowled. Then she turned serious. "I know that Morgan deserves to know the truth, but I'm scared."

"Of what?" Rosemary asked.

"Of her reaction." Mamie grabbed her purse. "I have some explaining to do, don't I?"

Deon and Rosemary nodded in unison.

Mamie looked away.

"I'll take you to get your meatloaf," Deon said, as he accompanied his friend into the kitchen to retrieve Rosemary's gift. As they walked towards the back door, Deon asked, "Are you still mad at me?"

Mamie stopped in the middle of the hallway and said, "Yes."

Deon grinned.

"I should have joined Third Baptist Church when I had the chance."

Deon's laughter echoed down the hallway.

"What's so funny?" Mamie asked, as she sassily leaned on one hip.

"I can think of at least three different husbands and their wives who would have objected to your membership."

"Oh, Deon," Mamie wailed.

Deon opened the back door and watched Mamie stomp across the parking lot. Then he strolled back towards his office, knowing with surety that Rosemary's intervention had been a directive from God.

CHAPTER 52

✝

JACOB READ THE REPORT AGAIN, BUT NOTHING NEW JUMPED OUT. R. K. INTERNATIONAL HAD experienced explosive growth for five solid years. During that time, Edward had relied less and less on his leadership team, and more on a particular financial consultant. Close associates attributed the company's success to this woman, his young African American muse.

Edward's divorce papers contained explosive information about her. Jacob messaged his throbbing temples. Various pictures of the couple lay scattered on his desk. According to court documents, Edward's generosity towards his lover had played a major role in his second divorce. Apparently, the whole sordid affair had been tried in the court of public opinion.

Jacob leaned back in his chair. There was no denying that Morgan, had almost singlehandedly catapulted the company's New York office into profitability. The woman was smart and an adept strategist. He'd heard about her accomplishments, but only in global terms. Now that he'd been in her presence, he understood her power. Unfortunately, if a quarter of what he'd just read about Morgan Harding was true, she wasn't fit to have contact with his daughter.

Jacob stuffed the report into his brief case. Like a computer, his logical mind filtered and sifted all the information that he'd just read. Now, he had another job to do, which was far more pressing than his current project. His mother had made a serious error in judgment. Jacob couldn't undo any of the damage that his late wife's drinking had caused, but he could definitely fix this problem. And he would, just as soon as he spoke with his mom.

Jacob cleared his desk. He'd spent the past few days arranging meetings and schmoozing government officials while Jeffery and Edward's legal teams worked behind the scenes to nullify Edward's contract. He'd scheduled two important meetings in Mexico over the weekend. The kind of work that he had to do now couldn't be done during normal business hours.

Jacob exited the elevator and walked towards his car. It was late, but under the circumstances, the one-hour time difference between Michigan and Illinois was inconsequential, so he dialed his mother. The call went directly to voice mail. He'd taken Petra's phone as punishment, so he couldn't call her. Then he tried his mother's landline. Surprised, but not alarmed when she didn't answer, Jacob continued driving towards home.

Two hours later, he punched his pillows and settled under plush bedding. Moonlight filtered in through sheer curtains that covered his floor to ceiling window. Jacob relaxed. Although he still hadn't spoken with his mom, he had a clear plan for handling both of his problems. Sleep came fast and hard.

CHAPTER 53

✝

"I TRIED CALLING YOU LAST NIGHT." JACOB WAS ALREADY SEATED ON THE COMPANY JET.

"I returned home too late to call back. What's the matter?" Rosemary asked.

"Why does something have to be wrong?"

"Because, you haven't called once since you left for Chicago and in less than twelve hours, you've dialed my number three times. What's going on?"

"I don't want Petra associating with Morgan any longer."

"Did you have her investigated?" Rosemary asked, knowing that Jacob had used a private investigator before.

Jacob flinched, not liking the implication. "Not directly."

"I'm surprised that you'd make such an important decision without speaking with her first," she said calmly.

"Ma, the information I have is indisputable."

"I'm sure that it appears truthful, but I still think that you're making a mistake."

"A mistake, if you only knew what I just read," Jacob yelled.

"I probably do," she interjected.

Jacob inhaled. "So you know about her past and you still gave her access to my daughter."

"Adjust your tone young man. I'm still your mother," Rosemary snapped.

"She broke up a marriage."

"If that's true, then it's none of your business. We'll discuss this after you've calmed down."

"No," Jacob yelled. Frustration was fueling anger. "Tell her that you made a mistake."

"Deliver the message yourself."

Jacob fumed. "The plane is about to take off, so I need to turn off my phone," he lied to his mother.

Rosemary sighed. "As usual, you're much too busy to handle what's most important. When will you be back?" she asked.

Jacob heard censure. "Next Wednesday."

"Please do me a favor and speak with Morgan after you've talked with your daughter."

Jacob seethed. He knew what was best for Petra. "I can't agree to that."

His mother sighed. "Jacob, have you prayed about any of this?" she asked.

He exploded. "I don't have to pray about ending my daughter's relationship with a whore!"

Rosemary gasped. "Jacob!"

"My decision is final. I'll see you on Wednesday." Jacob hung up. Unbridled anger choked any rational thinking. Morgan was immoral like her mother and his deceased wife. Jacob knew first hand how dangerous this type of woman could be.

CHAPTER 54

❦ ✝ ❧

DEON SHOVED ANOTHER FORKFUL OF EGGS INTO HIS MOUTH WHILE HE WATCHED HIS WIFE sashay around the kitchen. He enjoyed spending quiet time with Summer. When the house phone rang, she handed it to Deon.

"Good morning," he said to the caller.

"Morning Pastor, can Petra and I stop by today. I really need to speak with you," Rosemary asked.

"It shouldn't be a problem. What time?"

"We'll be there in about an hour."

"I'm home."

"Give Summer my love, I'll see you soon."

Deon ended the call.

"Who was that?" Summer asked.

Deon took another bite and chewed. "Rosemary, she'll be here in an hour. She sends her love."

Summer stopped washing dishes. "I wonder what's going on?"

Deon shook his head. "I don't know, but we'll soon find out." He finished eating and then said a quick prayer.

Forty-five minutes later, Cocoa began barking when Rosemary's car pulled into the driveway. Deon stood behind the screen door in the living room, watching Rosemary and Petra walk up the sidewalk. Rosemary wore crisp cotton slacks and a matching shirt. Her graying hair glimmered pewter in the sun. It was pinned into a neat bun. As usual, she was the epitome of casual elegance.

Petra bounded up the stairs, earphones dangling.

Deon smiled.

The teen held up a convenience store bag and his grin widened. "Pastor Deon, we brought you a treat."

"My granddaughter doesn't think I'm spontaneous," Rosemary joked.

Deon winked at the teen. "She isn't, so stopping at Meriwether's had to be your idea."

Rosemary rolled her eyes.

"Grandma is taking Morgan and me shopping in South Bend today," Petra said happily.

Deon's grin broadened. "Shopping," he said. Deon knew that Rosemary hated shopping malls.

Petra nodded and then bent to rub Cocoa's ears. The dog's tail wagged contently.

"Cocoa, take Petra to Summer," Deon ordered.

The dog gently nipped at the teen's pant legs.

Petra laughed. "Does she really understand?"

"She sure does. She'll take you directly to Summer." Deon and Rosemary watched the dog lead Petra across the expansive front yard. The dog and teen soon disappeared.

"So, what's so important that you drove all the way out here," he asked, ignoring formality.

Rosemary's eyes blazed. "That fool son of mine had Morgan investigated."

Deon shook his head and then peaked into the convenience store bag. He couldn't wait until they got back into the kitchen. "Want one?" he asked, remembering his manners.

Rosemary shook her head.

Deon grabbed another mug from the drainer and handed it to Rosemary. She held it out and Deon poured a liberal amount of coffee into her mug. Then he took a donut from the bag and bit into a chocolate covered fry cake.

"I really don't know how much more Morgan can take," Rosemary said, sipping her black coffee.

Deon couldn't imagine anyone actually enjoying coffee without flavored cream and loads of sugar. In gastronomical delight, he took another bite.

"This is the same hair brained foolishness that his father used to do and look where it got him, dead and buried in an early grave," Rosemary said furiously.

Deon savored the fried dough. "Pride comes before a fall," he said.

"You are absolutely correct. My late husband's prideful nature contributed to his early demise," Rosemary said sadly.

Deon swallowed and then took another bite.

"Both his grandfather and father died from heart disease. Even when truth was staring him in the face, arrogance and stubbornness kept him from doing anything about it." Rosemary glanced his way.

With neither high cholesterol nor high blood sugar, Deon ignored her insinuation and pulled another donut from the bag. "Do you want to split a donut with me?" he asked feigning innocence.

Rosemary shook her head. "Pastor, I really need your undivided attention."

Chastened, Deon placed the uneaten pastry on a napkin and pushed it aside. Then he focused on the conversation. "Rosemary, I'm not surprised by Jacob's response. Pride can take on many forms."

"It's so frustrating," Rosemary said.

"When your husband passed, I was newly ordained and spiritually immature. I missed an opportunity to effectively minister to your son," Deon said.

"Deeply grieving myself, I wasn't there for him either," Rosemary said miserably.

"Kids don't come with a training manual," Deon said, hoping to lighten the mood.

"Parenting would be so much easier if they did."

"Why are you really so angry?" he asked, trying to get to the core of her troubles.

"He's so much like his father."

Deon now understood Rosemary's angst. "If your son humbles himself and repents, then deliverance can occur."

"He's repeating his father's mistakes."

"From my experience in counseling, children rarely do what they're told, but always do what they've seen."

"It's so frustrating," Rosemary said.

"I can only imagine. Weeks ago, Summer and I offered help. We'll start fasting tomorrow," Deon said. He pulled his napkin closer, picked up his donut and took a large bite. Gooey chocolate frosting dribbled down his hand. Deon licked his fingers clean.

"Thanks Pastor." Rosemary said, as she finished her coffee.

"We've been friends for too long. Besides, I owe you."

Rosemary looked puzzled.

Deon smiled. "Your visit kept me from working at the farm stand today."

Rosemary grinned. "By the way, did Jerome get a hold of you last night?" she asked.

Deon nodded and his smile turned electric. "That boy finally proposed to Dana. Looks like, there's going to be a wedding."

Rosemary clasped her hands. "I'm so happy for them."

Deon stood. "Leave your mug on the table. I'll get it later." Then Deon led Rosemary back into the living room. While he held the front door open, she walked onto the porch. Deon leaned over the railing and whistled. Cocoa's barking echoed across the yard. Minutes later, the pair watched as Petra followed the dog across the front yard.

"You didn't eat all the donuts did you?" the teen asked, when she reached the steps.

Deon looked uncomfortable.

"Pastor Deon," Petra moaned.

"There's a vanilla buttercream left. Will that do?"

"I guess," Petra said.

Deon went back into the house and retrieved the crumpled convenience store bag. "I'm sorry, I didn't know that I was supposed to save one for you."

The teen took a big bite from the vanilla covered fry cake. Then she licked her top lip.

Rosemary handed her granddaughter a tissue from her purse. "Come on Petra, we don't want to be late."

"Are you meeting Morgan at the mall?" Deon asked.

Rosemary shook her head. "No, I'm picking her up at the cottage."

Then Deon had an idea. "Wait a minute," he said, while running back into the house. When he reappeared, Deon held a twenty-dollar bill in his hand.

"What's that for?" Rosemary asked.

He smiled. "There's a new candy store in South Bend that carries an amazing selection of chocolates. A box of chocolate covered peanuts will get me husband points."

Rosemary chuckled. "Consider it done," she said, reaching for the money.

Deon stood on the porch and watched Rosemary's car pull onto the road. Rosemary's concerns were valid. Pride always ended in death, destruction or despair. Jacob was going to fall long and hard if he didn't make some personal changes. Deon also knew that Morgan Harding was tough and that the younger McDonald was about to meet his intellectual match. Lillian had cowered under Jacob's chauvinism and control, but Morgan was cut from a different cloth. Deon walked back into his house, knowing that the next few days were going to be interesting and he couldn't wait.

CHAPTER 55

✢

PETRA STARED OUT THE PASSENGER WINDOW AS SHE AND HER GRANDMOTHER DROVE TOWARDS Morgan's cottage.

"Grandma, I'm sorry about being such a pain."

"What are you talking about?" her grandmother asked.

A wave of regret washed over the teen. "You hate shopping, but you're taking me anyway. I really don't deserve this trip."

Grandma Rosemary smiled. "Love forgives and forgets."

"But I don't always do what's right."

"Sweetheart, if God doesn't remember your sins, then why should I," she said, as she patted Petra's hand.

The teen's grin broadened. "I keep forgetting about that," she said.

Grandma Rosemary chuckled. "That's why I keep repeating the same scriptural principles over and over again. Eventually, they'll sink in."

"Grandma, can we stop by the gas station again?" Petra asked.

Grandma Rosemary glanced sideways. "We were just there, what do you need now?"

Petra thought quickly. "I didn't realize that Pastor Deon would eat all of the chocolate donuts. They're my favorite too," she said, groaning for affect.

Grandma Rosemary sighed. "Yes, I'll stop, but you'll have to hurry. I don't want to keep Morgan waiting much longer." Grandma Rosemary pulled into the parking lot of Meriwether's Convenience Store and Gas Station. She parked, but left the engine running. "Now hurry," she said, handing Petra a couple of singles.

The teen exited and walked towards the entrance. After pushing the door open, she perused the store. Then she stealthily approached her target. Shawn, the Meriwether's godson and part time employee was stacking can goods on a shelf. He was two years older. The kids had known each other for years. They usually sat together during youth ministry. Petra liked his quiet, serious nature, even though he was country stupid. Petra didn't care much for his father. The man was old and funny acting, but Shawn's stepmom was nice. He rarely mentioned his biological mother, so Petra didn't know much about her. What really bothered her was that Shawn's father rarely let his son associate with his maternal side of the family. She knew his grandmother and aunts. They were really nice people.

"Hey Stupid."

Shawn turned. "Weren't you just here?" he asked.

Petra nodded. "Yeah, I need more donuts."

Shawn followed her to the warmer. "Why?"

Petra sucked her teeth. "Because Pastor Deon ate all the good ones," she said exaggeratedly.

Shawn chuckled. "I should have warned you."

Both kids turned when they heard Mrs. Meriwether holler, "Shawn, I need you to carry a bag of mulch out to Mrs. Turner's car."

"Yes Ma'am!" he yelled back.

Petra followed him to the cash register.

"Mornin' again, Miss Petra," Mrs. Meriwether, the proprietor greeted the teen.

Petra placed her bag on the counter.

"Will that be all?" the woman asked.

Petra nodded.

"Shawn, after you finish with Mrs. Turner, go and sweep aisle four. There's been a spill."

The older teen quietly waited until Petra paid for her purchase and then he escorted her to the front door.

"You workin' all day?" she asked.

Shawn pushed it open. "Pretty much."

The kids walked side by side across the lot.

"Why are you always working?" she asked.

Shawn lowered his voice. "My parents think that I'm savin' for a car."

"You're not."

"Nope, I'm planning on visiting my mom in Chicago real soon."

"Why?" she asked.

Shawn slowed down. "Because I've got a few questions to ask her."

Petra now stood beside the passenger door of her grandmother's car.

"Mornin' Ms. Rosemary." Shawn leaned in through the open window and greeted the older woman.

"Good morning Shawn."

"Where are you guys off to?" he asked.

"If we ever get out of town, Petra and I are going shopping in South Bend."

Shawn stepped away from the car. "Well, have fun," he said, before turning.

"Bye Shawn, and don't forget about Mrs. Turner," Petra said. The older woman was standing by the main entrance, frowning

"Oh yeah, bye!" he said, before running away.

Shawn was a good friend and Petra didn't fault him for leaving her at the cottage. She wondered if her grandmother had ever suspected that he'd been her accomplice. Petra bit into her donut. "I can't wait to see Morgan's finished kitchen," she said, with food in her mouth.

"Petra, mind your manners," Grandma Rosemary admonished.

The teen rolled her eyes before licking gooey frosting from her fingers. "I bet it's as beautiful as the bathroom," she said, savoring the dark chocolate frosting.

"I really don't see how you can eat those things," Grandma Rosemary said, tolerantly.

"They're the best."

Her grandmother smiled. "I suppose they were, when I was your age."

Petra leaned back contemplatively. She just couldn't picture her grandmother being young. While they drove towards the cottage, she thought about Shawn's father. His dad was mean. She felt sorry for her friend. Petra glanced sideways. She was blessed to have a grandmother who loved her unconditionally. Since Shawn's father wouldn't allow him to visit his maternal grandmother, the teen had never experienced what she'd always taken for granted. Petra turned somber and then she became sad.

CHAPTER 56

✝

MORGAN WAITED PATIENTLY FOR ROSEMARY AND PETRA TO ARRIVE. A DUSTY BLUE SKY PEEKED through the treetops. Always amazed by the wonders of nature, Morgan watched a soaring hawk swoop down on an unsuspecting rodent. The bird's wings flapped mightily as it soared with the creature still hanging from its sharp talons. Morgan stood behind the screen door until she heard a car on the private road. She waved when Rosemary's vehicle pulled into the driveway.

"Morgan," Petra yelled from the open window.

Morgan smiled, truly excited to see the pair. "Good morning," she hollered as she stepped onto the porch.

Petra exited her grandmother's car and ran into her friend's welcoming embrace. "I can't wait for Grandma Rosemary to see your new rooms," the teen exclaimed.

Morgan waited until Rosemary climbed the front steps. Then the trio entered the cozy cottage. Excitement grew when she saw Petra's eyes enlarge as the newly renovated kitchen came into view.

"Wow, it's beautiful," the teen said approvingly.

Morgan smiled.

Rosemary clasped her hands together in delight.

Stone flooring, granite countertops, and stainless steal appliances glistened. Petra was correct. The room was exquisite, and definitely not out of place, in its humble surroundings.

"Grandma, come see the bathroom. I picked out all of the accessories,"

Petra said, grabbing her grandmother's hand. The teen led the older woman down the short hallway.

Morgan stood back and let the pair ooh and aah over the beautifully appointed space.

"Morgan, I have to tell you that I'm impressed. You've definitely given me a few new ideas for my old house," Rosemary said.

Morgan smiled.

"Grandma, your house is perfect the way it is," Petra interjected.

Morgan and Rosemary glanced at each other.

"Sweetie, sometimes change is good," Rosemary said.

Petra frowned, clearly not liking the idea.

"Come on you two, let's not waste another minute of this beautiful day. There's shopping in our future," Morgan said, grabbing her purse and jacket from the back of a chair. The three women exited. Rosemary and Petra stood to the side while Morgan locked the front door.

"Grandma, when are we having lunch?" Petra asked.

"You can't possibly be hungry. You just ate two whole donuts," Rosemary said.

Just then Morgan patted her growling stomach.

"Apparently, my granddaughter isn't the only one who needs food."

Slightly embarrassed, Morgan walked across the yard and opened the passenger door of Rosemary's car. Petra climbed into the back seat. Once everyone was settled, Rosemary backed from the driveway. Forty-five minutes later, the trio dined in a cozy restaurant. They consumed grilled chicken sandwiches and salads outside the city limits of South Bend, Indiana.

Rosemary placed two boxes of chocolates on the counter of the regionally famous chocolatier. The shop was impressive. Petra sat in the corner of the store, looking stuffed and miserable.

Morgan appeared content. "This is the most fun I've had in years," she said.

Rosemary smiled. The day was turning out quite nicely. The chili pepper flavored trifle that she'd just sampled had been surprisingly good.

"We'll have to come back at another time and dine in the café. The prices on the menu looked reasonable."

"Can we leave now?" Petra moaned. The teen looked stuffed.

"No one told you to eat so much. We'll leave as soon as Morgan and I are ready. Then, I'm going to find a bench in the center of the mall and let you girls go shopping."

Petra moaned. "Grandma."

"Don't grandma me, you only want me along so that I'll pay for your purchases. Morgan has young legs and I don't. She can accompany you."

"I'm actually looking forward to it," Morgan said.

The trio eventually left the shop. A short time later, Rosemary rested on a bench in the center of the mall while the girls went from store to store. When Morgan and Petra finally finished shopping, Petra gave her Grandmother's charge card back.

"By the size of your bags, young lady, you gave this card a work out," Rosemary said.

Petra grinned.

Rosemary noted that the teen's earlier discomfort was long gone and forgotten. The group eventually left the mall. While Petra slept peacefully in the backseat, Morgan and Rosemary quietly talked.

"Thanks for today," Morgan said.

Rosemary smiled. "Child, you've taken really good care of Petra these past several weeks. Buying you lunch was the least that I could do."

"I'm not talking about the meal."

Rosemary understood what remained unspoken. "You're welcome, truthfully, I wasn't sure whether the arrangement would work. Thank you for being receptive."

"Petra is an amazing young woman. I have really enjoyed myself," Morgan said.

"Are you moving back to Indigo Beach permanently?" Rosemary asked.

"I'm really not sure yet, but I do know that I want to complete graduate studies here in the states."

"I know that you've been working from home. Is that a long term option?" Rosemary asked.

"It could be." Then Morgan became pensive.

"Child, what's on your mind?" Rosemary asked.

"You've never judged my family. Why not?"

Rosemary smiled. "Because judging is God's job, not mine."

"I don't understand."

"Most people don't." By now, Rosemary was parked in front of Morgan's cottage. Darkness had descended and June bugs buzzed and zapped around the porch light that Morgan had left on.

"Folks have looked down on me my whole life," Morgan said.

"I know and believe me, it hasn't gone unrecorded. Most people don't understand that how they judge others is how God judges them. Promise me, that you'll forgive those who've hurt you."

Morgan's eyes lowered. "You're asking a lot."

"I know, but do it anyway," Rosemary said, squeezing the young woman's hand. Morgan opened the passenger door. "I'll think about it. Do you need me to watch Petra this week?" she asked, before exiting.

Rosemary shook her head. "No, since Jacob will be back on Wednesday, I'm taking Petra to Grand Rapids tomorrow. I want her to spend some time with her cousins before she leaves. They're going back to Chicago sooner than expected."

"So his plans have changed again," Morgan said.

"I'm afraid so." Rosemary peered at her granddaughter, who remained asleep.

"Please give Neville and his wife my regards. His wife and I used to be very close friends."

Rosemary nodded. "I remember."

"Then, I'll see you tomorrow morning at church, drive safely," Morgan said.

"Child, I have one more favor to ask of you. Please speak with your mother tomorrow. I know that she's made some mistakes . . ."

Morgan's eyes enlarged.

"I didn't say that they weren't major."

Morgan's face clouded.

"Your mother taught you principles that she learned from her mom. And God rest her soul, Grandma Grace was carnal to the bone. I'm sure you know that she ran the local juke joint and well, how should I say it . . ."

"You don't have to sugar coat anything. She ran an underground brothel," Morgan said emotionlessly.

Rosemary nodded. "I wasn't sure how much you knew."

"Adults sometimes forget that children have big ears."

Rosemary felt overwhelming sadness for the young woman.

"I'll be cordial tomorrow, but my mom and I really don't have much to discuss until she's ready to answer some pretty tough questions."

"What if she is?" Rosemary asked.

Morgan looked pointedly at Rosemary before responding. "Then I'll listen."

"Child, God is working things out for your good. Be patient," Rosemary said encouragingly.

Morgan stepped out of the car. "I'll try," she said, before shutting the door.

"Flash the porch light when your front door is locked," Rosemary yelled through the open window.

Morgan waved, acknowledging the directive.

Once Rosemary saw the front light flicker, she drove away. Would Morgan honor her request? Only God knew what her heart desired. All Rosemary could do was pray about the situation. So she did, all the way home.

CHAPTER 57

✧ † ✧

WANTING TO BE ALONE, JACOB HAD SHUNNED THE SHARED LIMO WITH HIS COLLEAGUES AND was traveling back into the city on the commuter train. Even though his train section was packed with other riders, anonymity gave him privacy. The forty-five minute ride also gave him time to decompress and reflect.

Intense negotiations had resolved Edward Rousseau's contractual problem, but the long days and even shorter nights had taken an emotional and physical toll on Jacob. Resting his head against the window, he watched city dwellings meld as the train whizzed by houses and landmarks. Jeffery had called often from Europe. Although fully capable of negotiating a settlement, Jacob had appreciated his employer's assistance. Interestingly, while in route to the Mexican airport that morning, his limo driver had driven through a picturesque stretch of mountainous terrain. While enjoying the views, he'd noticed a church that was perched high in the mountains. In all the times that Jacob had traveled to and from that same airport, he'd never noted the building or its uncanny resemblance to New Life Full Gospel Church before. Its pull was strong and clear. Was his mother correct? Had the enemy kept him so busily distracted, that he couldn't see God's truth when it was right in front of his face.

Jacob knew that it would take more than reading a few scriptures and one counseling session to resolve his problems. He sighed. He and his daughter would only have another week together in Michigan before they returned home. Once again, he wouldn't be able to honor his promise. Petra would eventually understand, although she might not forgive him.

He was glad that his mother had taken Petra to Grand Rapids. Neville was the last person in the world that he wanted to see right now. From the pictures that his mother was sending, everyone was having a wonderful time. His brother's parental success was a bitter pill.

The train passed a neighborhood where Jacob and Lillian had once lived. They'd been happy in their small apartment, or so he'd thought. Even then, his arrogance had masked low self-esteem. He saw his faults more clearly now. His judgment, sarcasm, hurtful words, and arrogance had eventually killed her love for him. His mother had once called him a bully and he'd become offended, but she'd been correct.

His constant negativity had eventually sucked the life from his wife and their marriage. His father had been overbearing, but because his mom knew her worth in Christ Jesus, she'd always let God's Word fight her battles. He'd witnessed his mother's uncompromising faith countless times. She was wise and Jacob knew that she was blessed.

Which was why her latest decision didn't make any sense. Even knowing all that she knew about Morgan and her family, his mother had given the woman access to his daughter. Just thinking about it caused his blood to boil. The last thing he needed was Petra becoming promiscuous, which the Harding women were known to be.

He and his departed wife had already done enough emotional damage to Petra. Protecting her was now his top priority and failure wasn't an option.

CHAPTER 50

✚

EDWARD READ THE REPORT ONE LAST TIME BEFORE HE RELAXED. A CATASTROPHE HAD BEEN averted. City lights twinkled below. The view of Paris was magnificent from high above the city, although Italy, his country of birth, would always be home. He'd met with a specialist today, suffering humiliation alone. Later that day, he'd assembled his personal attorneys. It was time to change his will. The life that he knew was fading faster than anticipated. He'd called both of his children to make amends, but sadly, neither had cared. Regardless, he'd put plans into motion. His legacy would continue with or without their assistance. His phone rang.

"Edward." He didn't recognize the caller's voice. His memory was so precarious these days.

"Hello," he said.

"Edward, it's Jeffery."

Edward smiled. "My friend," he said happily.

"I just wanted to make sure that you received the final report."

"I have it in my hands. Thank you for all of your assistance. I never meant to cause so much trouble."

"I know," Jeffery said.

"My purse is considerably lighter, but I'll be indebted to you for years to come," Edward joked.

"I'm just glad that everything worked out. How are you feeling today? You didn't look well yesterday," Jeffery asked, sounding sincere.

"As well as can be expected under the circumstances," Edward said cryptically.

"I was hoping that we could get together again before I leave."

Upon hearing Jeffery's request, Edward became anxious. He wasn't ready to discuss his health, just yet.

"I'm rather busy right now, but I'll call you later in the week once you're back in the states," he said, rushing Jeffery off the phone. *"Au revoir my friend."*

"Au revoir Edward," Jeffery said.

Edward looked down onto the busy street below. People scurried to and fro. Thick traffic clogged the narrow Parisian streets. He hated loneliness, but tonight, he relished solitude. There was much to celebrate this evening. Most importantly was that his memory wasn't entirely gone and he still had his independence. Edward leaned forward and continued enjoying the view. Life was short and sadly, his was becoming even shorter.

CHAPTER 59

✝

JEFFERY'S CHAUFFEURED CAR GLIDED ON WET PAVEMENT WHILE RAIN POURED FROM THE heavens above. He'd slept through most of his flight across the Atlantic Ocean. Even so, he was still jet lagged and tired. Although he owned multiple residences, Chicago was home. The "Windy City" held fond, yet bittersweet memories. The city was his late wife's birthplace. Twice, she'd undergone cancer treatment at a well-known university hospital. Soon after her initial diagnosis, the couple had rededicated their lives to Christ and ever since, Jeffery's belief in the power of God had remained unwavering.

Months of medical care had been exhaustive and difficult for the entire Kennedy family, but fortunately, their marriage had survived, in spite of some fairly insurmountable odds. Their love had deepened. Mona, only thirty years of age at the time, successfully fought the disease. She remained symptom free for over twenty-five years until its return. Towards the end of her second battle, she praised God for the extra days that He'd given her. She'd been able to raise their children and help Jeffery build a strong financial legacy.

Jeffery missed her counsel. Mona had been more than a business partner and wife. She'd been his spiritual advisor and friend. Their relationship had never been highly passionate, but maturity had a way of putting youthful expectations and folly into perspective. Forgiving by nature, his wife was a gem that Jeffery felt privileged to have known. Her love had made him a better man.

Jeffery stifled a yawn. He couldn't wait to climb into bed. First thing in the morning, he was driving to Indigo Beach. He and Morgan had business to discuss. Paramount was Edward's failing health. He'd seen fear and fatigue in his friend's eyes and it was concerning. Stakes had become too high. With certainty, the answers that he needed were in Michigan.

After a restful night of sleep, Jeffery drove along the toll road and into Indiana. Using this route usually reduced the travel time into Michigan by about thirty minutes. The dull gray sky above was ominous. A second day of rain had been forecasted, so Jeffery wisely kept the sunroof closed and he turned on the air conditioner to reduce the car's humidity. Although it was early, traffic was thick, but at least it was moving.

Since he knew that life's distractions often muted God's voice, Jeffery used his alone time wisely and quietly meditated on God's Word. A little over an hour later, he passed Napier Avenue and instinctively veered into the far right lane. The off ramp for 196 approached and he maneuvered onto the newly paved highway. Indigo Beach was just a few miles up the road.

In childhood, he'd frequently traveled back and forth between Chicago and his grandparent's farm, once located in nearby Covert Township. Indigo Beach was his second home. Excitement and apprehension caused his pulse to quicken. Returning to the area always had this effect on him. With reservations at a local inn, one that he and Mona had frequented often, Jeffery exited the highway.

Shaking off melancholy, he steered his car onto a country road, soon passing Meriwether's Convenience Store and Gas Station. Once he reached his destination, he parked. Jeffery grabbed a leather overnight bag from the back seat and strode towards the entrance. Then he walked towards the registration desk. "I'm here to check in," he said, placing his credit card and driver's license on the counter.

An employee looked at both. "Good Morning Mr. Kennedy, I hope that your drive was pleasant. Did you encounter any rain?" she asked.

Jeffery shook his head. "No, although, I expect that we'll get some later tonight."

The young woman smiled and handed him a paper. "If you would be so kind as to sign the registration form," she said.

Jeffery signed the document without reading.

Then she handed him his room key. "You'll be staying on the top floor, room 220, as requested," she said politely.

Jeffery smiled.

"Just take the stairs and turn right."

"I know the way," he said, as he picked up his luggage.

The employee's wide smile was friendly. "Well, if you need anything else, please feel free to contact us. We want your stay to be enjoyable."

Jeffery climbed the narrow staircase to the second floor. The hallway was just as he remembered. Local artwork covered its walls. Standing in the doorway of his suite, he glanced around the room, noting subtle changes. Since his stay in town would be short, he'd packed light. Jeffery placed a few personal items in a drawer and hung the rest of his clothes in the closet. Then he looked at his watch. It was much too early to visit Morgan or anyone else for that matter. Then his stomach rumbled. Jeffery patted his back pocket, checking for his wallet. He grabbed his jacket and umbrella before venturing out the door. Business could wait, but his stomach couldn't.

CHAPTER 60

✝

PETRA ROLLED ONTO HER BACK AND RUBBED HER EYES. NEITHER SHE NOR HER GRANDMOTHER had wanted to leave Grand Rapids the previous evening, but her dad was arriving today. Crisp morning air blew in through her open bedroom windows. Petra purred contently under her warm blanket.

Spending time with Uncle Neville had been fun. Although her uncle was opinionated, just like her father, the brothers were different in so many ways. Uncle Neville really listened to his kids and treated his wife lovingly. While staying in their home, she'd observed her aunt and uncle holding hands and expressing affection, which had been a rarity for her parents when her mother had been alive. But more importantly, her cousins really respected their dad. Her father could learn a lot from his older brother.

Petra plumped her pillow again and rolled back onto her stomach. Since her private high school began earlier than public school, she only had three weeks left of summer vacation. She was excited about her upcoming birthday and beginning her junior year. Being an upperclassman had perks. Turning sixteen also meant that she could date, drive, and enjoy a later curfew.

She was going to miss Indigo Beach. Although, she would never say it aloud, having Morgan as a babysitter had actually been fun. Petra rolled onto her side, wondering what she and her father would do when they went back to Chicago. He wasn't a good planner. Then she thought about Shawn.

He was seventeen and cute, in a weird sort of way, although he was dumber than rocks. His friendship meant a great deal to her. She was going to miss seeing him at church and at his godparents' convenience store.

The aroma of bacon wafted through the vents. Petra's stomach rumbled. Ignoring the unction to go downstairs, she burrowed deeper and pulled her blanket up to her chin. Then she went back to sleep. Sometime later Petra cried out in alarm.

"Wake up, wake up, sweetheart," Grandma Rosemary said.

Petra slowly opened her eyes.

Her grandmother's soft honey brown orbs peered into her own. Petra rubbed her eyes.

"Eating pizza before bedtime had the same affect on your father when he was your age," Grandma Rosemary said, leaning close. "Were you having a bad dream?"

Petra nodded.

"Tell me about it."

Petra scooted over and made room for her grandmother to sit. "I don't remember much, but two knights were dueling. One was scary. He wanted to kill me."

Grandma Rosemary stroked Petra's arm comfortingly. "The enemy's job is to steal, kill, and destroy. He plays to win. Use the sword of the Spirit for protection. Do you understand?"

Petra nodded. "The Word of God is all that I need," the teen said confidently.

"I'm glad that you learned something this summer. Now get your lazy bones into the shower. Your dad will be arriving soon," Grandma Rosemary said, before kissing Petra's forehead. "I love you."

"I love you too, Grandma." Petra quickly made her bed and padded into the bathroom. After brushing her teeth, she bathed in record time. Then the teen popped earphones into her ears and ran down the stairs. Listening to music helped drown out angry thoughts. She had to be careful. Negative thoughts often turned into sinful actions. This was another lesson that Grandma Rosemary had made sure that she learned.

CHAPTER 61

✝

JEFFERY SAT IN THE TINY CAFÉ THAT OVERLOOKED LAKE MICHIGAN AND REMINISCED. HE AND Mona had dined here often. Today, he watched booming waves roll ashore. Sea Gulls swooped low and wide over hardened sand and churning water. It was as if time had stood still. Memories also crashed and collided. He'd eaten breakfast at his favorite table. Morgan's assessment of her hometown was correct. Not much had changed over the years, but he had.

After paying his bill, Jeffery drove through town, enjoying the sights. Unconsciously, he traveled past his grandparents' old farm. The current owners had done a wonderful job of renovating the property. It looked different, yet the same. Fonder memories propelled him further up the road. Before long, he was parking in the lot of New Life Full Gospel Church. Noticing that a certain Lincoln was parked on the side of the building put a smile on his face. He walked to the church's back entrance, rang the doorbell, and waited.

"May I help you?" Deon's blustery voice came through the intercom.

"Man, you owned that same Lincoln the last time I was in town."

"It's paid for. Now, don't get nothin' started. I'm taller and wider," Deon said wittily.

The buzzer sounded. Jeffery effortlessly pulled the door open and entered. Deon met him half way up the hallway. The two men hugged, slapping each other's backs heartily.

"I wondered when you'd come calling."

Jeffery followed his friend down the darkened hallway and into the

171

outer office. "You of all people would," he said, still following Deon into his office.

"What's it been, four or five years since you were here last?" Deon asked. Jeffery nodded. "At least."

"How are you holding up?"

Jeffery sprawled across the worn leather sofa. "I still miss her," he said sadly.

"You always will," Deon said. He sat across from his friend.

Jeffery's eyes moistened. "I'm going to be a grandpa," he said enthusiastically. The men sat facing each other on the sofa.

"Congratulations," Deon said, sounding truly happy.

Jeffery stared out the office window. "How's your sister? Mary usually calls to check on me, but I haven't heard from her in a while."

Deon chuckled. "Mary and menopause ain't no joke! Pray for me!"

Now Jeffery laughed. "Man, you're crazy. Hey, what's that I see in your hair?" he asked, trying to start trouble.

Deon slowly rubbed his hands through his thick dark curls, which were lightly sprinkled with gray. "At least I've still got some," he said jokingly.

Grinning, Jeffery caressed his smoothly shaven head.

The men laughed raucously and when the levity subsided, Deon turned serious. "I'm sure, this isn't a social call."

Jeffery looked away, pulling his thoughts together.

Deon retrieved two water bottles from his mini fridge and handed one to Jeffery, who quickly unscrewed the cap and swigged. Then, Deon sat and leaned forward. "Why don't you start from the beginning?" he said compassionately.

Jeffery peered at a true friend, one who knew him well and had always refused to condemn. Then he slowly unburdened his heart.

CHAPTER 62

✝

APPREHENSION GREW AS JACOB NEARED INDIGO BEACH. CHOICES WARRED. HE COULD AVOID Morgan and never explain his position or end his daughter's involvement with the woman, by defending his decision. He chose the later, but as he drove towards the Valley, anxiety caused his breathing to become shallower. Again, he questioned whether his decision to confront Morgan was right. Jacob focused on the passing scenery. Although he no longer desired to live in rural Michigan, he still found the Valley's isolation attractive.

After parking in front of Morgan's cottage, the front door slowly opened. Dressed in running shoes, black leggings, and a sports bra, Morgan looked ready for a workout, with her hair clipped high on top of her head. Soft curly tendrils cascaded from a messy bun. Jacob exited his car and walked towards the front porch.

"Oh hi, did I forget that we were meeting?" she asked, holding the screen door open. Jacob climbed the front stairs and entered the parlor. "No, I gambled that you'd be home."

Morgan smiled. "When I heard your car, I thought that you were Destiny. She's really the only person who drives all the way out here unannounced."

Jacob coughed uneasily.

"Let me get you something to drink," Morgan said, leading him down the short hallway.

"Thank you," he said, following her into the kitchen. Jacob glanced around the renovated room. "Leroy did a wonderful job. However, my mother's description of his work didn't do it justice. This is truly spectacular."

Morgan handed Jacob a glass of water. "So, what brings you all the way out here?" she asked. The look she gave him was challenging.

"There's something I wish to speak with you about," he said, already questioning his decision. Jacob noticed papers on the table and graphing on Morgan's computer screen. "I should have called first. I can see that you're busy."

Morgan waved her hand, poo pooing his last statement. "Not at the moment. As you can see, I was about to go running on the beach. I've found that strenuous exercise usually clears my mind when numbers don't add up," she said, pointing towards the paperwork on the table.

Jacob placed his empty glass on the newly installed granite.

"Why are you really here?" she asked again.

Jacob spoke awkwardly. "I've made a decision that impacts your relationship with Petra."

Morgan's face remained passive. "You've got my full attention."

"I don't think any relationship with you is in my daughter's best interest."

Morgan's crossed arms rested serenely against her chest. "Why?" she asked.

"Because, I don't want your lifestyle negatively impacting her in any way," he said, feeling threatened and insecure by Morgan's calm demeanor. Her composure was unnerving.

"What do you think you know about me?" she asked.

"You broke up a marriage," Jacob said, feeling off balanced.

Morgan uncrossed her arms and stepped closer. "Is there anything else that you've uncovered, that makes me unfit to mentor your child?" she asked.

Anger simmered. "You're Grace Harding's granddaughter," he snapped. Morgan calmly leaned against the sink.

Jacob knew that the situation was spiraling out of his control.

"I see," she said softly.

The kitchen clock ticked rhythmically.

His heart pounded.

Morgan's face remained passive. "Since, I'm well aware of my pedigree, your concerns are understandable."

"Does my mother know about your affair?" he asked, purposely goading the woman standing before him.

"She knows, and she didn't care."

"Well, she's far more forgiving than I am," Jacob said, pushing tolerance aside. Morgan remained unfazed. "Is there anything else that you wanted to say?" she asked.

Jacob stared disbelievingly as Morgan turned and walked towards the front of the house. Holding the door open, she gestured for him to leave.

"Jacob, your daughter is a wonderful child. I wish you both the best."

Stunned by her blatant dismissal, Jacob stepped onto the porch. Then the door slammed in his face. He heard the dead bolt slide into place. Hands clenched, Jacob strode angrily towards his car. *Screw Morgan and every woman like her,* he thought as he drove towards his mother's house. Consuming rage churned. God urged him to turn around, but once again, Jacob ignored the Holy Spirit's directive. Out of control, he barreled towards town.

CHAPTER 63

✝

DEON GRINNED AT JEFFERY WHEN HE HEARD SOFT FOOTSTEPS TRAVERSING THE BACK HALLWAY.

"Is that Rosemary?" Jeffery asked.

Deon nodded. "Rosemary, I have someone in my office who wants to see you," he yelled.

Seconds later, his administrative assistant stood in the doorway. Jeffery turned slowly and Deon watched Rosemary's eyes sparkle in recognition.

"Jeffery," she said, greeting him warmly.

"Rosemary, it's been ages."

"What are you doing in town?" she asked, clearly surprised and pleased at the same time.

Jeffery stood and Rosemary walked into his open arms. Deon observed their friendly embrace from the couch.

"I'm in town on business and decided to visit my dearest friends first," he said, before releasing her.

"We've been discussing old times," Deon said. Then he winked.

"Oh, really," Rosemary said, pulling a chair from the corner of the room. She now sat, facing the two men. "I can't wait to hear the lies that the two of you have been telling."

Deon chuckled.

"Rosemary, to your recollection, has Deon ever beaten me at anything?" Jeffery asked. His eyes glittered mischievously.

Grinning, she clasped her hands together. "Sorry Pastor, but I'm going to have to say no."

Deon harrumphed.

Jeffery smiled self-assuredly.

Then the trio burst out laughing. Minutes turned into hours as the three friends talked and shared.

Finally, Rosemary stood. "Jeffery, it's so good seeing you, but I have an inbox full of work to do."

He nodded.

"Did Jacob make it back safely?" Deon asked, before Rosemary left the room.

"I left him staring out the kitchen window. Apparently, his meeting with Morgan didn't go well. Petra was still in her room with earphones stuck in her ears.

Jeffery shook his head. "I remember adolescence well."

"No parent can forget it." Then she turned. "Jeffery, I may need your help. Jacob is really making a mess of an already bad situation."

"I know he is, but pride won't let him seek help. You raised a fine boy and he's an excellent employee, but he's never wanted nepotism hanging over his head. He keeps our relationship strictly professional and me at arm's length. I can't tell you how many times, I have wanted to shake some sense into your son's thick head."

"He acts just like his father."

Stepping closer, Jeffery grasped Rosemary's hands into his own. "I respect his privacy, but I've been concerned for quite some time about his relationship with Petra. How is she fairing?" he asked.

Rosemary answered slowly. "Better, but her pain goes deep."

Jeffery sighed. "I'll pray."

"Thank you," Rosemary said, as she exited the room.

Then Deon stood.

"Before I leave, I need an answer about something that has stumped me for over a year. Did you beg Summer to marry you?" Jeffery asked, teasingly.

"I sure did," Deon said. His eyes danced.

Jeffery clasped Deon's hand. "I would have done the same thing, my friend. Then Deon led his childhood friend from his office. He held the back door open and watched Jeffery walk across the parking lot. Deep in thought, Deon walked back towards Rosemary's desk.

"I can only imagine what your son said to Morgan."

Rosemary looked up. "By the look on his face, Morgan had the last word," Rosemary said, before she resumed typing.

Deon walked back into his office. With no other pressing appointments, he sprawled face down on the carpeted floor and travailed for his flock.

CHAPTER 64

✝

MORGAN SAT AT THE KITCHEN COUNTER AND STARED. FOR HOURS, SHE'D BEEN UNABLE TO MOVE. Her cheeks were now raw from crying and her back hurt from remaining immobile for so long. Shame burned intensely. Her grandmother's colorful past had been mostly forgotten by the time that she'd been born, but her mother's adulterous lifestyle was still hot gossip in the small beachside community. Grandma Grace had shielded her granddaughter's tender heart from local gossip as best that she could, but a childhood filled with infamy and embarrassment along with unexplained abandonment, had produced deep bitterness.

Mona had penetrated Morgan's protective wall. Brick by brick, she'd chiseled away at the stronghold, helping her mentee see its destructive influence. She'd offered Morgan unconditional love and solace, without condemnation or ridicule, but then she'd gotten sick again and died. Deeply grieving from another personal loss, Morgan's resentment slowly returned. This time, it was directed towards her mother.

Morgan had exuded calm professionalism throughout Jacob's verbal assault, but she was inwardly seething with indignant fury. How dare he judge her family! His rejection cut deeply. After sitting for hours, unfiltered rage finally exploded. Morgan threw her coffee mug. Shards of pottery splintered and dark liquid splattered against the newly painted wall. Then coffee slowly dripped onto the floor. Unconcerned, Morgan watched liquid pool on the travertine tile.

Her mother was to blame for every failed relationship and rejection that she'd experienced in life. Mamie's lies were inexcusable. Grabbing her purse, Morgan stormed from the house. Today, she would get answers. Gunning her car's engine, Morgan careened down the road. Eyes blazing, she sped towards her mother's house. Stomach acids churned. Nerves were taunt and sensitive. Morgan drove erratically, as indignation burned.

CHAPTER 65

✝

HUMIDITY WAS HIGH. THE CLOUDS ABOVE HAD GROWN ANGRIER AND DARKER WHILE JEFFERY visited with Deon and Rosemary. A storm was fast approaching. Although he was older than Deon, their bond had been unbreakable for more than forty years. Rosemary's husband had been another childhood friend whom he'd held in high regard. Bishop McDonald's death had left a void in his life that remained unfilled. Rosemary was the sister that he'd never had. Now, he drove towards another friend's house. This person had preoccupied his dreams for a lifetime.

Toys littered the front yard of her tiny house. Smiling, Jeffery exited his car. The front door was partially open, although the screen door was closed. He saw movement at the large picture window. Then he heard muted voices inside the house as he walked up the gravel drive. Mamie soon appeared in the doorway, smiling broadly. His grin widened. Quickly scaling the front steps, Jeffery was soon engulfed in an openhearted hug. Her soft warmth was as intoxicating as fine wine. Time stood still.

"You should have called first," she said.

He kissed the top of her head, before they separated. "And what would have changed?" he asked.

"You're right! I'd still have grandbabies and toys scattered about."

Jeffery hugged her again.

Flustered, Mamie disengaged and quietly led him through the house and into the kitchen. Three children were seated at the table eating peanut butter crackers and drinking from juice boxes.

Jeffery leaned against the counter, silently observing. "How many grandchildren do you have now?" he asked.

Mamie smiled proudly. "Seven."

Jeffery grinned. "My first is on the way."

Her eyes twinkled. "Parenting is much better the second time around. When I'm tired, I just send them home to their mothers," she joked.

Watching Mamie move around the tiny kitchen brought back wonderful memories. Shaking off nostalgia, Jeffery suppressed longing. The children soon ran off to play.

Mamie wiped the table clean and motioned for him to sit. "Can I get you anything to drink?" she asked.

He shook his head. "No, I'm still full from breakfast, but thank you," he said, still bewitched by her beauty.

Mamie hung her wrinkled apron on a wall peg.

When she turned, he looked to see if her shapely legs were still unshaven, as he liked.

Catching him staring, Mamie blushed. "That look means trouble," she said.

His unbridled laughter filled the room.

Her eyes sparkled. Mamie was aging gracefully. Laugh lines beautifully contoured her face.

"It used to," he bantered.

"Gwandma, somebody is here!" One of her grandchildren yelled from the living room.

"I wonder who that could be," she said, excusing herself.

Jeffery watched Mamie's hips sway rhythmically as she walked back down the hallway. He heard the front door slam, hard. Then heated words followed. Raw, ugliness floated down the hallway. Resigned, he walked slowly towards inevitability. With tears streaming down her face, Morgan stood angrily before her mother. Jeffery had heard her impassioned plea.

"Morgan, please!" Mamie said, trying to calm her daughter.

Morgan looked up when he entered the room. "Jeffery, what are you doing here?" she asked. Confusion clouded her emotion filled eyes.

Heart aching, deep regret burned within him. In that moment, Mona's deathbed request became haunting. She'd always wanted this wrong, righted, but pride had gotten in the way. Mamie looked on helplessly, imploring Jeffery to speak. But first, he addressed one of her grandchildren who'd just entered the room. "Son, keep an eye on your cousins. We don't want to be disturbed."

The child quickly turned and ran back into a back bedroom.

Then Jeffery stared into Morgan's anguished eyes.

"What's going on?" she asked, demanding answers.

Jeffery had often wondered how this drama would end.

"Morgan, I think your father should start first," Mamie said softly.

Morgan's head snapped up.

Jeffery lowered his eyes shamefully, as his daughter glared.

"Father," she mumbled, sinking to the couch.

No one said a word.

Shakily, Morgan took deep calming breaths. Then she looked up, peering quizzically at both of her parents. Collecting her thoughts, she finally said, "You both have some explaining to do."

Jeffery watched color drain from Mamie's face. Through tear soaked eyes, Morgan looked questioningly at him. Watching Mamie cry was unsettling, but strangely, for the first time in a long time, Jeffery felt unparalleled relief.

CHAPTER 66

✝

FURIOUS WITH HER FATHER, PETRA PACED BACK AND FORTH IN HER BEDROOM. HE'D BEEN ignoring her for hours. Adding insult to injury, he'd just left his room, without uttering one word of apology and was now seated beneath the weeping willow tree, out back. Frustration boiled over. Petra marched out of her grandmother's house and stomped across the backyard.

"What are you doing out here?" she asked.

Jacob stared at his daughter. Petra's hair hung long and free.

"New outfit?" he asked.

She rolled her eyes. "Yeah, Grandma took Morgan and me shopping last Saturday," she said, petulantly.

"It looks nice. How much did it cost?"

Petra glared, already tired of the senseless conversation. "Why?" she asked.

"Because, I need to repay your grandmother. You're my responsibility." Petra moaned.

"Why are you looking at me like that?" he asked.

"Because Grandma didn't buy this outfit. Morgan did."

Jacob stared. "Why did she buy you clothes?" he asked.

"Maybe, because she likes me and we're friends."

Jacob looked away.

Petra glared, hoping to provoke a response from her father.

"Honey, we need to talk," he said, patting the seat beside him.

Petra moved closer, but continued standing. "What do you have to say?" she asked.

Jacob sighed again. "Certain lifestyle choices can make a person unsuitable to mentor children."

Petra leaned on one hip and stared at the swaying branches above. She definitely wasn't going to make things easy for him.

"It's my job to protect you," he said.

Petra stared at her nails and sucked her teeth.

"Morgan and I spoke this morning. We've, I mean . . . I've made a decision," he continued.

Totally indifferent to her father's discomfort, Petra watched a butterfly land on a leaf.

"You won't be seeing her any more," he said.

Stunned, Petra peered at her father. "You make it sound like I'll never see her again," she said, totally confused.

"She isn't the kind of influence I want for you," Jacob explained.

Petra scowled. "Oh, I get it, you're worried about the affair that she had with her boss. Are you concerned that I might grow up and do the same thing?"

"How do you know about that, young lady?" Jacob asked.

A lone tear fell. "I know about it, because she isn't a liar, like you," Petra yelled before turning and running towards the house.

Jacob stood, shouting. "Petra, get back here. Now."

Her father's words barely registered as she ran through the back door and up the stairs. After slamming the bedroom door shut, Petra flung herself across the bed. Minutes later, her dad entered her room. Ignoring him, she focused on the wall.

"The fact that she told you about her affair is precisely why, I don't want you hanging around her."

Petra stubbornly looked away. Angry tears flowed onto her wet pillow. The room was silent except for her father's heavy breathing. When her bedroom door finally closed, she exhaled. Her father was responsible for everyone leaving, first her mother and now Morgan. He didn't understand the kind of love that Pastor Deon preached about. He was selfish and self-centered and he just didn't listen.

As Petra lay across her bed, with her arms tucked securely behind her head, she formulated a plan. She was leaving Indigo Beach, but she had to do it before her grandmother got home. Petra got up and stuffed her backpack with a few personal items. Grabbing cash, her music, and house keys, she crept silently down the staircase and out the front door. She knew where she was going, but not quite how she'd get there. She had to get to Shawn. Besides Morgan, he was the only friend she had in town. She felt certain that he would help, because he owed her for not ratting him out.

CHAPTER 67

✝

PETRA SAW SHAWN LONG BEFORE HE RECOGNIZED HER. GRAVEL AND DUST SCATTERED AS SHE walked along the shoulder of the road. Weeks earlier, they'd met under similar circumstances as he'd walked home from work. That day, Shawn had carried two six-packs of beer. She'd readily accepted his invitation to drink at Grace Harding's old cottage. Petra had never blamed him for leaving her. She knew that he would've been beaten if he'd stayed out past curfew.

"Long time no see," he said.

Her backpack hung loosely over one shoulder. "Yeah, right," she said caustically.

"Where are you heading?"

"Home," Petra said, kicking a rock.

"Chicago?"

She nodded.

"Who pissed you off this time?" he asked.

Petra rolled her eyes. "My Dad, who else?"

"I totally understand. My old man is the worse."

"Wanna come?" she asked, impulsively. Petra kicked another rock.

"Depends, how are you getting there?" he asked.

Petra shrugged. "I need a ride to Michigan City."

"Why?"

"Dummy, there isn't a train that goes to Chicago from here."

"Why are you really going home?" he asked.

Petra's eyes watered. "To get some peace. I just want some peace," she yelled. Ignoring her rant, Shawn stared off towards the station. "See that blue car over there, the one with the Indiana license plate," he said.

Petra looked across the gas station's lot.

"Go ask the driver if she will give you a ride. Offer her twenty dollars," he said.

Petra looked doubtful.

"I see hitch hikers doing it all the time."

Petra glanced at the car again, noticing that a young female driver was seated behind the wheel of an older model Ford. Steeling her nerves, she walked across the lot and approached the stranger. They spoke through the open passenger window.

"You drivin' back towards Chicago?" Petra asked.

The skinny girl shook her head. "I'm not going that far."

"Can you get me to Michigan City?" Petra asked.

The girl smiled. "Sure, it's not too far out of my way."

Petra handed the girl a twenty-dollar bill.

"Do you need more?" she asked.

The girl grinned.

"Nope, twenty sounds fair."

Petra smiled.

"Hop in the front seat," the driver said.

Petra quickly opened the passenger door and slid into the seat. She waved at Shawn, who had resumed sweeping. He nodded. Then she watched two older boys exit the convenience store and walk towards the Ford. Already regretting her impulsive decision, Petra's eyes widened fearfully. The boys looked more like grown men. Her great idea was fast becoming a nightmare. The taller of the two guys, swung open the back door and crawled in. Petra stared hopelessly at Shawn. Looking concerned, he leaned the broom against the building and quickly ran over to the vehicle. Then he leaned in through the open window.

"You got room for one more?" he asked. Shawn's appearance caught the young men by surprise.

"You goin' to Valparaiso too?" one of the teens asked from the back seat.

"I'm going where ever she is," Shawn said, pointing at Petra.

The boys grumbled, but made room for one more. Shawn slammed the back door shut. Petra's stomach lurched and tumbled as the late model sedan pulled from pump seven. Soon, the car loaded with five passengers exited the lot and within minutes was traveling fast on the interstate. Petra never took her eyes off the road.

CHAPTER 68

✝

JACOB TRIED RELAXING, BUT HE COULDN'T. HIS MOTHER HAD GONE GROCERY SHOPPING AFTER work and he was expecting her home within the hour. Once she arrived, he would happily step aside and let her address Petra's rude behavior. Until he got his anger under control, he refused to go back upstairs and confront his daughter. Her conduct on top of Morgan's dismissiveness had pushed him over the edge.

While he rocked, Jacob reflected on three observations that Pastor Deon had made during their counseling session. At the time, he'd rejected all of them, but now he wasn't so sure that the pastor hadn't been correct. He did expect blind obedience, mercy, and unconditional love, yet routinely disobeyed God, judged others and loved conditionally. Jacob was starting to realize just how deeply he'd dug his hole. It would take a miracle to get him out.

He rocked harder. The rhythmic movement was physically soothing, even though his mind remained unsettled. The slight breeze that the rocking afforded was at least a little respite from the clinging humidity.

CHAPTER 69

✝

PETRA AND SHAWN WERE FINALLY BOARDING THE COMMUTER TRAIN. SHE HOPED THAT THEIR clothing didn't reek of marijuana. The boys in the back seat had smoked the entire trip. "Why'd you come with me?" she asked Shawn. They were finally able to speak.

Shawn slouched in his seat, attempting to get comfortable. "I didn't like the way those guys looked."

Petra peered out the window, thankful for his intervention. "Are you going to be in a lot of trouble?"

"Probably," he said.

Worried, she looked at her feet. "Maybe my grandma will be able to help. She's good at fixing things."

Shawn's half grin was comforting. "It's okay, remember, I was planning on visiting the city anyway."

Petra perked up. "Are you going to call your mom?"

"Yeah," he said lazily.

Petra smiled. "We'll go there first thing in the morning."

"Sounds good," Shawn said, gazing out the window.

Petra began relaxing once she saw familiar landmarks pass by.

"Do you have your phone," Shawn asked.

Petra shook her head. "No, my dad still has it."

He frowned. "I don't have mine, either. It's in my locker at work."

"It's just as well. Your folks could have tracked us if you did. One of my

191

girlfriends got caught at her boyfriend's house that way. You aren't scared are you?" she asked. Petra looked closely for signs of fear.

"Naw, I just don't like being unplugged."

"Me neither," she said, before leaning against the hard vinyl seat. Petra became pensive. She really regretted breaking her promise to Morgan.

"Are you scared?" Shawn asked.

"No, everything is cool." She quickly looked away. Now she'd added lying to her growing list of sins. Petra used her backpack for a pillow and then leaned against the window. Pretending sleep, she kept her eyes closed so that Shawn wouldn't ask any more questions.

As she silently prayed, the train bounced and jiggled while it zoomed towards Chicago. More people got on at each stop until their section was full. Excitement grew. She watched Shawn sleep, gladdened that they were traveling together. She couldn't wait to get home and sleep in her own bed. Her bedroom was her sanctuary, the one place in the world, where she felt alive and secure.

Its walls had been a blank canvas, a backdrop for color and vibrancy. With her mother's full approval, she'd decorated the space based on feeling not rules. It was a beautiful mix of modern, whimsy, and function. She'd boldly rebelled against her father's control and hypocrisy.

Once the train whizzed past East Chicago, anticipation increased with each passing stop. Shawn groggily awakened when they pulled into the Randolph Street station.

"Get up, we're here," Petra said excitedly.

He stood and yawned. "That was fast."

Hoards of people exited the train.

Petra's smile grew as they stepped onto the platform. "Follow me," she said. Then she led Shawn through the crowd. They climbed steps. Excitement pulsed. Freedom from tyranny felt liberating. She was scared, but rebellion always came with a price.

"Are you sure that you're okay?" Shawn asked.

Petra giggled. "I've never felt better," she said, as she led him to the busy street above.

CHAPTER 70

✝

JACOB HEARD HIS MOTHER'S CAR COMING UP THE STREET, LONG BEFORE SHE PARKED IN THE driveway. Grocery bags dangled from each of her arms. Jacob snuck up behind her and kissed the top of her head.

"Jacob!" she yelped.

He chuckled. "Let me take these bags," he said.

Rosemary swatted his hand. "Grab the rest of the groceries from the backseat of my car."

After gathering everything from his mother's car, Jacob followed Rosemary into the house. He dumped his items on the kitchen counter.

"Thanks, now call Petra down. I'm going to need her help," Rosemary said.

Jacob looked away.

"You still haven't spoken with your daughter?" his mother asked. Rosemary walked down the hallway and hollered from the base of the stairway. "Petra, come downstairs and help me put away the groceries."

Jacob waited for his daughter's response. He also watched his mother's irritation grow when his daughter didn't respond.

"I'll handle this." Rosemary marched up the stairs. Minutes passed before she yelled, "Jacob, get up here."

Jacob stood at the bottom of the staircase. "What's the matter?"

"Petra isn't here."

"What do you mean?" He climbed the stairs two at a time.

"I've looked for her in every room," Rosemary said.

Jacob walked into his daughter's empty bedroom.

His mother sat on the edge of Petra's bed. "When did you see her last?" she asked.

Jacob tried remembering. "Not since early afternoon, I guess."

"What time?" Rosemary's voice was edgy.

"Around noon, maybe one o'clock," he stammered.

"She's probably been gone for at least five hours." Rosemary stared crossly at her son.

His frustration quickly turned into defensive anger. "So this is my fault?" he yelled.

Rosemary tapped her foot. "Lower your voice in my house," she said, walking out of Petra's bedroom, visibly disgusted.

Jacob's rage grew darker.

"Drive over to the beach and see if she's there," Rosemary ordered.

Scared, Jacob raced down the stairs and retrieved his car keys.

His mother followed closely behind. "Don't forget to check the bluff and then go by the dairy. I'll call Summer, on the outside chance that Petra went over there and then I'll contact Morgan," she said, fully in control.

Jacob pivoted. "If that woman has my daughter, I won't be responsible for what I do." His words came out deadly.

Rosemary calmly looked at her second born son. "If Petra walked over to the Valley, then you better thank God for protecting that silly girl and then thank Morgan for providing a safe haven, am I clear?"

Jacob ignored his mother's stern rebuke and stormed out the door.

CHAPTER 71

✝

MORGAN HEARD DESTINY ENTER THE HOUSE. EMOTIONALLY DRAINED, SHE SAT ACROSS FROM Jeffery at the kitchen table sipping lukewarm coffee. Her sister hollered from the living room.

"Hey Ma, I'm here to pick up the kids."

"We're in the kitchen," Mamie yelled back.

Morgan heard children squealing and then soft footsteps traversed the hallway. Soon, Destiny was standing in the doorway. Morgan peered at her sister through red-rimmed eyes.

"What's going on?" she asked hesitantly.

Morgan shrugged. "Meet my dad," she said, pointing towards Jeffery. He stood.

Destiny stared. Then a gappy grin spread across the younger sister's face.

"Hello young lady, I've heard so much about you," Jeffery said.

Destiny addressed their mother. "Ma, I'm going to take all of the kids to my house."

"Sara's too?" Mamie asked.

Destiny nodded.

Morgan followed her younger sister into the living room and helped gather the children's belongings.

"What's really going on?" Destiny whispered.

Morgan placed toys in a toy box. "I'm finally getting answers."

Destiny hugged her older sibling.

"What's that for?" Morgan asked.

"I'm happy."

"About what?"

"I'm happy for you," Destiny said merrily.

"Just be prepared. Momma's secrets are messy," Morgan cautioned.

"Sin usually is."

Morgan hung her head, thinking of all the skeletons that were hanging in her own closet.

"I love you," Destiny said, while ushering the kids from the house.

Morgan smiled and followed the small group to her sister's car.

"Call me later. I want to hear all of the juicy details."

"Aren't you breaking a couple of laws?" Morgan asked, knowing that her sister had more passengers than car seats.

Destiny rolled her eyes. "Hey, I'm tryin' to help."

Morgan laughed heartedly. "It's appreciated," she said, closing the passenger door. Morgan watched her sister's car drive from sight. She was finally getting answers and she hoped with all of her heart that her sister would too, someday soon.

CHAPTER 72

✥

THE TEENS STOOD ON MICHIGAN AVENUE. SKYSCRAPERS DOTTED THE SKYLINE, WHILE THE Chicago River flowed under a gigantic bridge.

"Wow," Shawn exclaimed.

Petra's eyes sparkled. "Cool huh," she said.

He nodded.

"My friends and I hang out downtown all of the time."

"Is it always this busy?" he asked.

"Yes," she said, as they resumed walking. "I live about a mile away. Our condo faces the lake."

"On Michigan Avenue?" Shawn asked.

"No, a few blocks over," she said. Petra stopped walking and gave Shawn more time to view the river.

"Man, this is awesome!" he said, hanging over the railing.

"Come on. I want to show you North Michigan Avenue. It has the coolest buildings.

Shawn's stomach growled.

Petra began laughing. "You must be starved. What do you want to eat, fast food or frozen pizza?"

"Either is fine," he said, following Petra across the bridge.

The two walked side by side, in silence.

"What's the matter?" she asked, noticing his reticence.

"Indigo Beach can't compete with Chicago. I'm sure it's why my mom doesn't visit often.

197

"Indigo Beach is special too," she said, hoping her words helped.

"You were raised here. I don't expect you to understand."

Wisely, Petra kept her mouth shut.

"Well maybe she'll let you live with her," Petra said.

Shawn shook his head. "She won't let any of us stay with her."

Petra stopped walking. "You have siblings?" she asked.

He nodded. "Yeah, there are two more."

"I didn't know," she said, now realizing that there was more to Shawn's story.

"My brother and sister are being raised by relatives back home."

"Different fathers?" she asked.

"Yes, and they're much younger. I don't see them all that often." Shawn stood in the middle of the sidewalk, peering up at skyscrapers. "You know, I've been really naïve," he said, frustration boiling over.

Petra clenched her fists and screamed. Her shouts echoed between buildings. Other pedestrians stared, but she ignored their glares and began giggling. Then she started running down the sidewalk. Shawn gave chase. Soon, the teens stood in front of a tall high rise.

"Is this where you live?" he asked, peering up.

She nodded. "Uh-huh, but we can't go through the front door."

"Why not?" he asked.

"Because the doorman knows me. We'll enter from the parking garage."

Shawn followed Petra down a back alley and over a railing.

"It looks like you've done this before," he said.

Petra grinned. "A time or two, I know where all of the security cameras are hidden," she said, pointing to one mounted on a wall.

Shawn looked up. "So you aren't as innocent as you pretend?" he teased.

"It's not what you think. My Mom didn't want my dad keeping tabs on her." Shawn looked confused. "It sounds like she was hiding something."

Petra stopped walking. "I never thought of it like that," she said, reflectively. Shawn's stomach rumbled again. This time, much louder.

"You need to eat," she said, using a card to access the private elevator. The doors opened immediately.

Shawn followed her inside. "Are cameras in here?" he asked.

Petra shook her head. "No, they're only in the service elevator," she said. The elevator began moving. When the doors opened, the kids exited into the condominium's foyer. Using the cleaning lady's code, Petra disarmed the alarm system. Then the kids entered the condo. An expansive window, the height and width of an entire wall anchored the room.

Shawn pressed his face against the window and peered through fog. A lake was visible below.

"So, what do you think?" Petra asked.

"Is that Lake Michigan?"

Petra also pressed her forehead against the glass, "Yes."

Shawn continued staring. "It looks different from this angle," he said.

Petra faced her friend. "I know." Then she led Shawn into the kitchen. After washing and drying her hands, Petra preheated the oven. Opening the freezer, she grabbed a box of frozen pizzas and placed two pies on the counter.

Shawn stood transfixed. "You know how to cook?" he asked.

"Sure do, I can make just about anything," she said. Petra placed the unwrapped pizza pies on round pans. Then she peeked into the refrigerator. "It's empty!" she said, not surprised. "But pop and snacks should be in the pantry." Holding the door open, she grabbed beverages, chips, and a jar of peanut butter.

Shawn snatched a box of crackers from the shelf before Petra closed the door. Once the timer buzzed, the pies were placed into the oven. Forty minutes later, the kids ate pizza and drank pop, while they watched a movie.

"Thanks for coming with me," Petra said, as she dried the pizza pans and placed them in a drawer. The friends had just finished watching their favorite super hero action flick.

"No problem, I felt badly about leaving you earlier this summer and swore that I'd do things differently, if I ever had the chance."

"That's nice," Petra said, realizing that Shawn wasn't as lame as she'd originally thought. She smiled. Then she turned off the kitchen light.

"Wanna watch another movie?" Shawn asked.

"Sure, but this time I get to choose." Petra led Shawn back into the living room. While he nestled under a blanket, she used the remote to scan the movie channel. Once she made her selection, Petra leaned back and relaxed. Being home felt really good, but she was well aware that the sentiment might not last.

CHAPTER 73

꣖ † ꣖

MORGAN'S HEAD POUNDED FROM STRESS. TAKING PAIN RELIEVER HADN'T HELPED, SO SHE HOPED the cool compress plastered across her forehead would. She was still at her mother's home, trying to sort out the jumbled stories that her parents had shared. It was all so overwhelming. Then her phone rang. She recognized the number and answered.

"Hello."

"Morgan, is Petra with you?" Rosemary asked.

"No, why?"

"She's run off again and I was just hoping . . ."

Morgan quickly sat up. "I've been with my parents all afternoon," she said.

Rosemary gasped, "Your parents."

"Yes, they've finally come clean."

"Oh Morgan, I'm so happy for you. Now I feel badly about calling."

"Don't, you couldn't have known."

Rosemary sighed. "I feel just terrible about how things have turned out."

"You have nothing to apologize for. And one day, I might even thank your son."

"You'd thank him for being rude and acting ill raise," Rosemary said.

"Yes, because after he left my house, I came over here and Jeffery's presence forced both of them to tell me the truth."

"So God worked everything out for your good."

"Just like you promised."

"Can you think of where Petra might have gone? Jacob is checking the beach and dairy," Rosemary asked.

"No, not really, how is he holding up?" Morgan asked, truly concerned.

"His anger is misguided as usual, but he'll be fine."

"I'll tell momma and Jeffery about Petra," Morgan said.

"I'd appreciate it."

"You know that I'll help in any way."

"I do, thanks for being an angel."

The call ended. Morgan walked into the kitchen and peered out the window. Mamie and Jeffery were seated out back. Dusk was descending. Smoke from yard torches kept the mosquitos away. Rain had come and gone, but humidity remained. Her parents had maintained a secret for thirty-four years. Misguidedly believing that their actions were justified.

She felt sorry for Jacob. It would be years before he realized how his actions had affected his daughter. Feeling a strong urge to speak with Pastor Deon, Morgan dialed Summer's number. The First Lady answered on the second ring.

"Good evening, this is Morgan Harding."

"Well hello, what can I do for you?" Summer asked kindly.

"I apologize for calling Pastor Deon on your phone, but I'd like to share some wonderful news with him."

"Hold on, I'll see if he's available."

Morgan waited patiently until Pastor Deon got on the line. "I could really use some good news right now," he bellowed.

Morgan chuckled. "I have some, I know who my dad is."

"Praise God, it's about time Jeffery and Mamie did the right thing," Pastor Deon barked.

"You knew?" Morgan asked.

"I've always known that my old friend was your father. How do you feel about it?" he asked.

"Different, but whole," she said.

"Good, now tell your parents that I want to see the three of you in my office before Jeffery leaves town."

Morgan chuckled. "I'm not sure that I can use that tone of voice with either of them."

Deon harrumphed. "I've put up with their foolishness long enough. Tell them to show up or else."

Morgan laughed merrily. "Pastor, are you aware that Petra is missing?"

"Yes, and I'm tired of grown folks behaving like children and then getting upset when their kids emulate their behavior. One of Mrs. Meriwether's godsons also walked off the job today."

"Which one? She's godmother to half the county," Morgan said, growing concerned.

"Charmaine Hutchinson's boy, Shawn is missing."

Color drained from Morgan's face. "Oh my, Pastor we need to talk," Morgan stammered.

"What's going on?" Pastor Deon demanded.

"Petra and Shawn are probably together," she said.

"I was just thinking the same thing. Where are you?" he asked.

"Momma's house."

"Meet me at Rosemary's house in fifteen minutes. We'll talk there."

Then the line went dead. Morgan quickly opened the kitchen window and hollered, "Momma, Petra and Shawn are missing."

"What do you mean, the kids are missing?" Mamie yelled.

"I'll explain later, come on, we've got to go." Morgan leaned against the kitchen sink and prayed. The kids were smart, but young. After grabbing her purse, she ran down the hallway and out the front door.

CHAPTER 74

✝

JACOB RECOGNIZED THE LINCOLN IN THE DRIVEWAY AS SOON AS HE PULLED UP. HE PARKED ON the street. Defeated and scared, he'd spent fruitless hours searching for his daughter. Then he'd gone to the police station and answered countless questions. Hours had dragged by without any word from Petra.

Deon and Summer were seated in the kitchen, when he entered the room. His mother was drinking tea. Jacob approached the group. "I can't activate an Amber Alert because she's a runaway," he said, slamming his fists on the table.

Deon and Summer glanced at each other.

Jacob looked at his mother's guests, who were calmly seated and frustration boiled over. "So, the three of you are going to eat sandwiches and drink coffee all night, while my daughter is missing," he snapped.

Ignoring the outburst, Deon spoke calmly, "We've prayed and our faith is in God."

Jacob glared, "Forgive me for having doubts, but it's dark outside and Petra doesn't have a cell phone."

"Why not, she had one earlier in the summer," Summer asked.

"Jacob thought that my punishment was insufficient," Rosemary told her friend.

"You took her phone away for the whole summer?" Deon asked, staring at Jacob in disbelief.

The room went silent.

"I planned on giving it back this week, but I left it at home," Jacob said, trying to explain.

"Sweetheart, remember that child from Mount Calvary," Summer said, glancing at her husband for confirmation. "The parents used his phone to find him."

Deon harrumphed.

His wife's implication went unspoken.

"Heavy handed punishments rarely work," Deon said sternly.

Jacob stormed from the kitchen, intending to go out back. But Sheriff Jones was standing on the other side of the back porch door. He motioned for the officer to enter.

Deon, Summer, and Rosemary looked up.

"Good evening everybody, I thought I'd stop by before heading over to the Hutchinson's place. I've got an update."

"Sheriff, I haven't had time to tell Jacob about Shawn's disappearance," Rosemary said, turning towards her son. "One of the Meriwether's employees walked off the job today and hasn't been seen since."

"What does this kid have to do with my daughter?" Jacob asked angrily.

Sheriff Jones stepped forward. "Shawn and Petra got into the same vehicle. We believe that the runaways are together."

Jacob exploded, "She's with a boy."

"Thank you Jesus," Rosemary cried out.

Sheriff Jones looked confused.

"The kids are in youth ministry together. They're friends," Deon said, sounding equally relieved.

Just then, another car was heard pulling into the driveway.

"Morgan is here, and just in time. I asked her to stop by," Deon added.

The small group quickly followed Deon out the back door. A lone porch light illuminated the yard. Dusk had turned to darkness. Morgan and Mamie were practically running across the grass. Jacob never noticed the third person that followed closely behind them.

"I sure hope that Morgan can shed light on the situation," Deon said, to the sheriff.

For Jacob, seeing Morgan was the last straw. The small group stood helplessly as he unleashed uncontrolled fury, verbally accosting Mamie and her daughter.

"Jacob, just shut up. I won't take your bullying," Morgan yelled. Threateningly, he moved closer. "Oh yes you will," he hollered, infuriated that she was so near.

"No she won't," Jeffery said, moving Morgan aside.

Jacob looked up. Chest heaving, he peered at his employer bewilderingly. "What are you doing here?"

Placing protective arms around Morgan's shaking shoulders, Jeffery spoke, "I'm taking up for my daughter."

Jacob gasped! Disoriented, he stared. "Your daughter." Jacob looked at his mother for confirmation.

Rosemary nodded.

"And you won't disrespect her ever again," Jeffery said sternly.

"Well, it's about time, you stepped up to the plate," Deon barked.

"Deon," Summer snapped.

Ignoring his wife's outburst, Deon held the door open as the group silently filed through. Everyone eventually congregated at the dining room table.

"Morgan, we'd be grateful for any information that you can share," Deon said. She nodded.

"Am I missing something?" Sheriff Jones asked.

"Sheriff, Shawn Hutchinson is my nephew," Morgan said.

"Your nephew, how?" he asked.

"He's Sara's oldest boy," she explained.

Rosemary quickly handed Mamie a cup of tea.

Jacob stared in shock.

"How well do the kids know each other?" the sheriff asked, taking notes.

"Extremely well, Petra got caught drinking earlier this summer, but she never snitched on Shawn."

Jacob slumped in his chair, realizing just how much he didn't know.

Sheriff Jones appeared relieved. "Now we're getting somewhere. I don't believe in coincidences," he said, radioing dispatch with the update.

"Do you have any idea where the kids might be?" he asked.

"They're probably in route to Chicago," she said decisively.

Jacob struggled to breathe.

Sheriff Jones jotted a few notes and then looked up. "Young lady, start from the beginning."

Morgan slowly began her tale, telling the Sheriff details that neither Rosemary nor Jacob knew.

Later, after Sheriff Jones left the house, Jacob sat on his bed drowning in remorse. He'd let pride and anger cloud his better judgment. Satan had made a fool of him once again.

CHAPTER 75

✝

"I'M SORRY THAT YOU GOT CAUGHT UP IN MY DRAMA TODAY," PETRA SAID, HANDING SHAWN AN extra toothbrush and a pair of her dad's sweat pants. "When you finish showering, throw your dirty clothes into the washer, they stink."

Shawn's face turned a funny shade of pink.

Petra stifled laughter.

"Sorry," he said, before slamming the bathroom door.

"Cleanliness is next to Godliness," she shouted, through the closed door.

"Who told you that?" he yelled back.

"My grandmother, who else."

"Well then, you better take a soak too," he said.

Petra sniffed under her arms and moaned, "Oh my gosh." Mortified, she raced down the hallway.

After her bath, Petra lay across her bed and watched television alone.

"I'm going to bed," Shawn yelled from the living room.

"Did you finish folding your clothes?" she asked.

"Yes."

"See ya in the morning," Petra yelled back.

The teen used her remote and turned off her TV. Then she reflected on the information that Shawn had shared earlier that evening. Chances were probably slim to none that his mother would allow him to stay in Chicago with her. All because of her, her friend was in a boatload of trouble.

Their home situations were completely different. When she and her dad were finally reunited, he'd ground her for life, but his bark was far worse than his bite. Morgan and her grandmother would be disappointed, but they would soon forgive. Shawn's dad was abusive. Folks at church suspected that Mr. Hutchinson beat his wife.

Petra prayed and asked God for help.

CHAPTER 76

✝

AS THE SUN ROSE, JACOB QUIETLY DRANK COFFEE IN THE KITCHEN. HIS MOTHER WAS UPSTAIRS sleeping. Jacob still couldn't believe how shamefully he'd acted the night before. Jeffery had witnessed a side of him, few ever saw. Would he ever be forgiven? Once again, his anger had made a bad situation worse.

On top of everything else, Old Man Hutchinson held him personally responsible for Shawn's disappearance. The man had cursed his poor wife and Jacob unmercifully when the couple arrived. Fortunately, Sheriff Jones had calmly intervened. Pastor Deon was then able to minister to the man's distraught wife. It was glaringly obvious that she was battered, forcing Jacob to acknowledge his own horrible behavior. The realization was sobering.

Hearing a knock, Jacob walked towards the back door. Pastor Deon stood on the other side, holding a bag of donuts and two large coffees. Jacob held the door open.

"Mrs. Meriwether sends her love," the minister said, walking past Jacob. "Is Rosemary still sleeping?"

Jacob nodded.

"Good, we can talk privately," Pastor Deon said, placing two donuts on two separate napkins. He slid one towards Jacob. Then he grabbed a container of coffee. "Cat got your tongue?" he asked.

Jacob finally spoke, "My daughter lied to me."

Pastor Deon licked chocolate from his sticky fingers before speaking. "She's got talent. Who'd she learn it from, you or your wife?"

Jacob lowered his head.

209

Deon chuckled, "Son, I didn't drive all the way over here to make you feel bad or to mess with you. Repent and crucify your flesh. The Holy Spirit will help. You definitely can't do it alone."

Jacob hung his head. "You make it sound easy."

"Walking in righteousness becomes easier with practice. Getting started is the hardest part. God loves it when we repent and change our ways." Pastor Deon reached across the counter and pulled Jacob's uneaten donut towards him. "Have you asked God for help?"

Once again, Jacob lowered his head.

"I thought so, you can't keep relying on others to do what God expects of you."

"The kids are out there somewhere and I'm worried."

Pastor Deon frowned. "Why, Petra is smart and resourceful and Shawn is level headed by nature. God is protecting them."

Jacob looked doubtful. "My mom said the same thing last night."

"Listen to her. Your father never regretted a decision that Rosemary helped him make, and for your information, the church did not kill your dad. Your mother tried for years to get Deacon McDonald to change his diet. High blood pressure and clogged arteries caused your father's untimely death," Pastor Deon said, between bites.

"I hate waiting," Jacob said.

Pastor Deon chuckled, "That's part of your problem. Stand on the Word and watch God do His thing," Pastor Deon said, before taking another bite. Then he gulped coffee. "Call me when you hear from the kids."

Jacob stood. "You sound confident, that they'll call."

Pastor Deon grinned. "I am."

Minutes later, Jacob stood in the doorway, watching Pastor Deon drive away. Once gain, the country minister had given him something to think about.

Then Jacob walked into his father's old study. His mother still kept his father's Bible prominently displayed. He picked it up and interestingly, the book opened to Matthew 6. Verses nineteen through twenty-three were already highlighted. Jacob began reading. "But lay up for yourselves treasures in heaven, where neither moth nor rust doth corrupt, and where thieves do not break through nor steal. For where your treasure is, there will your heart be also." Tears fell as he read the scripture over and over again. When he finished readying, Jacob wept.

CHAPTER 77

✝

PETRA MICROWAVED FROZEN SAUSAGES WHILE WAFFLES TOASTED.

Shawn was trying to locate a bottle of juice in the pantry. "I don't see cranberry. Are you sure it's here," he yelled.

Petra leaned over his shoulder and pointed. "It's right there," she said, rolling her eyes.

Unperturbed, he grabbed the bottle off of the shelf. Unscrewing the lid, he poured the beverage into glasses that were filled with ice.

"How many waffles can you eat? Petra asked.

"The whole box," he said truthfully.

"Geez, you're greedy," she said, popping four more waffles into the toaster. Shawn heaped his plate with food.

Petra scowled, "Don't forget to say grace."

He set his fork down.

Petra moved him aside and then thanked God for their meal. She also prayed for Shawn's mother.

He appeared surprised. "So you think that we'll find her today?" he asked.

Petra smiled confidently. "With God's help, it shouldn't be too difficult."

Then she flicked on the television that hung high above the stove.

"So, tell me about your siblings."

Shawn stopped chewing. "There really isn't much to tell. They're just kids."

"How old are they?"

"Nine and six," Shawn said, as he poured syrup over his waffles.

"Do they ever visit?"

He shook his head. "No, my dad won't let them come over. He says that it's too hard on my stepmom. She's never been really good with small children."

Petra wondered whether that statement was true. "Your stepmom doesn't seem mean," she said, between bites.

Shawn's eyes clouded. "She isn't, but my dad is."

"I thought that he stopped drinking."

"He did, but it didn't change how he treated us."

Petra pushed her dish aside. "Don't you ever worry about your stepmom?" she asked.

Shawn lowered his head. "It's one of the reasons why I haven't left."

Petra's heart hurt. She grabbed a sausage link from the platter, took an angry bite, chewed hard, and then swallowed.

"Hey, you took the last one," Shawn said.

Petra scowled and then took another bite.

Shawn picked up the remote and channel surfed, settling on a cartoon station.

"You're so lame," Petra moaned.

"This is my favorite show."

She turned pensive.

"What's on your mind? You seem preoccupied this morning." Shawn asked.

"I'll feel better, once we locate your mother. I'm hoping that she'll be able to help. You're going to be in a lot of trouble because of me."

"What's done is done, so don't worry. Do you really think that we'll find her today?" he asked.

"Yes, as long as you have an address."

"I hope that you're right."

Petra did too, for Shawn's sake.

CHAPTER 78

☙ ✝ ❧

MORGAN WATCHED JEFFERY EAT. THE PAIR WAS SEATED IN THE INN'S DINING ROOM. YESTERDAY, parents and child had talked and cried together. This morning, food was a top priority for the father and daughter. Jeffery was chowing down on a breakfast skillet filled with eggs, fresh vegetables, sausage, and cheese. Morgan had already finished a tall stack of pancakes dripping with locally made maple syrup and topped with fresh whipping cream. Stomach bulging, they pushed away from the table at the same time.

Morgan chuckled, "How many times have we done this?" she asked.

Jeffery smiled, "Two many to count."

For the first time ever, Morgan noticed similarities in their features. "I always wanted you to be my father."

"Really!"

"I dreamed about it," she said, as the waitress removed their dishes from the table. Morgan watched the woman pour more coffee into their cups.

"I'm sorry about all of the lies and deception. Until the day she died, Mona begged me to tell you the truth," Jeffery said apologetically.

"She always treated me like a daughter."

"Because you were."

"When did Mona find out about the affair?"

"She knew about it from the very beginning. Quick money and spiritual immaturity is never a good combination. I was prideful and unrepentant. Mona tolerated my adultery. I still regret, how I treated her, but I've never regretted having you. As your mom and I explained yesterday, we've loved each other since adolescence, but my parents wouldn't allow us to marry. Frankly, your mother wasn't interested in marriage. So, I'm not so sure that she would have accepted my proposal anyway. I financially supported you with Mona's full knowledge. We eventually purchased the cottage in the Valley, so that you'd always have a home. Mamie and I decided that Grace would raise you there, although our well-intentioned decision wasn't thoroughly thought out. Can you ever forgive us?"

A lone tear trickled down Morgan's cheek. She quickly wiped it away. "I already have," she said, as more tears fell. "But I wonder what your other kids are going to say?"

"They already know."

Shocked, Morgan stared back.

"Mona told them about you before she died. Wisely, she felt that our other children needed to hear the facts from her. They've been waiting on me to make the next move."

"How did they take the news?" Morgan asked.

Jeffery smiled, "Jeffery Jr. didn't take it well at all. I think he had a crush on you, but surprisingly, the girls were open to having another sister. Let's face it, by the time that they found out, we'd all spent a great deal of time together."

Morgan grew somber as the conversation slowed.

"You must have been so disappointed with me when I moved in with Edward?" she said, finally acknowledging the elephant in the room.

Jeffery answered slowly, "When I contracted the head hunter to recruit you, I never realized that I was opening Pandora's box. As soon as I found out about the affair, I demanded that Edward end it and he did. I was disappointed, but truthfully, I still haven't forgiven myself. My lies have caused so much pain."

"That part of my life is so embarrassing. I've made so many mistakes," Morgan said regretfully.

Jeffery waved, scoffing at her comment. "We all have and you've done nothing that God can't forgive, but forgiving ourselves is more difficult."

Morgan dried her eyes with a table napkin.

"Edward isn't doing well, is he?" Jeffery asked.

Morgan shook her head. "It's time that I told you everything."

Jeffery leaned back in the antique chair. "I've got nothing but time," he said, placing his napkin on the table.

Morgan did the same, took a sip of coffee, and then told Jeffery the truth.

CHAPTER 79

✠

"YOU SMELL NICE," PETRA SAID.

"It must be the fabric softener," Shawn said, following her down the hallway.

"When does your cleaning lady come?" he asked.

Petra stopped walking. "She stops by every couple of days, but cleans once a week, why?"

"Well you better empty the trash or she'll know that we're here."

Realizing that Shawn was right, Petra ran down the hallway and grabbed the kitchen garbage bag. She then gave her bedroom a once over for good measure, throwing dirty clothes into the closet before shutting the door.

Leaving the condo in the same condition as when they'd arrived, the teens rode the service elevator down to the parking garage. Petra threw their trash into the dumpster.

"Where's the bus stop?" Shawn asked.

"A few blocks away."

"We aren't going to get lost, are we?" he asked playfully.

"I know where we are going."

The pair climbed over a railing and jumped to the pavement below.

"How often do you speak with your mother?" Petra asked, truly curious. Walking side by side, the duo proceeded down the street.

"Not often enough, we're supposed to be one big happy family, but we aren't."

Petra heard sarcasm. "What do you mean?" she asked.

"For some reason, my dad gets really angry when I contact her."

Petra stopped walking and faced Shawn. "My dad used to get jealous of my relationship with my mom too. We were really close."

Shawn kicked a piece of chipped concrete aside.

"Have you ever asked your grandmother about why your father won't let your siblings visit?"

"I spoke with Aunt Tonya once, but she didn't know the reason."

"What about Morgan?"

"I haven't seen her in years."

"Well, I know her and she's really cool," Petra said.

The teens arrived at the bus stop.

"Have you ever ridden a city bus?" Petra asked.

Shawn shook his head.

"Man, you're country!" she teased.

After paying their fairs, the kids found seats in the back.

Petra listened to music while Shawn peered out the window. It felt really good to be home.

CHAPTER 80

✝

JACOB STAYED ON THE LINE WHILE HIS HOUSEKEEPER ENTERED THE CONDOMINIUM.

"Is she there?" he asked.

"No, Mr. McDonald, the place looks just like how I left it, but I'll look in her bedroom just in case."

Jacob nervously waited on the phone while the woman did a walk through.

"Mr. McDonald, her room looks the same," she said.

Jacob's heart sank. Neither teen had been seen on lobby surveillance tapes. He'd hoped with all his heart that Petra had gone home.

"Thank you anyway, I really thought that she would be there." Jacob's worry increased.

"I can stop by tomorrow, if you'd like," she said.

"No, that won't be necessary."

"Call me with any news," the housekeeper said.

"I will." Jacob hesitated before asking his next question. "Mrs. Sanchez, you probably know Petra better than most. If she's in Chicago, where would she go?" he asked.

"When your wife was still living, she and Miss Petra spent a lot of time with a friend."

"Can you remember her name?" Jacob asked.

"I believe it was Phillips, Mrs. Phillips," she said.

Jacob became more frustrated. He'd never heard of the woman.

"Do you know her?" she asked.

"No, but thank you anyway," he said, before disconnecting.

"What did you find out?" Rosemary asked. His mother was standing in the doorway.

"She didn't go home."

Rosemary walked into the room and motioned for her son to sit. "Let me tell you a story."

Jacob sat.

"Before you were born, your father and I wrestled over your name. I wanted a biblical name and your father eventually agreed. Even though your namesake had a few character flaws, he was a man of great importance. Start honoring the name that we gave you."

"I've never thought much about my name," he said frankly.

"We gave it to you for a reason, and just like your namesake eventually realized, personal failure doesn't negate God's calling on your life. Believe in God's Word."

Jacob contemplated his mother's words. "So, you really believe that Petra is safe?"

"Yes I do," Rosemary said.

Jacob searched her face for doubt. "You're asking me to believe in something that I can't see and to give up total control."

Rosemary grinned, "Son, that's the definition of faith."

Jacob finally understood. "I've never been in charge, have I?"

Rosemary smiled, "Only in your mind, seek God first. Like Abraham before you, just believe."

Jacob watched his mother leave, understanding why his father had relied so heavily on her wisdom. He began praying. The calming presence of The Holy Spirit soon dampened anxiety and for the first time ever, Jacob gave all of his cares to God.

CHAPTER 81

✝

EVEN THOUGH IT HAD BEEN YEARS SINCE SHE'D WALKED DOWN THIS PARTICULAR STREET, PETRA remembered the route well.

"I told you that I knew how to get here," she said.

The teens walked up the trendy well-maintained avenue.

Petra pointed towards a large historic mansion that was still beautifully preserved. "When my mom was alive, we used to visit that house often."

Shawn looked at the number above its door. "That's where my mother lives."

"Are you sure? What's your mom's name?" Petra asked.

"Sara Harding."

"Mrs. Phillips lives in that house now," Petra said, totally confused.

Shawn grinned, "That's her, she married some old guy who died a few years ago. He left her the house and a whole lot of money. My mom's name is Sara Harding Phillips."

Petra plopped on the steps.

Shawn knelt beside her. "So you know my mom," he asked.

Petra felt out of sorts. "I guess, she and my mom used to uh, hang out together."

Shawn looked questioningly. "What does that mean?"

Avoiding his stare, Petra tried explaining, "Sometimes, my mom worked for your mother. She helped her entertain really important clients."

Shawn looked confused.

Petra refrained from saying more.

"Is she nice?" he asked.

Petra contemplated his question. "She's different, but nice. When you see how she lives, you'll understand."

Petra stood. Then she and Shawn climbed the massive concrete stairs together. Even though, the old mansion had been updated, it still retained much of its original charm. Petra rang the buzzer and waited.

"I guess no one is home?" Shawn said, after a moment.

Petra shook her head. "Mrs. Phillips, I mean your mom is probably still in bed. She, uh, works nights."

This time Shawn pushed the buzzer.

A sultry voice filtered through the intercom, "Can I help you?"

Petra quickly responded, "Mrs. Phillips, it's Petra McDonald, Lillian's daughter."

"Darling, it's been too long. Please come up."

The buzzer rang.

Shawn held the door open. Then he followed Petra up the stairs.

Sara Phillips stood at the top of the staircase, draped in a flowing peignoir. "Petra, who is behind you?" she asked.

"Ma, it's me."

The teens advanced to the landing.

Sara Phillips looked from one to the other. "Interesting, well give me a hug," she said to Petra.

Walking into the woman's embrace was like stepping back in time. Mrs. Phillips smelled familiar, just like her mom used too. Hearing Shawn's cough, the teenager disengaged. Then Petra watched the older woman embrace her son. The pair rocked to music of their own making.

"Well, this is a surprise. Come in and tell me how the two of you met and why you're here."

Petra followed the woman into the room, choking back memories and tears.

"Are you ill?" Mrs. Phillips asked.

"No, just remembering."

Sara smiled. Then she sprawled on a luxurious chase lounge. Astute eyes peered closely at the kids. "Now speak up," she said.

Petra gulped. Shawn's mother was dangerous. The teen knew secrets about her that a child shouldn't know.

"Petra," the woman said darkly.

Petra began her story, but she started from the day of her mother's accident, which was truly the beginning of the winding tale.

CHAPTER 82

✝

DEON AND SUMMER WAITED FOR ROSEMARY TO ARRIVE. HE'D TOLD HIS ADMINISTRATIVE assistant to take the day off, but she'd refused. Summer was seated on his couch flipping pages in a magazine. Hearing movement, Deon turned and faced the door.

"Rosemary is that you," Deon yelled.

"Yes it is, good afternoon Pastor, hello friend," Rosemary said, poking her head through the office door.

Deon offered his administrative assistant a seat.

She walked into the room and sat on the opposite end of the leather couch.

"Is there anything that I can get for you?" Summer asked. She then leaned forward and hugged her friend.

"Girl please, I began praising God, right after I got out of bed this morning."

Deon beamed proudly. He could always count on Rosemary's unwavering faith.

"I knew you'd come skipping in here," he said.

She smiled, "You've known me too long, to have any doubt."

"How's the rest of the family holding up?" he asked.

Rosemary sighed, "As well as can be expected. Not all of my children are as faithful as others."

"What am I smelling?" Deon asked, knowing full well, that whatever it was involved something delicious.

Rosemary smiled, "I stopped by the diner and picked up a thank you gift."

"You shouldn't have," Summer exclaimed.

"I know, but I wanted to," she said sincerely. Rosemary quickly left Deon's office and returned with two large bags. "I've never known either of you to forgo peach cobbler or pulled pork."

"The diner's onion rolls are sinful," Summer said happily.

Deon patted his stomach. "Honey, grab plates from the storage closet."

Rosemary began taking plastic containers out of bags while Summer grabbed eating utensils.

"Deon, nobody should get this excited over a meal," Summer said, scolding her husband.

Ignoring his wife's comment, he waited impatiently until the ladies fixed their plates. Then he made his.

"Is Jeffery still in town?" Rosemary asked, once she was seated on the couch.

"Yes, we spoke earlier. He and Morgan had a breakfast meeting, and from what he shared, it went exceptionally well."

"I'm glad, I always knew that the truth would set them free. Unfortunately, Mamie's morning hasn't gone as well. She's worried sick about Shawn."

"The Meriwether's are equally anxious. They just left," Deon said, shaking his head. Barbeque sauce dripped from his fingers.

Summer shook her head.

Deon ignored his wife's nonverbal censure.

"How's Jacob?" Summer asked Rosemary.

"He's scared, but God has him right where He wants."

"Amen," Deon exclaimed.

"Honestly, even my faith was tested yesterday," Rosemary said.

"But not for long," Deon said, filling another onion roll with pulled pork.

"Having been a single parent, tribulation and I are old friends," Rosemary quipped.

"I'm just glad that my spiritual maturity deepened as I got older," Summer said, laughing.

Rosemary grinned, "Mine deepened too and so did my wrinkles."

Deon chuckled at Rosemary's deadpan expression. The Word of God was true. Laughter was good like medicine.

CHAPTER 83
꧁ ✝ ꧂

"GOOD MORNING MRS. LEWIS, I'M PETRA'S DAD AND I WAS WONDERING IF MY DAUGHTER IS AT your house?" Jacob asked. The Lewis's were neighbors and it was sheer luck that Jacob had found their phone number.

"Why no she isn't, what's going on?" the woman asked.

"Petra ran away from my mother's house in Michigan and I was hoping that she'd returned to Chicago."

"Oh my, I haven't seen Petra since the winter. Our daughters aren't as close as they once were."

Jacob exhaled, "I didn't know. I spend a lot of time on the road."

"I know," the woman said.

Jacob heard judgment and being on the receiving end of it hurt.

"Have you spoken with Brenda Connors? I believe her daughter, Alyson and Petra are friends."

Jacob hung his head. The list of friendships that he knew nothing about was increasing. "Do you have her telephone number?" he asked.

"Why yes, just give me a minute to find it," she said.

Jacob waited until the woman returned to the phone. "Well thank you for your time," he said, after she'd given him the number.

"I'll call if I hear anything," she said.

"Thank you again, it would be appreciated," Jacob said, before disconnecting. He'd contacted everyone that he knew and no one had seen or heard from the teens. The kids had completely vanished.

Old Man Hutchinson had just left and it had taken every ounce of self-control to refrain from slugging the man. Apparently, a good night's sleep hadn't changed the elder Hutchinson's disposition.

Jacob sprawled across the bed and buried his head under a pillow, hoping to quell the enemy's voice. When it didn't, he got up and went back downstairs. Earlier, he'd watched his mother walk calmly out the front door, refusing to harbor fear. Her faith was resolute.

So with nothing else to loose, Jacob ventured back into his father's old office. Again, he opened his father's Bible and began reading. Hours passed. Burdens melted and then a flame of hope started burning again.

CHAPTER 04

✠

A STAFF MEMBER ADDED VEGETABLES TO PETRA'S PLATE. LUNCH HAD JUST BEEN DELIVERED from a service that Petra's mother had regularly used.

"More water?" Mrs. Phillips asked.

Petra nodded.

The woman poured sparkling liquid into stemware.

Bubbles popped and sprayed from Petra's glass. The carbonated beverage was a rare treat. "I haven't eaten chicken like this since my mom died," Petra said, between bites.

"That's why I ordered it today,"

"You know that my mom hated cooking and cleaning," the teen said.

Mrs. Phillips chuckled. "I'm well aware that your mother loathed housework, although, I never quite understood why she complained so much. She had plenty of help. Her life was enviable."

Petra had heard these sentiments before, but no one really understood the pain that her mother's smiles masked. "My mom and I loved coming here," the teen said.

"And I enjoyed having you both around."

"Mrs. Phillips, can Shawn stay with you?" Petra blurted.

Shocked, Shawn looked up.

The woman answered slowly, "Petra, darling, I had Shawn when I was about your age, so you're both old enough to hear the truth. There's a huge inheritance at stake and some very angry people that don't want me to have it. My late husband's family doesn't know about my children. It would greatly alter their perception of me, if they did," she said, lowering her voice.

Shawn remained unnaturally quiet.

His mother looked directly at him. "Charmaine has done a fine job of raising you. It would be best if she finished," she said.

Petra glanced at Shawn, whose jaw was rigid.

He grew defiant.

Mrs. Phillips placed her empty glass on the table. "I've truly enjoyed having lunch with you, but I have a business to run."

Shawn glanced between Petra and his mother. He appeared confused by her comment.

"Shawn, your mom dates a lot," Petra said, trying to explain.

The teen's eyes locked and then a blush slowly covered his face.

Mrs. Phillips had the decency to look away.

Petra resumed chewing.

"Now, do you understand why you can't live with me?" she asked.

He nodded, "Can I at least visit from time to time," he asked.

"Absolutely and I'll travel to Michigan more often. Your stepmom and I have a wonderful relationship. Your dad and I, on the other hand, well, let's just say that we have an understanding."

Shawn's face turned stormy.

Petra coughed.

Mrs. Phillips stared at the teens. "What aren't you telling me?" she asked, looking between the two.

"Shawn's father beats him," Petra said, violating his trust once again.

Mrs. Phillips eyes darkened.

Shawn lowered his gaze.

"And he beats his wife," Petra said, for good measure.

Mrs. Phillips drummed her manicured nails on the antique mahogany table.

Petra knew that Shawn was angry with her, but she didn't care. He needed an advocate.

"Why haven't you told me?" his mother asked.

"You call, maybe three times a year. When was I supposed to tell you?" he shouted.

Mrs. Phillips looked away. "I can handle your father. I always have."

Shawn peered back, disbelievingly.

"She can," Petra said.

Shawn continued glaring at his mother.

"Sweetheart, your father won't ever hurt you again." Mrs. Phillips words were softly spoken, but lethal. "Who else knows that you're in Chicago?" she asked.

Again, the teens glanced at each other.

"I figured as much," Mrs. Phillips said, before picking up her cell phone. Then she speed dialed a number.

Petra resumed eating.

"Hello darling, I need a favor. Can you drive me to Indigo Beach later today? Naughty boy, it won't be that kind of trip."

Petra munched on a dinner roll while Mrs. Phillips conducted the kind of business that was comfortably familiar.

"And by the way, bring your friend. I have a small job for him to do. I'll tell you all about it when you arrive."

Petra lathered butter on another dinner roll.

"We'll leave for Michigan in a few hours," the woman said. Then her conversation ended.

"I don't want to go back to my grandmother's house," Petra said angrily.

Mrs. Phillips frowned. "I'm sure that you don't. I don't want to go either, but we must," she said. The woman stood and her gown flowed gracefully as she left the room.

Petra scowled.

Shawn swallowed the last bite of chicken. "The lemon sauce was really good," he said.

Petra rolled her eyes. "I do not want to see my father," she wailed.

Shawn shrugged, "Get over it, I don't want to see mine either."

Petra leaned back in her chair, pouting. Adults were so stupid, even the grownups that she liked.

CHAPTER 85

✞

WAVES CRASHED AND WATER SPRAYED AGAINST MORGAN'S FACE AS SHE WALKED ALONG THE beach. One perk of living near the Valley was its accessibility to Lake Michigan. This stretch of land was a hidden jewel. A bright azure sky was the perfect backdrop for the rocky stonewalls and the ragged bluff above. The view was amazing. Morgan felt her phone's vibration long before she heard the buzzing. She answered.

"I was hoping that you hadn't changed your number." Sara's voice was low and sultry.

Morgan stopped walking. "Sara?" she said, caught off guard.

"So you're visiting for the summer and you didn't call."

Morgan's pulse raced. "I've been busy."

"We all are," Sara said irritably.

"Did Momma call you about Shawn?"

"No, but my beloved son and his darling friend are in my living room watching television at this very moment. I've already spoken with our mother."

"They're with you?" Morgan asked.

"Yes, I'll be bringing the kids home in a few hours."

"Oh Sara, this is wonderful news."

"I can't wait to hear your version of this truly amazing story. Petra shared that the two of you have become fast friends."

"I'm in a different space, emotionally and spiritually."

"It sounds like you've been spending a lot of time with Destiny," the second born sister crooned.

Morgan chuckled, "Yes I have."

"I don't talk to her all that often, that Jesus stuff was getting rather old."

"I used to feel the same way, but no more." Morgan's words were boldly spoken.

"Since something is clearly in the water, don't expect me to drink anything when I arrive."

Morgan laughed loudly. "I can't wait to see you." The two sisters had once been close.

"Likewise darling, we'll be there in a few."

Morgan and her younger sister were alike in so many ways, but different where it most counted. Sara's heart was hardened by hardship and vice. She survived by her wits and impenetrable resolve. Morgan had always respected her sister's drive and tenacity, but never her personal life choices.

Reaching down, she picked up a flattened rock and skimmed it across the water. Then she threw three more stones and watched them jump. She'd planned to walk into town, get a bite to eat, and return. But knowing that the kids were coming home changed everything. Morgan dialed her mother. "Ma, I just spoke with Sara."

"Child, ain't God good?" Mamie said happily.

Smiling, Morgan walked towards stairs that were bolted to the side of the bluff.

"I just got off the phone with Rosemary," Mamie said.

Morgan began climbing. "I'll be over as soon as I shower and change," she said, climbing the steps.

"Be safe. I'll see you when you get here."

"Momma."

"Yes, Baby."

"I love you," Morgan said, truly meaning the words.

"I love you too. Now get off the phone. I've got a few more people to call before you arrive."

Morgan ended the call. Then she placed her phone in her back pocket and gingerly traversed the winding stairs that led towards home.

CHAPTER 86

✛

"MA, I CAN'T BELIEVE THAT PETRA MADE IT ALL THE WAY TO CHICAGO," JACOB SAID, AS HE watched his mother put a stuffed turkey into the oven.

"Your daughter is extremely resourceful. Don't ever forget it," she said, never glancing up.

"I get angry all over again, when I think of what could have happened."

"But it didn't because while you were worrying, some of us were praying."

Jacob guiltily looked away.

"Son, sit down. We need to discuss a few things before Petra arrives." Rosemary wiped her hands on a dishtowel and then sat at the counter. "I loved Lillian dearly. She was a wonderful daughter-in-law, but I knew that something was wrong when she began distancing herself from family and friends. Sin helped turn her away from God and from those who truly loved her. Her new friends provided acceptance and excitement. If you'd been more focused on your family's needs, you might have seen the trouble that was lurking. You ignored my concerns, so I stopped mentioning them."

Jacob looked away again. His mother's words were true.

"Begin appreciating Petra's gifts and talents. You remade Lillian into someone that she hated and then you despised. Don't make the same mistake with your daughter."

"Ma, I only wanted the best."

"The best according to whom? Definitely not God. It isn't too late to fix things with Petra."

Jacob nodded.

"Also, Sheriff Jones called while you were upstairs."

"What did he want?"

"He wants to speak with the kids when they arrive."

"I guess I have some apologies to make," Jacob said.

"Yes you do," Rosemary said, picking up a potato peeler.

"I probably need to start with Morgan."

"Sounds about right."

"God is undoubtedly unhappy with my behavior," Jacob said thoughtfully.

"That's a pretty good bet," she said, placing a peeled potato in a pot of water.

"You aren't going to play nice, are you?"

"I'm your mother. I don't have too."

Jacob left the kitchen and walked out back. The security of the weeping willow tree beckoned. He sat in the metal glider and rocked. He'd sent his daughter to Michigan, hoping that his mother would teach her a lesson or two. But the tables had turned. It was he, not Petra who really needed instruction and this knowledge was another hard pill to swallow.

CHAPTER 87

✢

ONCE THE TRIO LEFT THE CITY, THEY TRAVELED IN VIRTUAL SILENCE. NOW, THE SLEEK BLACK limo cruised the open highway. Petra peered out the window, daydreaming while Shawn slept. Her stomach was knotted. An hour and a half later, the vehicle passed Meriwether's Gas Station and Convenience Store.

Once they got closer to Shawn's house, Petra shook him awake. He looked scared and truthfully, so was she. Then she glanced at Mrs. Phillips, whose face was devoid of emotion. Even though the woman was casually dressed in jeans, a cotton top, and jewelry, her presence was still commanding. Naturally silky hair flowed long and straight. Eye makeup hid dark circles. In spite of physical exhaustion, the woman was still enviably beautiful. Petra had always questioned her ethnicity, but no more.

Her mother's friend smiled, but it never reached her eyes. From a young age, Petra had heard whispers about the woman's character and alliances. Mrs. Phillips associated with men of power and prestige. Many were pillars in their communities. Some controlled their empires from the shadows. Others wore respectability like a well-made suit. Mutual friends had warned Lillian about Sara Phillips, but she'd ignored their advice.

Petra had never told a soul about her mother's business relationship with Mrs. Phillips or about her late night trysts. She'd instinctively understood that mentioning anything about her mother's meetings could be dangerous. She'd always felt that something more sinister had forced her mother off the road that fatal night and that Shawn's mother was connected in some way.

Keeping a dead woman's secrets was exhausting. The vehicle slowly pulled into the Hutchinson's driveway. Petra's stomach ached from worry.

"Everything is going to be just fine," Mrs. Phillips said to both teens.

The woman comfortingly patted her son's hand and gave him an encouraging smile.

Petra felt sick. "How mad will he be?" she asked.

"Very," Shawn said.

The woman sighed, "I just wish that I'd known." She leaned over and kissed her son's cheek. Shawn appeared stunned by the gesture.

Movement, outside the tinted windows caught Petra's attention. Charmaine Hutchinson stood on the porch. Mr. Hutchinson was walking towards the parked car. The limo driver opened the door and Petra followed Mrs. Phillips and Shawn out.

Without provocation, Mr. Hutchinson backhanded the right side of his son's face and Shawn fell to the ground. His wife screamed and ran down the porch steps. But within seconds, the limo driver held Charmaine Hutchinson back as another man exited the car. This man punched Shawn's father in the stomach. Petra watched in horror as the older man went to his knees.

Unfazed, Mrs. Phillips approached Shawn's stepmother. She tilted the woman's face upward. Makeup couldn't hide the splotchy, bruised skin. "Darling, just drag that piece of garbage around back and make sure he understands that his wife and son aren't punching bags."

Struggling for release, the man was dragged away.

"Let's talk inside," Mrs. Phillips said, draping her arms around Charmaine Hutchinson's shoulders.

Amazed that he'd taken the slap without uttering a sound, Petra helped Shawn stand.

Grunts and groans were heard from the backyard.

"They won't kill him? Will they?" Petra asked.

"Not unless I tell them too," Mrs. Phillips said.

"Sara, please tell them to stop," Charmaine Hutchinson begged.

Mrs. Phillip's eyes turned steely. "Not until my point is made."

Visibly shaken, Shawn pushed the front door open and stepped aside so that the women could enter.

"Charmaine, you should have told me about the abuse years ago," Mrs. Phillips said, clearly aggravated.

"It's so embarrassing," the woman said. Tears now flowed down her face.

Shawn hugged his stepmom tightly.

Petra's stomach was on fire.

"Shawn, go into the kitchen and get Petra something to drink. The poor child looks sick," Charmaine Hutchinson said, looking closely at the teen.

Muted sounds could still be heard from the back yard. Petra desperately wanted the beating to end. Minutes later, Shawn handed her a glass of water.

"Sara, please," the woman begged again.

Mrs. Phillip's held up a well-manicured hand. "I've neglected my responsibility. Handling this matter is the least that I can do."

"Thank you for bringing the kids home," Charmaine Hutchinson said, between sobs.

"There is no need. They're my children too, but I have two more stops to make, so I can't stay long. Do you have any questions for the teens before Petra and I leave?"

Both kids squirmed.

Charmaine Hutchinson addressed her son first. "Why did you leave?"

"I couldn't let Petra travel alone."

"I don't understand," she said.

"Petra was going to hitch hike by herself. I'm sorry."

"I'm sorry too," Petra said, feeling horrible for causing so much trouble.

"You kids aren't to blame for this mess," Charmaine Hutchinson said bitterly.

"What do you mean?" Petra asked.

"Darling, my grandmother made a bad situation worse with her meddling," Mrs. Phillips said, shaking her head.

Then Petra gasped.

"What do you know?" Shawn asked.

Petra's face colored. "Um, nothing," she said, glancing from one adult to the other.

"Darling, say what's on your mind," Mrs. Phillips said. Her voice was smooth, yet commanding.

237

"You were a teenager when you had Shawn."

"Yes, I was sixteen," Mrs. Phillips said.

"But Mr. Hutchinson is really old."

Charmaine Hutchinson's tears flowed harder.

Mrs. Phillips stared shrewdly at Petra.

"You weren't old enough to date him," the teenager said.

Shawn's eyes got wider. "I never thought of that."

Mrs. Hutchinson slumped beside her son on the couch.

"You're definitely Lillian's daughter, too smart for your own good. I wasn't mature enough to understand that adult decisions come with grown up consequences. Grandma Grace gave Shawn to his father."

"No, she blackmailed my dad," Shawn said, looking at his stepmother.

Charmaine Hutchinson lowered her head shamefully. "I didn't know that you knew," she said horrified.

"I've always known. I just never understood why, until now."

Shawn's mother stood. "My grandmother's heart was hardened. She was mean and no one challenged her authority. Come Petra, your family is waiting," Mrs. Phillips said, pushing the screen door open.

Petra followed. Stories that her mother had shared were finally making sense. As she walked out the front door, she saw that Mr. Hutchinson was leaning against the side of the garage. His eyes were horribly swollen. He staggered towards the limo. Protectively, the driver guarded his employer.

"Sara, I love you. I've always loved you," the old man cried out.

Mrs. Phillips pushed Petra into the vehicle. "You don't know the first thing about love," she said, before stepping into the vehicle. Then Morgan's sister leaned back against the soft leather interior and offered Petra a crooked smile. "Unfortunately, I won't be able to handle your father so easily," she said, as she snapped open a mirrored case and reapplied her lipstick.

Petra gazed out the window, dreading their next stop. Tears fell. In deep mourning, she ached for Shawn and his family. Then she remembered Grandma Rosemary's truthful words. *Dirty deeds done in darkness, always come to light.* Her grandmother was correct again, but she should have added that when they did, people got hurt.

CHAPTER 88

✝

DEON WAITED PATIENTLY ON THE PORCH. CHARMAINE HUTCHINSON HAD JUST CALLED, SO everyone knew that the limo was in route. He just couldn't stop grinning.

"I tell you, God puts people together for a reason. I can't believe that you didn't know about Sara Phillips or that she was Mamie's daughter."

"Lillian didn't talk much about her friends."

Jacob's weak excuse didn't deserve a response, so Deon ignored it. "I've seen God weave people and circumstances together for His glory many times." Just then, a long limousine turned the corner and slowly approached. "They're here," Deon shouted, as he ran down the steps. Jacob followed closely behind. The two men stood on the front lawn until the car parked. "Open the door, Man, you're taking too long," Deon barked. Then Petra sprang out the door and into her father's arms. The driver assisted Sara while a second man stood off to the side. After assessing all of the occupants of the vehicle, Deon motioned for the group to follow. "Come, we can talk inside."

Soon, family and friends congregated in the dining room.

Deon sat at the head of the table. "So the prodigal child returns," he said to Sara.

"Please forgive my husband," Summer said, as she kicked his leg under the table.

Deon reached down and rubbed his shin.

"Hello Jacob, I feel as if I know you." Sara's voice was low and sensual.

"I'm at a disadvantage, Lillian never spoke of you."

Her eyes glinted amusingly. "Your wife was private by nature. It's what I liked most about her."

Petra interrupted the conversation. "Mom and I used to go over to Mrs. Phillips house all the time."

Deon watched the exchange with interest.

Sara's eyes remained blanketed. "Darling, your father doesn't want to hear about any of that," she said softly.

Petra quieted.

"Oh, I'm sure he does, but now isn't the time," Deon said. Then he faced Jacob. "I just can't believe that you've never met Sara."

Summer kicked her husband's shin again.

Scowling, Deon repositioned his chair. "As I was saying . . . "

Jacob raised his hands in surrender. "I know what you were saying and I agree, there's no excuse."

Deon beamed smugly.

"We can become acquainted, once we're back in Chicago?" Jacob said to Sara.

"I'd like that."

Petra grinned.

"Young lady, you have some explaining to do, but it can wait until after we've eaten. I need your help in the kitchen," Grandma Rosemary said, as she stood inside the doorway.

Petra left the room. Minutes later, Rosemary placed platters of food on the sideboard while Petra and Summer set the table. Within the hour, a turkey dinner with all the trimmings was served.

"Let us pray." Deon glanced around the table, making sure that everyone's eyes were closed. "Lord, thank you for keeping the kids safe. We especially thank you for deliverance and restoration. God bless the food that we are about to eat and the hands that prepared it, Amen."

Salt and pepper shakers passed from hand to hand. Summer poured copious amounts of freshly made punch. Nosily, Deon addressed the limo driver who sat beside him.

"How was traffic?"

"Smooth," the man said, without further comment.

Undeterred, Deon turned towards the other gentleman. "Are you and Sara friends?" he asked.

The man nodded, but said no more.

"Deon, let Sara's guests eat in peace," Summer chastised her husband.

Miffed by his wife's censure, Deon stuffed a fork full of turkey into his mouth. Then he caught Sara's sly grin and winked.

"Pastor, I've heard wonderful things about you and your church," she said.

Deon noted how tired the young woman looked. Maintaining her grandmother's business was taking a tremendous toll. He said a quick prayer.

"You need to call your mother," Deon said, not mincing words.

"Deon," Summer snapped. He peered at Sara innocently.

"I usually do when I'm in town."

"Your mother realizes her mistakes," he said, offering hope.

Sara stopped chewing. "I'm not sure that I can forget or forgive."

"You probably don't want too, but it doesn't mean that you can't," he said.

"Do you know my father's identity?"

Deon's heart ached for the young woman seated before him. He shook his head.

"I just wondered," Sara said. She pushed away from the table and stood.

"Mrs. McDonald, thank you for your hospitality, but we must get going. I still have one more stop to make."

Deon also stood. "I'll walk you to the door." Deon led Sara and her guests from the house.

"Thank you for helping my sister. Momma told me everything."

"But she hasn't shared what matters most to you."

Sara's laugh was hard. "I'm happy for my sister. Since her dad is rich, maybe mine is famous," she said.

"Never lose hope. God is faithful," he said, as they neared the limo. The driver stood beside the open door.

"Can I pray for you?" Deon asked.

Sara shook her head. "Say a prayer for someone more deserving."

"Child, you're no less worthy, be blessed," he said, before closing the limo door. Deon watched the vehicle pull away. Then he slowly walked back towards Rosemary's house. Four sets of eyes looked up expectantly when he entered the dining room.

"Is she okay?" Summer asked.

Deon sat and placed his dinner napkin across his lap. "No, but she will be," he said, as he shoveled a forkful of turkey into his mouth.

Summer smiled perceptively at her husband. Then she said, "Amen!"

CHAPTER 89

✝

FIREFLIES ZAPPED AND BUZZED AROUND A LIGHT POST NEAR THE ROAD. CICADAS SCREECHED. The sounds of summer were familiar and comforting. A warm breeze gently caressed Morgan's bare arms. She swatted a mosquito. Mamie came onto the porch and joined her daughter on the swing. The swing swung rhythmically.

"Have you heard from Jeffery?" Mamie asked.

"Yes, he made it back to Chicago safely."

"I'm glad that you had time to talk privately."

"Me too."

"Have his other children been told?"

Morgan nodded, "They already knew."

"I didn't know."

The creaking and groaning of the swing was soothing.

"Is he still going to purchase another home in the area?"

"Yes."

The women sat in silence.

"Why are you so quiet?" Mamie asked.

"Just thinking."

"About what?"

Morgan paused, "My life."

"What part specifically?"

Morgan smiled, "I've been wondering why the cottage was really purchased? I know there's more to that story than what Jeffery shared."

Mamie steadied the swing.

Morgan waited for her mother's reply.

"Momma made him."

"I thought so, Grandma Grace was nickel slick."

Mamie chuckled, "You've described her perfectly."

"Did she try extortion?" Morgan asked, expecting to hear the worse.

Mamie exhaled, "She tried, but since Mona already knew about the affair, the ploy didn't work. Jeffery and Mona purchased the cottage in your name and allowed your grandmother to live there until she died. Your father sent money for you every month until you graduated from high school."

"He told me about my college fund," Morgan said.

"I didn't even know about it until your senior year."

"So the scholarship that I supposedly earned was another lie?"

Mamie sighed, "I'm afraid so."

Morgan peered at the stars that dotted the dusky sky. Jeffery had been a part of her life from the very beginning and she'd never known. "Do my sisters know any of the details?"

"Yes."

Now, Morgan understood why no one had questioned her inheritance.

A limo slowly approached.

"She's here," Mamie said excitedly.

Morgan stood and leaned against the railing.

Mamie waved wildly.

Morgan watched the vehicle park and then its driver opened the passenger door. Sara exited. With assistance from another man, her younger sister walked up the gravel driveway.

"Sitting on a porch is so country," the younger sister yelled.

Morgan smiled, "Sister Dear, despite your expensive clothing, you still have a little country left in you too."

Sara rolled her eyes, false eyelashes fluttering. "Momma, when are you going to pave the driveway? I've just ruined a pair of ridiculously expensive heels."

Mamie laughed heartedly. "You should have worn flats."

The driver deposited Sara at the bottom of the porch. After tipping his hat towards the women, he walked back towards the car.

"Darling, show a little respect," Sara addressed her older sister.

Morgan stepped down and hugged her sibling.

Sara's body was stiff and unresponsive.

Disappointed in her sister's reaction, Morgan pulled away.

"You girls come inside," Mamie said, oblivious to her daughters' comfortableness.

Sara and Morgan followed their mother into the living room.

"Momma, I can't stay long," Sara explained.

Mamie appeared hurt.

Morgan frowned.

Sara shrugged indifferently.

"How did it go at Rosemary's house?" Morgan asked, hoping to change the subject.

Sara plopped into a chair. "Jacob wasn't what I expected," she said, slipping off her shoes.

Mamie sat next to Morgan while Sara got comfortable.

"Tell us everything," Morgan said.

Sara chuckled, "Pastor Deon sure is nosy," she said, beginning her tale.

CHAPTER 90

✝

THE HOUSE WAS FINALLY EMPTY AND PETRA WAS SLEEPING UPSTAIRS. JACOB HANDED HIS mother a dish to wash.

"Ma, tell me about Dad."

Rosemary turned towards her son. "What do you want to know?"

"What was he really like?"

She smiled, "Your father was loving and kind, but he was also hard headed and stubborn."

Jacob chuckled, "So I got it honestly?"

Rosemary smiled, "I'm afraid so, but your father got it from his dad. So, it's really Great Grandpa McDonald's fault."

Jacob hooted, "I remember your mother being a pistol too."

"So maybe you received equal dosages from both sides of the family," Rosemary joked. "What else do you want to know?"

Jacob hesitated, "Pastor Deon says that I'm like him a lot."

Rosemary nodded, "You are, but in ways that you might not realize."

Jacob leaned closer.

"Your father was the smartest man that I've ever known. You get your book smarts from him. He was also a great negotiator."

"I never knew."

"You never asked."

"You forgot to mention that I'm competitive."

Rosemary took her hands out of the dishwater and faced her son.

"Your competitiveness started out innocently, but grew over time into ridicule and judgment. Arrogance hid your insecurities from others, but not from me. My heart ached for Lillian. When you wouldn't accept responsibility for her pregnancy, even though you were most definitely present when Petra was conceived. I knew then, that pride was hardening your heart."

"She knew that I didn't want children," Jacob argued.

"Then you should have practiced celibacy or used better protection. The enemy tried using that unplanned pregnancy to abort both of your futures. He succeeded in killing Lillian. You could be next, if you don't humble yourself before God."

"Was Lillian's death my fault?" Jacob asked the one question that haunted his dreams at night.

"It's complicated, the consequence of unrepentant sin can be either spiritual or physical death. Only God knows why Lillian died. You aren't responsible for her drunk driving, but you did create a toxic home environment. It was your responsibility to set the spiritual tone of your home."

Jacob listened intently, finally understanding where he'd gone wrong.

"Is there anything else that you want to know?" she asked.

"No," he said somberly.

"Ask God to reveal your faults, and when he does, thank and praise Him for His honesty. He is going to turn this situation around for your good. I just know it. Now, get out of my kitchen. It's been a long day and your questions are keeping me from finishing my work."

Even though Jacob knew that his mother hated the gesture, he kissed the top of her head.

"Jacob!" Rosemary shouted.

Laughing loudly, he exited the room. Then he climbed the stairs two at a time. After entering his old bedroom, Jacob stretched out across the bed, contemplating his mother's brutal, yet truthful words. She was right as usual. Lillian had paid the ultimate price for disobedience. He would too, if he didn't change his ways. Only with the Holy Spirit's help, could he right the terrible wrong that he'd committed.

Jacob quickly undressed and readied for bed. Then for over an hour, he stared at the ceiling. Deeply repentant, he cried out to the Father again and again before finally succumbing to sleep.

CHAPTER 91

⊷ † ⊶

MORGAN LANGUIDLY SIPPED COFFEE AT HER MOTHER'S KITCHEN TABLE, WHILE SARA AND MAMIE chatted. Morgan had successfully talked Sara into staying a little while longer.

"What do you think Rosemary puts into her dressing? I've been trying to figure out her recipe for years," Mamie asked.

Sara propped her feet on a kitchen chair. "I'm not sure, but it tasted wonderful."

"Can I offer you anything else?" Mamie asked.

"No Momma, I have to get back to Chicago. You know that I have a business to run."

Morgan watched sadness envelop their mother.

"I bet Deon and Summer were glad to see you," Mamie said, changing the subject.

Sara smiled, "First Lady was gracious as usual."

Mamie looked pleased. "Summer is special. She's real genuine."

"I ran into one of her daughters recently."

Morgan stopped drinking and looked up.

"Which one?" Mamie asked.

"The oldest, she's very pretty."

"Leave her alone," Mamie snapped.

Sara rolled her eyes. "She's grown and can make her own decisions."

"Please," Mamie asked, imploringly.

"For goodness sake, if she means that much to you . . ."

Morgan became grieved, but remained silent.

"I'm glad that you stopped by today," Mamie said.

Morgan knew that her mother wanted to say more, but Sara's hardened expression ended further discussion.

"Well, I must be going," Sara said. The younger sibling stood. "Sister Dear, will you escort me outside?" Sara stood and reluctantly hugged their mother.

"It would be my pleasure," Morgan said. Then she led Sara back down the hallway.

The women exited the house and descended the porch steps. Locking arms, Morgan supported Sara as they gingerly tiptoed towards the limo.

Sara giggled.

Morgan felt young and free.

Mamie stood on the porch, watching.

Sara's driver waited patiently for the women to approach. He opened the vehicle's door.

"Momma looks good," Sara said.

"Outside of your coloring, you both could be twins," Morgan said.

"Me, you've got her smile," Sara said, holding her sister's arm tightly.

Morgan chuckled, "Girl please, you're gap has always been wider than mine." The two sisters playfully bantered.

Then Sara quieted.

Sensing her sister's mood change, Morgan waited for the inevitable.

"You didn't call at all last year," Sara said.

Morgan knew that Sara's explosion masked hurt. "Are you raising your children yet?" She brought up the topic that they'd last discussed.

"I support them," Sara said defensively.

"It's not the same and you know it."

"You can't judge me," Sara hissed.

"Momma gave us away and you're repeating the same tired story!"

"Honey, there's nothing wrong with my lifestyle or my kids."

"You didn't even know that Shawn was being beaten."

"I took care of it today."

"But the damage is already done," Morgan said, as calmly as she could.

"I don't want to talk about it," Sara said, through clenched teeth.

Morgan exhaled, "You haven't been the same since Grandma Grace sent you to Chicago."

"I'm fine."

"No, you're not." Morgan refused to accept her sister's lie.

"I've been on my own since I was sixteen."

"Grandma Grace and Momma were wrong to abandon you."

"Sister Dear, I don't need anyone." Resentment shimmered in her cynical orbs.

"You're street smart. I'll give you that, but what about your future?" Morgan asked.

Sara shrugged, "I have plans," she said, standing by the open car door.

"You can't hustle forever. Even Grandma Grace and Momma stopped."

Just then, Sara's phone rang. "Excuse me, but I have to take this call."

Morgan felt overwhelming sadness. Once again, she and Sara were arguing. Her heart ached further as she listened to her sister's conversation.

"Darling, it's been too long. No, two o'clock is perfect. We'll party until dawn. I'll see you then," Sara purred into the phone.

"Sara, I worry about you," Morgan said.

Sara lifted her chin, defiantly. "Our lifestyles are similar, even though you don't see it. My clients pay handsomely for my services, no differently than your lovers.

"I'm done living like that," Morgan said passionately.

"So you say."

Overwhelming sorrow enveloped Morgan. Sara was right. Their lifestyles had been similar, but no more.

Sara stepped into the limo and paused. "So tell me, how does it feel to know your father's identity?" The question came out huskily.

"A wound is finally healing."

"I'm truly happy for you. I really am," Sara said.

"Sara, I don't want to fight anymore."

The air thickened.

"It's what I do best.

Morgan gathered courage.

"What's on your mind? I have to leave," Sara asked.

"Was Lillian's death really an accident?"

Sara's eyes clouded. "I'm not so sure anymore." Why do you ask?"

"Because, I don't believe that it was."

"And you might be right," the younger sibling said. The driver closed the door.

Morgan watched the vehicle leave. Then she walked back up the driveway, whisking tears away.

CHAPTER 92

✝

DEON SNUGGLED CLOSER TO HIS WIFE. HER SOFT WARMTH WAS COMFORTING.

"I'm exhausted," Summer said.

"Me too," he said, burrowing deeper under the covers. Deon kissed his wife's ear.

Summer purred.

"Your ears are my weakness," he crooned.

His wife chuckled, "Honey, I want to discuss something."

"You want to talk now?" Deon asked.

"Yes."

He glared.

"Do you think that Rosemary knew about Sara and Lillian's relationship?"

"Probably not, but it sure explains a lot," he said, shaking his head.

"How is Jacob?"

"He has large shoes to fill," Deon said innocently.

Confused, Summer turned towards her husband. "What are you talking about?" she asked.

"Israel was a rebellious nation, constantly worshipping other idols and operating in disobedience. Hosea 12:2-6 says . . ."

Summer swatted her husband's arm. "I'm not talking about that Jacob!"

Deon grinned. Then he sensed his wife's intent, but she was quicker. Her pillow hit its mark. "Woman, don't do it again or I won't be responsible for what happens next," he barked.

Summer threw another pillow.

Laughter filled the room.

"I told you that this was going to be an interesting summer," she said, before turning out her light.

Deon kissed his wife's forehead.

"Really Deon, I only get a kiss on the forehead."

"Stop talking and go to sleep," Deon said, still smarting from his wife's sneak attack.

Summer leaned over and kissed her husband tenderly.

Very happy and extremely content with his life, Deon turned out his light.

CHAPTER 93

✛

PETRA LICKED ICE CREAM FROM HER FINGERS. WATER TICKLED HER LEGS AS IT SPRAYED AGAINST her shins. Her legs were dangling over the side of the pier. Jacob was seated beside her, munching on an ice cream sandwich.

"Are you enjoying yourself?" he asked, between bites.

Petra nodded. "I haven't had this much fun all summer," she said. The teen licked her cone.

"I thought that you would enjoy spending your final days in town on the beach."

"Daddy!"

"What, baby girl?"

"I'm really sorry about everything," Petra said, for the hundredth time.

"I know that you are. So, we're going to put this episode behind us. I'm sorry too."

Petra looked up, shocked.

"Don't look so surprised," he said, laughing.

"I'm not used to hearing you apologize," she said, between licks.

"I know how, even if I haven't done a lot of it," he said remorsefully. Jacob took another bite of his sandwich.

"We haven't discussed my driver's training class. Are you taking that away too?" Petra asked.

"You'll be able to attend the classes, as planned," he said.

Petra grinned. "Thank you Jesus," she exclaimed loudly. The teenager happily chewed on the remainder of her waffle cone.

Jacob shook his head. "Promise me, that you won't keep any more secrets." Petra peered out at the rolling waves, knowing that she couldn't honor his request.

"I'll try, will you spend more time at home?" she asked.

"I'll try."

Petra nodded, understanding what each of their responses really meant.

"Can I visit Mrs. Phillips?" she asked.

Jacob stared out across the lake. "She's welcome in our home."

Petra smiled. She would gladly take his concession.

"Thank you."

"So, you really like her?" he asked.

"Yes," she yelled, over the roaring waves.

Jacob glanced at the water again. "God doesn't hold our past against us, so I'm going to be open minded."

Petra's eyes welled. "Daddy, I love you."

"I love you too," he said, grabbing her hand.

"Yuck, they're sticky."

Petra giggled. "Come on. I'll race you."

The pair left the pier and walked onto the beach. Sea gulls swooped high and low, looking for food. The turquoise colored water shimmered. Indigo Beach was packed with vacationers and locals, enjoying a respite.

Petra took off running.

"No fair," Jacob yelled, from behind her.

Wind caressed her face as she zoomed past prone bodies and children who played along the shoreline. She picked up speed. Hearing her father's labored breathing she knew that he was close, but she put her head down and concentrated on winning. Her calves burned, but she kept running.

"Petra!"

She heard her father yell. He was close, but he hadn't passed her yet, so she plowed towards the finish line. The boulders were in sight.

"Okay, okay, you win!"

She heard him shout from behind. Petra ran past the erosion barriers and slowed to a jog. Tears welled from exertion. Water moistened her face and body. She looked back and saw her father bent over and breathing hard. He was grinning.

"You've gotten faster." he said, surprised.

Petra jogged towards her dad. "No, you're getting old," she said, matter-of- factly.

"Old!" he yelled.

Giggling, Petra took off again, with her father in fast pursuit. " You're ooold!" she yelled, running towards their car.

Jacob reached it first. "I am not old," he said, clutching his chest. "I got here before you."

"I let you win," Petra said.

"Do you really think that I'm old?" Jacob asked incredulously.

She smiled, without commenting further. Then, Petra entered her father's car and leaned against the soft leather seating. She was happy and hopeful, because God was turning everything around for her good, just like Grandma Rosemary had promised.

CHAPTER 94
☩

SARA GLANCED AROUND THE EXQUISITELY DECORATED BEDROOM. HER INTERIOR DESIGNER HAD done a remarkable job of creating a sensual, yet sophisticated chamber. She never entertained clients here. This floor of the old mansion was off limits to everyone, except close personal friends.

She lounged on her chaise. The file that she was reading had remained unopened for many years. Grieving deeply at the time, she'd originally accepted the private investigator's report, but now she wasn't so sure that his assessment was accurate. Uneasiness had her stomach fluttering. Morgan was correct. Lillian's death didn't feel right, but truthfully, it never had.

Petra had shared information that posed more questions than answers. She'd always known about Lillian and Jacob's argument, but now Petra had confirmed that Lillian had also argued with someone else that day. Sara knew the man's identity. Lillian had an admirer and he was no gentleman. Her headstrong friend had ignored her warnings. Sara speed dialed a number.

"Hello darling."

"Two calls in two days, I feel special."

"I could be calling, just to talk."

The man chuckled. "But you aren't, so tell me what you need. His voice was craggy and imposing.

Once, they'd been very close. Now, they were business partners.

"I'm calling about Lillian."

"I thought so, her daughter's comments are really bothering you."

"You know me well."

"I keep my enemies close," he said.

Sara wasn't offended by the remark. This man had experienced her wrath before. The remembrance brought a smile to her face.

"Lillian was seeing Rico on the side. Can you investigate him without his knowledge?" she asked.

"It can be done, for a price."

"Lillian was like a sister. I couldn't live with myself, if I didn't investigate her death."

"Then, I'll make it happen."

"I knew you would and I'll pay your usual fee," Sara said.

"I have one question," the man asked.

Sara knew what he was thinking, before he spoke.

"What will you do if he's responsible?"

She laughed. "Darling, you know that I never discuss business details over the phone."

The man chuckled.

"That's why I like working with you," the man said, before hanging up.

Sara reclined. She was tired. Her last client had left around six o'clock that morning. Plus, the trip to Michigan had been emotionally draining. Her mother had been gracious and accommodating as always, but spending time in a house that she'd been forbidden to inhabit was always difficult. Being exiled to Chicago at such a young age had left scars that still hadn't healed.

She had really enjoyed seeing her older sister. They'd been close once. Sara had leaned heavily on Morgan for financial and emotional support after the births of her two youngest children. She'd only sent her babies to Michigan after Morgan had relocated to New York. Parenting was hard, but hustling with children was even harder. The decision to send her children away, had strained their relationship. They were now estranged, but not a night went by, that Sara didn't regret this decision, her subsequent marriage or that she and Morgan were no longer close. If she were truly honest, she missed her older sister's meddling. Morgan had always cared, which was more emotion than Mamie had ever expressed towards her.

Sara stared off into space. Morgan was prettier than she remembered. Free of make-up, her complexion was youthful and vibrant. Then she peered at herself in the full-length mirror that hung behind her bed. Expensive lighting couldn't mask the ravages of late nights, hard living and excess.

Sara didn't understand why Morgan had accepted Christ as her personal savior. She didn't understand why anyone would. How could a Heavenly Father care, when her biological father hadn't? She thought about Destiny, her Bible thumping younger sister. Loving God hadn't put any more money into her pockets. Destiny had argued that self-respect was worth having less, but Sara didn't agree.

For now, sleep beckoned. Having never experienced peace, Sara closed her eyes and hoped for the best. At least hope was free, because the mortgage and the rest of her bills needed to get paid. That's why she worked so hard.

CHAPTER 95

✝

IT WAS EARLY. JACOB WATCHED THE SUN RISE FROM HIS BEDROOM WINDOW. PETRA WAS STILL sleeping. Mrs. Sanchez would arrive within the hour to begin her workday and see Petra off to school. Yesterday, he'd kissed his daughter's forehead before she'd left for school. Later that evening, they'd eaten dinner at her favorite restaurant and then gone to a movie. Her sixteenth birthday celebration had been a rather low-key affair.

Jacob walked into the kitchen. He was starting to love this room. Since Petra was doing most of the cooking these days, he'd taken his mother's advice and allowed her to personalize the space. Fuchsia colored cookware now hung above the stove. The once immaculate and orderly room was awash in color.

Jacob shook his head, while holding up a yellow potholder. He quickly placed it in a drawer. Admittedly, the kitchen exuded warmth and he was going to miss it while he was gone. He turned off the light and walked back towards his bedroom.

His packed luggage set neatly by the door. Jeffery had been out of the country for the past three weeks. So the men hadn't spoken, but he planned to meet with his boss today before he flew out later this morning.

Jacob undressed and stepped into the shower. Once his toilette was completed, he quickly dressed and was out the door in minutes. City noise, stop and go traffic, and its orderly chaos were energizing. Steering his car past skyscrapers, he arrived at work and parked in the underground garage.

Then he exited and strode purposefully towards the elevator, which took him up to the top floor.

"Good morning, Mr. McDonald," one of the office managers said when he walked past her desk.

Jacob greeted the employee and then proceeded to his office. Once inside, he placed his briefcase on a desk. Then he stood in front of his corner office window and enjoyed its breathtaking view. The hum of office busyness mingling with muted voices on the other side of his closed door made him smile. He loved his job. His office phone rang.

"Mr. Kennedy is ready to see you," his administrative assistant said.

Jacob left his office and walked down a long hallway. Cubicles lined the inner space. Jeffery was speaking on the phone when he arrived, but motioned for him to enter. He closed the door, giving them privacy. Jacob sat quietly until Jeffery's conversation ended. While he waited, he stared out of the window.

"I love the view too," Jeffery said, once his conversation ended. What time is your flight?"

"Eleven."

Jeffery glanced at his watch. "Good, we have time to talk. How's your mother?" he asked.

"She's fine."

"And Petra?"

"She's doing well in school."

The room became uncomfortably silent. Jacob straightened his back and looked at his boss. "I want to apologize for my behavior a few weeks ago. I wasn't at my best."

"Neither was I, you had no way of knowing that Morgan was my daughter." Jacob looked contrite. "It shouldn't have mattered. I was disrespectful and demeaning towards her."

"I won't argue with you, but knowing that you have already apologized to her is the only reason that you still have a job."

"I know."

Jeffery chuckled. "Have you heard from Sara?" he asked.

"Yes, she took Petra shopping last week."

"Are you going to accept Deon's offer?" Jeffery asked.

"I already have, we started counseling two weeks ago."

"Good, I've always felt that spiritual counsel is beneficial."

"How are you and Morgan doing?" Jacob asked.

His boss leaned forward. "The last few weeks have been humbling. I allowed sin to hurt those closest to me. I have a lot to make up for."

"Me too."

"Whom the Son sets free is free indeed," Jeffery said, quoting scripture.

Jacob smiled. "I'll try and remember that."

"All things do work together for our good," Jeffery said.

"I've heard that scriptural principle a time or two."

"Deon said it to me, just this morning."

Jacob smiled. "So you're in counseling too?"

Jeffery nodded. "A thief asked Jesus to remember him as he hanged on the cross. If he could get delivered in that final hour, then I've still got time to get things right."

"Thanks for not firing me."

Jeffery's smile was crooked but sincere. "I can't say that I didn't think about it. Keep me apprised of how the Argentinean negotiations unfold and don't budge on the numbers."

"Did you get a chance to look at the charts I sent?" Jacob asked.

"Yes, but I want to make a few changes."

The men adjourned to the large mahogany table in the room and began working.

When the briefing ended, Jeffery escorted Jacob to the door. "Have a safe flight."

"I will."

Jeffery hugged Jacob paternally.

Then Jacob walked out the door.

CHAPTER 96

✝

JEFFERY LOVED EVERYTHING ABOUT CHICAGO, BUT INDIGO BEACH HELD A SPECIAL PLACE IN HIS heart, one that he couldn't ignore any longer. His assistant interrupted his thoughts.

"Mr. Kennedy," she said.

He acknowledged her presence.

"Your next appointment is here."

"Send her in."

The woman left and minutes later Morgan appeared.

"Did you see Jacob?" he asked.

"No, I just missed him."

Jeffery hugged his daughter, wondering whether Jacob and Morgan would ever bridge their differences. "You're early."

"I didn't expect traffic to be so light. I made really good time on the freeway."

Jeffery sat beside his daughter at the conference table.

"Stop smiling at me," she said, appearing embarrassed.

"I don't want to."

"Listen, I've got great news," Morgan said excitedly.

Jeffery waited for the pronouncement.

"I've been accepted into graduate school."

His chest swelled. "Congratulations, where?" he asked.

"Here, in Chicago." Morgan handed her father a folder.

"Well, this is good news," Jeffry said, as he lowered his reading glasses. Then he began reading a letter from the file.

"The acceptance letter came yesterday. My cohort begins in January."

"Will you commute?" he asked.

"I'd like to stay with you, if that's possible."

Paternal love, overflowed. "I'd be honored, by the way, I also have an announcement."

Morgan looked up.

"I'm going to purchase property at McGregor's Corner. I told your mother about it this morning."

"What did she say?" Morgan asked.

"She wasn't enthusiastic, especially when I told her that I wasn't going to live alone."

"Oh my," Morgan said, in shock.

Jeffery grinned. "You know your mother. She got so riled up, I had to ask for her hand in marriage, just to shut her up."

"You did what?" Morgan exclaimed.

"She hasn't accepted my proposal yet, but I'm hoping that she will? How do you feel?"

"I think that it's a wonderful idea, but it's going to take a lot of persuasion to get Momma to agree to marriage."

Jeffery chuckled. "I know, but I'm going to enjoy ever minute of the chase. Now let's get to work."

Seated side-by-side, the pair compared a variety of prospectuses. They analyzed and debated financial options, and Jeffery had never been happier.

CHAPTER 07

✝

PETRA READ A TEXT. MORGAN HAD JUST CONFIRMED THEIR DINNER DATE. ALTHOUGH THEY talked often, she'd only visited twice during the past month. Both times, they'd dined with Mrs. Phillips. Afterwards, the women had either gone shopping or back to the mansion. Petra loved listening to the sisters' colorful stories.

As she sat on the bus, a text from Shawn came through. The teens talked and texted daily. Mrs. Sanchez thought that he was handsome, even though his milky colored skin, pale green eyes, and sandy colored hair were an interesting blend. Since Shawn and his mother shared similar skin and hair coloring, his exotic features now made sense. His mother had always been able to pass for white. So far, her dad was tolerating their relationship.

The bus stopped. With her backpack slung over one shoulder, Petra stepped off and waited patiently at the corner before crossing the street. Her dad was flying to Argentina today. This was his first trip abroad since they'd returned from Michigan. Their relationship was getting better. Petra walked past the concierge and waved. The man smiled back. Then she rode the elevator up to her floor.

"Petra, is that you?" Mrs. Sanchez yelled, from the kitchen.

"Yes," she hollered back. The teen dumped her backpack on expensively laid hardwood flooring. Then she walked towards the kitchen.

Still drying her hands on a dishtowel, Mrs. Sanchez met her half way. "How was your day?" the housekeeper asked.

"Good," Petra said.

"Do you have time to explain your grandmother's meatloaf recipe to me? I want to take a loaf to my daughter. She has her hands full with her new baby."

"Sure, just let me wash my hands."

"I purchased everything on your list," Mrs. Sanchez hollered through the powder room door.

Once Petra entered the kitchen, she made sure that all of the necessary ingredients were on the counter.

Mrs. Sanchez held a two-pound package of ground beef in her hands. She was also frowning.

"What's the matter?" the teen asked.

"I'm a house cleaner, not a cook and I've never liked the feel of ground beef between my fingers."

Petra rolled her eyes. "Geez, you're making this difficult. You'll just have to get over your dislike because mixing the ingredients by hand makes meatloaf juicy and flavorful," she said, as she donned an apron.

Mrs. Sanchez smiled indulgently.

Then Petra closed her eyes. When she opened them, the housekeeper looked concerned.

"Petra, are you okay?"

Petra giggled. "I'm better than okay." And she was!

EPILOGUE

✝

WALKING BRISKLY PAST SECURITY, JEFFERY TRAVELED DOWN A LONG HALLWAY. THEN HE quickly climbed the stairs. Staff worked in silence. He waved to a few that he knew. A nurse dressed in starched white clothing sat outside his friend's bedroom. She stood and opened the door when he neared. Jeffery walked into the room and silently observed his business partner.

Edward was dapperly dressed and seated in an expensively embroidered armchair. Books and magazines lay scattered on top of an antique table. Edward turned and his smile grew expansive when he saw Jeffery. "My dear friend, I was told that you were in town," he said stiffly.

Jeffery motioned for Edward to remain seated. The nurse quietly closed the door, giving the men privacy. Then he leaned down and hugged his business partner and friend.

"*Bonjour mon ami*," Edward said.

"*Bonjour*," Jeffrey said, patting Edward's back.

Edward appeared youthful, almost childish. "How is Morgan?" he asked.

Jeffery realized that Edward's appearance was misleading. The man's eyes were glazed and vacant. "She will graduate in six months," he said proudly.

Edward beamed. "I'm happy for her. We learned a lot in grad school," he said. Then he became confused.

"Are you still mad at me?" Edward asked, in a childlike voice.

Jeffery shook his head, now realizing that Edward needed rest.

"You know that I never would have begun a relationship with Morgan, if I'd known that she was your daughter. I tried making things right," Edward said. His words were slurring.

"I know," Jeffery said, feeling the weight of regret.

"Good, because I don't want anger to stand between us."

Jeffery watched his friend struggle for words.

"Thank you for coming today," Edward said.

More than a year had passed since Jeffery's last visit. Edward's condition was worsening. Medication maintained lucidity for short spurts of time. Alzheimer's was slowly robbing his friend of reality.

"Why are you in town?" Edward asked.

"We recently purchased another distributorship in Switzerland. Once Morgan graduates, she'll manage that operation."

"She is a great asset."

"Yes, she is a rare treasure indeed," Jeffery said.

Edward excitedly clapped his hands together again. "Enough talk about business. How many grandchildren do you have now?" he asked.

"I have a grandson and another grandbaby is due any day now."

"Excellent!"

Then Jeffery shared stories about his family that his friend would never remember, but it didn't matter. Someday in the future, Edward's brain would forget to tell his body to breathe and their association would come to an end.

Soon, Edward tired. Jeffery left his friend's bedroom and walked back down the winding staircase. He left the house through the kitchen. Then he entered a limo, which was parked in the huge attached garage. He waited until the driver shut the door before speaking.

"How was your visit?" Morgan asked.

Jeffery remained reflectively quiet. "It went as well as could be expected."

She nodded.

Jeffery's eyes moistened. "Alzheimer's is a terrible disease."

Morgan handed him a tissue.

"You look puzzled, what's on your mind?" he asked.

"I just got off of the phone with Sara."

Jeffery grew concerned. "There is a seven hour time difference between Chicago and Paris, whatever she called about, must be important."

Morgan nodded. "It looks like Lillian's death wasn't accidental."

Jeffery sighed. "Is she sure?"

"Yes, she wants to meet with us as soon as we land."

"Does Jacob know about your concerns?" he asked.

"I've never mentioned them to him."

"Has Sara spoken with him?"

"No," Morgan said.

Jeffery glanced out the limo's window and meditated on the information that he'd just heard. Finally he said, "I'll help in any way. My personal resources are at your disposal. We'll have plenty of time to strategize on the plane, but first, tell me about your meeting."

Morgan grinned. "It went very well."

Jeffery opened a dossier that she handed him. He quickly scanned the contents. "What are you recommending?"

"I believe that two million dollars is a fair asking price."

"I agree." Jeffery looked up. "Your work is excellent as usual."

"It's in my DNA."

Jeffery smiled. "When we get back to the states, I have another project for you. You'll be working with Jacob."

One eyebrow rose on Morgan's face. "This sounds interesting."

"It will be."

The limo picked up speed.

"Will he work with me?" she asked.

"Jacob is a professional, but can you handle him?" he asked.

"My last name is Harding. I'm looking forward to it," she said.

Jeffery chuckled delightedly, knowing that truer words had never been spoken.